LIKE. LOVE. HATE.

ALSO BY CATHRYN GRANT

LIKE. LOVE. HATE.

A PSYCHOLOGICAL THRILLER

CATHRYN GRANT

ISBN: 978-1-943142-85-9

This book is a work of fiction. References to real people, events, establishments, organizations, or locales are intended only to provide a sense of authenticity, and are used fictitiously. All other characters, and incidents and dialogue, are drawn from the author's imagination and are not to be construed as real.

Visit Cathryn online at CathrynGrant.com

Cover design by Lydia Mullins Copyright © 2024

For my Mother,
Who has read every word I've published.

And has managed to live a delightfully social life
without engaging in social media.

PROLOGUE

ANONYMOUS

I thought about taking a photograph of the blood.

It would have been gruesome, but eye-catching, pooling on the white concrete path that wound through the trees in the park. If I really wanted to push things to the edge, I could have taken a shot of the place where the bullet had entered the body. Posting those images on social media would have attracted so many eyeballs.

How many likes would it collect? Would there be more loves or likes? Would it go viral? That's the burning desire of every person posting a picture, a reel, a little peek into their life.

Wasn't that the image everyone was searching for? The content everyone craved? Something shocking and new, something never posted before? Of course, I knew they didn't *really* want to see a gunshot wound, a dead body. I still thought about it though, because it seemed ... appropriate.

In the end, I didn't. But I wanted to. I really, *really* wanted to.

And I thought about it a lot. I couldn't stop thinking about it. Part of me regretted not doing it, but taking those pictures and posting them would have given me away.

CHAPTER 1

BLYTHE

*T*he tripod was positioned on the poolside table. Blythe stood in the shade. Even though she was wearing sunglasses, she didn't want to have even the slightest squint as she posed for her selfie.

She needed to strike the perfect balance between easy, confident, and attractive without looking as if she might be trying to look even slightly seductive. Her sea green bikini wasn't at all skimpy, and she'd tried a hundred different positions in front of the mirror, tested countless photographs before deciding on the right pose to be sure she looked serene, *not* seductive.

After ten rapid clicks of her remote, she was finished. She looked at the results. Three shots were definitely usable. Her shoulder-length strawberry blonde hair framed her face with thick, loose waves. Mostly, she wanted people to see her body. That everything she promised her potential fitness coaching clients was true — her low-key approach to nutrition and exercise, to overall good health, worked. She had a story to tell and she told it every day on social media.

It was fun. It was satisfying. Telling that story was almost as rewarding as the coaching itself. She loved helping women feel good about themselves. She enjoyed helping them feel at home in their own skin. She wanted everyone to feel like they could enjoy their lives without constantly obsessing over how their bodies looked, always counting calories. It broke her heart to see women slinking around, covering themselves up as if they were ashamed to exist, turning away from food as if it were poison. That wasn't how it was supposed to be.

She took the camera off the tripod.

"What are you posing for?" Kelsey's voice carried across the swimming pool from the open bifold doors leading to the family room. Her eldest-by-thirteen-minutes twin daughter stepped outside, holding an open bag of pita chips. She took a chip out of the bag and bit it.

"Something for my social media."

Kelsey finished the chip. "You look a little bit like a fool, TBH."

Blythe felt a pinch in her throat. More like a stab. Her daughter's words occasionally cut like the blade of a sashimi knife. Kelsey never softened her opinions. Never. Blythe loved that about her. But sometimes …

"Your bikini days ended a decade ago." Kelsey ate another chip.

"I think I look great for a woman my age."

"The key word," Kelsey licked her lips, moving around the edge of the pool until she was only a few feet from Blythe, "is your *age*."

She gave Blythe a charming smile. It was probably meant to be kind.

"It's a little sad. Putting that on the social stream."

"It's my brand. I'm a fitness —"

"I know, Mom." Kelsey grinned.

"People need to see evidence that I know what I'm doing. It's not about showing off, if that's what you think."

"I don't think anything. I'm just pointing out that a bikini is kind of drawing attention to things you might not want to draw attention to." She shoved her hand into the bag and brought out two chips at once. She delicately nibbled on the largest one.

"That's cruel."

"I'm being honest. Don't you want me to be honest? To tell the truth?"

"Yes."

Kelsey smiled. She stepped closer and kissed Blythe's cheek. "Love you, mom. You look great and you could accomplish the same thing in your workout clothes. That's all I'm saying."

"Mmm," Blythe said.

"Just be prepared for not all the responses to be super positive. Make sure you have your tough skin on. 'K?"

"I'll keep that in mind."

Kelsey disappeared into the house as quickly as she'd materialized. She was always that way. Seeming to appear out of nowhere, speaking her mind, and walking away. Blythe's twins couldn't be more different, even though they looked so much alike. She'd spent hours staring at them when they were infants, searching for differences so she would always know who was Kelsey, who was Kate. As they'd grown, she'd wondered how she'd ever doubted her ability to know.

She packed up the tripod and went into the house. Kate was in the living room, curled at the end of the sofa, reading a novel on her tablet, her long pale hair covering most of her face.

"Do you have a minute for me to show you something?" Blythe asked.

Kate looked up. She let the tablet fall onto her lap and tucked her hair behind her ears. "What?"

Blythe held out her phone. "Does this look too showy? Or ... I don't know, inappropriate?"

Kate shrugged. "Not really."

"It's for my social media. To show people I can help them get a summer body."

"It's already summer. Isn't it a little late?"

Blythe laughed. "But people are thinking about it, so it's a good time for getting new clients."

Kate shrugged.

"So it's okay?"

"Sure. Summer body, though?" She shivered slightly. "Kind of ... yuck. Women aren't fashion dolls."

"I'm not too old for a bikini?"

Kate smiled. "Women shouldn't live by rules like that. Wear whatever you want." She picked up her tablet.

Blythe wasn't sure Kate had answered the question, but she suddenly no longer wanted her daughters' input. Solicited or not. She looked good. And Kate was right about that. Women her age, any age, had a right to wear whatever style swimsuit they chose and feel good without worrying about being compared to twenty-something girls. This was absurd. She was overthinking it. She flopped into the armchair, loaded the photo to all her profiles, adding seven hashtags and a comment she hoped was witty—*Fine food doesn't have to be fattening. Focus on fitness and frolic freely in the sun.*

It wasn't that witty, but the alliteration would stick, even if it was clunky.

She posted it and saw an immediate heart.

Jenna Dale.

Of course. Jenna was always first. It seemed as if Jenna spent the day staring at her phone, waiting for something to happen. And with Jenna, if something didn't happen, she was likely to find a way to *make* it happen. Jenna had been that way since she was thirteen years old. She craved excitement and action, always wanting things to be happening.

More likes followed Jenna's. Blythe smiled as a few comments were added.

Soon, her photograph would be spreading across cyberspace, finding new followers, attracting attention, getting positive feedback. It made her feel good. She knew it was a false feeling of happiness. Everyone knew that, but it still felt good. Everyone knew that, too. It was satisfying to know people appreciated what you had to say, that they enjoyed your photographs and videos. It was natural and normal.

She should appreciate Jenna for always being ready to kick things off, always ready to be first with the comments and likes. She wouldn't give in to the vague feeling of guilt that Jenna evoked. If Jenna wanted to spend her day on her phone, making sure she was always the first to boost everyone's posts, that was her choice.

She would not give into that whisper of guilt. She was tired of it.

CHAPTER 2

*a*s Blythe walked down the hall, her phone vibrated with notifications. The photo was obviously a winner.

Kelsey's bedroom door opened. "You posted it after all."

"I did."

"Such a brave mama bear."

Blythe laughed. "Not brave. It's just business. But thanks." She gave her daughter an air kiss and continued down the hall and up the stairs.

As she entered the bedroom, Garret stepped out of their bathroom, dressed in jeans, his hair wet and uncombed.

"How was your run?" she asked.

"Good."

She held out her phone to him. "What do you think of this?"

"You look hot." He handed the phone back. "But hotter in real life." He slid his arm around her waist and began fiddling with the back of her swimsuit top.

She moved away. "It's not about looking hot."

"But you do."

"Thanks. I just did it to show that strength training and healthy eating—"

"I know." He leaned over and brushed his lips across hers.

8

"Kelsey said my bikini years are over." She laughed, regretting the hint of neediness in her tone.

"Not nearly." He pulled her close again and wrapped his arms around her. His skin, still hot from running and the shower, was warm and soft against her own.

"You really do look great," he said in a low voice.

"Thanks, but it's really, *really* not about that."

"I know. I just hope you're being honest with yourself."

"I am. I want potential clients, and even my existing ones, to see. How else can I show my muscle definition? It's not a seductive pose."

"You're right, it's not." He kissed her again. "It shows you're worth hiring." He kissed her more deeply.

After a moment, they moved away from each other.

He ran his finger along her cheekbone toward her ear. "But I also hope it won't attract the wrong kind of attention."

"So if some creep comes along, it's my fault?"

"That's not what I'm saying. I was thinking about that troll Jenna keeps complaining about. The one making weird comments on her posts."

"Oh." Blythe sighed. "She needs to block him and stop letting it get under her skin."

"She's a little scared."

"There are all kinds of bots and weirdos on social media. That's why they have a block feature. She needs to use it and move on."

"I don't want some freak saying rude things about you in a bikini, that's all."

"I'll hide it and block them if that happens. I'm not letting the dark side of social media dictate what I do."

He went into the closet and came out, pulling a dark blue T-shirt over his head. "You can't pretend it doesn't exist."

"I also won't let it control what I do. This is my business, and I need to promote what I have to offer new clients. We can't let the bad guys control us. That's what I told Jenna. I *won't* let them."

Garret tugged his shirt down and came toward her. He folded

his arms around her again, making her feel safe. Some imagined tweaker behind an anonymous screen name couldn't hurt her. Jenna was being too dramatic. Knowing Jenna, a tiny part of her probably liked the attention. She might not realize it, but it wouldn't be surprising.

CHAPTER 3

*B*lythe's appointment with Lacey Abbott was scheduled for eleven. They were meeting at the gym where Blythe had been a member since before the twins were born. Lacey was one of her complicated clients with blurry boundaries. She was a close friend, a part of Blythe's group of business-minded moms, and a client.

Blythe and the others had created their informal support group when their children were infants, all of them deep in diapers and breastfeeding, but looking toward a future when they'd begin building their home-based businesses so they could follow the slightly mythological path of having it all. They would be mostly available for their children while launching careers that would carry them into the middle of their lives. They would be fulfilled in all areas. They dreamed of earning money that was more than just a side gig, and achieve satisfying success as entrepreneurs.

Lacey had floundered for a long time, trying to figure out what it was she wanted to do. For a few years, she'd operated a small child-care center, then offered pet sitting services. After that, she'd set up a business that hired college students to run errands for the elderly.

Recently, she'd started selling coffee mugs and T-shirts, hats and tote bags with pop art designs and clever sayings, although most of her sayings weren't original to herself.

Blythe worried Lacey was going to get called out at some point for a copyright violation. Was that a thing, when you took a pithy saying that twenty or thirty people had repeated and put in books and journals and posted online and even if you Googled it, there wasn't always a clear answer as to where it had originated? She wasn't sure, but she worried about it, for Lacey's sake.

For now, Lacey was doing well. She sold a lot of mugs and T-shirts. A lot. People loved smart, amusing quotes that made them feel better about themselves, comments that made them smile every time they took a sip of coffee, or looked in a mirror.

Lacey was ten minutes late for her workout. That wasn't like her.

Blythe took a long sip of water. She did a few stretches and checked her phone. No messages. She checked her last social media post, unable to stop basking in all the positive comments. She hadn't gone back to check and compare, but she had a gut feeling it had received the most comments of any post in the past three or four months. That photograph had definitely been the right choice, despite the doubts her family had stirred. They were only trying to protect her. She smiled and tucked her phone into the pocket of her leggings.

It was eleven fifteen when she saw Lacey walking toward her. Blythe bit the inside of her cheek. Their session was forty-five minutes long. She wasn't sure what she should cut to get the most out of the time left.

Lacey gave her a hug. "I'm a little tired, so I hope I can keep up with my torture today."

Blythe smiled. "It shouldn't feel like torture."

"Just a joke."

"It should feel easier anyway since we only have half an hour."

"Why?" Lacy tugged on her ponytail to make it tighter.

"It's eleven fifteen."

"Oh? Is it?" Lacey pulled out her phone and glanced at it. "Well, I don't have anything. I can stay until noon."

This was the problem with having friends as clients—they assumed the rules didn't apply. Should she lie and say she had an appointment at noon? Or allow the extra time? She sighed and opened the profile for Lacey's workout on her phone. "Let's get started."

"You looked amazing in your swimsuit." Lacey tugged on her sports bra. "I'd never post a picture of myself in a bikini. To be honest, I don't like posting selfies period." She laughed. "I don't mind pictures of me and Miles, or with the kids. But by myself? Ugh." She laughed again.

"Don't say that. You're gorgeous."

"I'm an acquired taste."

Blythe laughed. "That's clever. But really, you look great. I've told you a hundred times. We're not competing with each other and we're not trying to reach some form of imagined perfection. My goal, and I hope yours, is to be healthy. To get stronger, and to feel good in our own skin."

"Yup. I know. But you can post a bikini pic and I will not do that. Ever. I wouldn't wear a bikini in my own backyard. I'll never look like you, sweetie."

Blythe felt her earlier confidence dissolve. Was the photo a mistake? How could one simple photograph cause so much second-guessing? She'd wanted to inspire people. She'd wanted to show women they could be proud of their bodies and not feel as if they had to look twenty when they were decades into adulthood, moms of teenagers. Why did it have to be so complicated?

"Let's start with the bench press," Blythe said.

They stayed until five past twelve, then went to lunch. Lacey ordered a Reuben sandwich. Blythe wondered if she imagined a defiant gleam in her friend's eye as she took her first bite, as if daring Blythe to make a suggestion about eating half the sandwich and saving the rest for another meal. Was the coaching session over?

Were they just two friends enjoying a relaxing lunch, or coach and client? It was so confusing sometimes.

CHAPTER 4

*W*hen Blythe arrived home after lunch, she went for a leisurely swim, did some bookkeeping, and chopped veggies she put in the fridge for dinner. Garret had said he'd fire up the barbecue, which sounded even nicer now that the temperature had hit eighty-six.

She went outside and sat on the lounge chair. She took a sip of sparkling water and checked her email, then her social media. It was time to post something new, but she'd given zero thought to it. Usually she had her posts planned out a week or two in advance, but the end of the school year had thrown her out of her routine.

At the top of one feed was a post from Lacey. A selfie. The thing she'd insisted she would never do, which was both funny and shocking because when Lacey said she would never do something, she was true to her word.

Should she be alarmed? A selfie didn't seem like something to be alarmed about, but this ...

It was a photograph of Lacey with her hair mussed as if she'd just woken. Her eyes were made up more heavily than usual. She wore a halter top that showed her bra straps. She stood slumped against a tree in her front yard, which emphasized the extra flesh around her armpits. Because it was a full-length shot, her hip cocked to one side, the pose also emphasized the swell of her belly and the roundness of her thighs in her very short, cut-off denim shorts.

She looked gorgeous, as Lacey always did, but she seemed to be going out of her way to feature the parts of her body that were starting to show age.

To make things worse, Blythe was absolutely certain she'd tilted her head and done her best to give the impression of mirroring the pose Blythe had presented in her bikini shot, but with a less flattering angle.

Worse, the caption felt like a punch to her gut.

I'll never have a perfect body, and why would I even want one? Because what IS perfection? I'm an acquired taste.

She'd added hashtags about body positivity. Below the hashtags was a comment added by Lacey.

That sounds like it belongs on a mug! LOL! If you want to pre-order a mug with your I-love-myself-as-I-am image and my aha moment from the gym (I won't go so far as to call it a revelation, but it kind of was, TBH), hit me with a comment.

In the single hour since Lacey had made the post, there were over three thousand likes. Below the image were over four hundred comments. As Blythe flicked through the string of comments, many of them filled with words of delight about her self-acceptance, praise for her confidence, kudos for her boldness, and echos of self-love, were easily a hundred and fifty people requesting mugs.

Blythe put her phone face down on her lap. She leaned her head back and closed her eyes. In the yard next door, someone fired up a leaf blower—not what she needed to calm her thoughts. She was overwhelmed by a thundering waterfall of conflicting emotions.

The leaf blower roared louder, a monster of gas-powered clamor that was destroying the tranquility of the garden around her pool that she lovingly cared for on a weekly basis.

She felt guilty and misunderstood at the same time. Everything she did to help people get healthy was being misconstrued. She was angry at Lacey for taking her good intentions and turning them into something that felt mean-spirited and critical. She felt undermined and attacked, as if Lacey was almost deliberately trying to sabotage her business, even though she knew in her logical mind this was absolutely not true. For the most part, Lacey's post had almost nothing to do with her. She also felt inexplicably lonely.

She opened her eyes and took a sip of water, letting the cold carbonation soothe her, then picked up the phone vibrating on her belly. As she'd expected, it was a text from Jenna.

> Jenna: I don't get it! A selfie where she looks meh at best, and it blows up!

She'd added four sobbing emojis. Another text followed quickly.

> Jenna: I don't get it! Why don't my posts blow up? Ever?!? And from that, she's selling hundreds of mugs? She hasn't even produced them yet. My work is exquisite. Everyone says that, but it's so hard. It's so f&@$(*# hard!

There were now ten crying and despairing emojis. Blythe texted back:

> Blythe: We've talked about this fifty times. Her mugs cost fifteen bucks. Everyone uses them and gives them as gifts. Handmade jewelry is expensive. And it depends on your taste. You know this!

> Jenna: It's not fair. And did I tell you the stalker is back?

> Blythe: He's not a stalker. You need to stop catastrophizing it.

> Jenna: I need positive comments. Not this!

> Blythe: Block and move on.

Jenna: I did. It keeps happening. He keeps coming back with new user names.

Blythe: Block. Block. Block.

Jenna: Why are you so unsympathetic?

Blythe: It happens to everyone. Creepy guys wanting to chat. Scams. Bots. It's all the same. You have to ignore it.

Jenna: This is different.

Blythe: If you obsess over it, they win.

She couldn't muster up any energy to offer more sympathy to Jenna right now. They'd already had this conversation. And right now, all she could feel was the ache in her stomach from Lacey's words. *I'll never have a perfect body.* It felt like they were directed at her. But she'd never, not once, suggested anyone should have a perfect body. She wanted to cry.

CHAPTER 5

JENNA

*J*enna left her phone in the bedroom and walked down the hall. As she passed by, she closed the door to her workroom, hard. Not slamming it, just closing it firmly. Although the framed photograph of herself, Oliver, and Naomi was turned crooked by the force. She left it that way.

She rounded the corner and stopped outside Naomi's room. The murmur of voices came through the door, but she couldn't make out any of the words. Naomi was in there with Cooper. She wasn't too worried about it. Cooper was nineteen to Naomi's sixteen, home for the summer after his first year at college, but they'd always been good friends, nothing more. Ever since they were little kids. All her friends' kids were friends to one degree or another, but Naomi and Cooper had always clicked. Two outsiders, maybe.

Oliver didn't like Naomi to entertain boys with her bedroom door closed, but Jenna didn't see the big deal. Teenagers were gonna do what they were gonna do. She preferred to educate her daughter rather than police her. Jenna wished she'd been treated that way by her parents. She also figured it was somewhat unlikely Naomi and Cooper were going to have sex while Jenna was in the house. Not impossible, but unlikely. Mostly, she just didn't get that vibe from the two of them.

She continued down the hall to the kitchen, poured a small glass of wine, and took a sip. She carried her glass back to the bedroom and picked up her phone. She shouldn't keep checking what was going on but it was so upsetting, some masochistic part of her made her look. She knew this was entirely different. Comparing apples and oranges, but that didn't reduce the hurt. Why on earth were a bunch of factory-made mugs printed with kitschy messages wildly popular, while her stunning, carefully crafted jewelry was so difficult to sell?

It wasn't that she sold nothing. She sold quite a lot of her jewelry. But it was feast or famine, a rollercoaster ride. Just when she thought her work was poised to become really popular, she would face three or four months during which she sold almost nothing. She knew her bracelets and necklaces were pricey, but people bought lots of expensive things online. And everyone loved her jewelry. Rather, the people who commented on her social media posts *said* they loved it. The people who bought her pieces loved them. They came back and bought more.

Her last post had been a photograph of her hand with a fresh manicure—pale mauve nails—a single silver ring on her middle finger, and three bracelets. She'd written a heartfelt comment, almost poetic, about people taking their hands for granted. They used them every moment of the day, but rarely, if ever, stopped to notice the magnificent intricacy of them.

She'd thought her words would touch people, make them pause and think. She'd *thought* it might make them want one or two of her beautiful bracelets to remind them to gaze at and appreciate their incredible, unique, beautiful, useful hands. It hadn't turned out that way at all.

Oliver appeared in the bedroom doorway, coming to a sudden stop. He looked as shocked to see her as she was to see him. She hadn't heard his car, hadn't heard the door, or his footsteps approaching their bedroom. It was a little frightening to think he could enter their house and come this close without her having any awareness of his presence whatsoever. She shivered.

"The house was so quiet," he said. "I thought you might be out back or next door."

"I'm right here. Watching thousands of people buy tacky mugs, while a total of three people consider purchasing handmade jewelry."

He sighed. He came to the bed and sat beside her, placing his hand on the back of her neck. He massaged it, pressing his fingers into her muscles.

She moved her head, feeling her body relax, fully aware that her mind would not follow, feeling it rush in the opposite direction, getting more upset as he tried to calm her.

After a few minutes, she thought she might scream from the silence. It made her thoughts seem louder, billowing with envy and frustration, although she couldn't say for sure what she envied. She certainly didn't want to sell mugs, not ever. Finally, Oliver spoke. "Please, don't compare yourself to her. Or whatever you're doing."

She straightened her shoulders. His hand fell away from her neck, flopping onto the bed as if to chastise her hypocrisy for not appreciating the amazing capabilities it possessed. "I'm trying to help out here!" Jenna wailed. "You have so much pressure at work. You don't know if you'll be impacted by the layoff, and I'm trying to get my business to take off once and for all so we can have a viable second income. You act like it's no big deal."

"I appreciate that." He put his arms around her and tried to pull her onto his lap.

She stiffened, making it impossible for him to comfort her further. "I pour my heart into my work, and it's so hard when I can't attract more attention."

He put his hand on her leg, rubbing it gently.

A moment later, she stood and left the room. In the kitchen, she realized she'd forgotten her wineglass on the nightstand. She probably shouldn't have any more. One glass with dinner would be nice.

She took out a clean glass, splashed in a small amount of wine, and took a sip.

Did her friends see how unfriendly and unsupportive social media was? They'd vowed to promote each other's businesses, but over the years, things had become unbalanced. She did her part, but it wasn't returned with equal passion. It wasn't as if she kept score. She didn't intend to keep score. The others seemed to view it more casually. Maybe because they weren't artists, they didn't feel it as deeply. It was hard to know.

Lacey sold her mugs and T-shirts, Blythe had her wellness coaching, Evie promoted her parenting podcast, and Scarlett sold hand-painted greeting cards. That was art, in a way. Yes, it was definitely art, but the cards were inexpensive.

Figuring it out made her want more wine. After a glass or two of wine, her brain didn't work so hard. It slowed down, she felt calmer. Her thoughts weren't as frantic.

She'd told her friends about the troll who kept changing user names, coming onto her posts and making comments about her jewelry being for rich b*#$%&es. Sometimes, he posted rude emojis without making a comment—the barfing face or the eye roll. No one seemed concerned. A few times there'd been comments that only privileged b*#$%&es could afford to play around making "art" all day. They knew she was rich because she lived in such an expensive part of California.

The only one who thought the comments were scary was Garret. The others sounded like a song on constant replay—*Block it. Report it. Hide it. Block it.*

No one ever asked—*Are you okay?*

No one said—*That must really hurt.*

No one said—*I'll be sure to put lots of extra comments so those get buried!*

No one hugged her and asked—*Aren't you scared?*

CHAPTER 6

BLYTHE

*D*espite telling Jenna, lecturing Jenna, if she was honest with herself, that Jenna needed to stop obsessing over the troll who kept popping up on her social media posts, Blythe couldn't stop herself from doing the same thing. She was now obsessing over Lacey's comments about never wanting a perfect body. She was imagining Lacey's tone, Lacey's gaze locking onto hers, suggesting she was superficial.

Lacey hadn't mentioned Blythe or said anything about having a fitness coach. But she'd said those things in the past. She'd tagged Blythe's pages multiple times, promoting Blythe's recipes and talking about her workouts. She'd made light-hearted jokes about the grueling strength training. Jokes that Blythe now thought might not have been as light-hearted as she'd thought at the time.

Against her better judgment, Blythe started clicking back through Lacey's posts. Reading them now, they sounded harsher than she'd noticed before.

Was this commentary about body *perfection* going to damage Blythe's coaching business? Did people remember that Blythe was Lacey's coach? Had they been following Lacey's fitness and healthy eating journey? It wasn't as if it was a theme on Lacey's social media, but this wasn't the first time she'd put an amusing comment about body image on one of her mugs or shirts.

Four or five months ago she'd introduced a line of T-shirts printed with the beloved meme that lifting a wineglass to her lips was her workout and she was thinking she needed to work out more often. She'd tagged Blythe's page with a series of laughing, winking, and psychotically winking emojis. It had seemed like it was all in good fun.

Was it, really?

Lacey was a good friend. Surely she wasn't trying to sabotage Blythe's career. What was she doing? Was this all frustration because she wasn't happy with her progress? What was going on?

Once again, Blythe worried the bikini picture had been a mistake. Maybe there was a better way to show that strength training had enabled her to develop muscles that made her feel strong, that increased her energy level and helped her feel more capable. When she'd discovered strength training, she'd stopped feeling like she was dragging herself around, tired all the time.

Was that the wrong message?

She'd never, *ever* suggested anyone should have a so-called perfect body. That wasn't her own goal, and seeing women strive for that sickened her.

"You're looking at your phone again," Kate said. "We're supposed to be playing Monopoly. You're the one who picked the game."

"I just needed to—"

"It's a no-phone zone," Garret said. "That's our agreement."

"I'm not socializing. It's business."

"I'm not working," he said.

"Your work is confined to business hours," Blythe said. "I have to stay on top of this twenty-four-seven. You know that."

"You don't *have* to." He moved his marker eight spaces, tapping the board so hard, the tiny houses and hotels jumped on their foundations.

"Lacey's post about not needing a perfect body is blowing up like you can't believe. It's had over three hundred shares now. I'm worried it's—"

"Stop obsessing over it," Kelsey said.

"I'm not obsessing."

"You are," Kate said. "You're the *definition* of obsession." She laughed and tapped her marker on Blythe's phone. "C'mon, Mom. Dad's right. It's your rule! No phones on game night. It's chill time."

"I've never seen something so silly blow up like this. Her photo gives the impression she's trying to look ... not great. On purpose." She picked up her phone again and opened it, staring at the image of Lacey. Over seven thousand likes. It was incredible.

"It'll be over in two days. Less than that," Kate said. "It'll drown like everything. Why are you so worried about it?"

"It's like you're addicted," Garret said.

"I'm not addicted." Blythe slid her phone into the back pocket of her jeans.

They played for another half hour. Each time her phone throbbed, Blythe felt an echoing ache in her stomach. When Garret got up to refill the bowl of popcorn, she pulled out her phone. Her daughters were doing the same. Since they were taking a break, it was allowed, even though she was setting a bad example. She was undoing years of careful screen management in a single evening. But she couldn't stop herself. Maybe she *was* addicted. This was the very definition of addiction—she couldn't stop herself.

She unlocked her phone.

At the top of her feed was Jenna's post from a few days earlier. Why had that reappeared? She scrolled down. The top comment was from the troll. At least she assumed it was the same creep.

If you want to sell over-priced jewelry, find a model with better looking hands. Those hands look like they belong to an old witch. No one would pay good money for that stuff if it's going to make their hands look veiny and dried out.

It had been posted nearly two hours earlier. There were already ten comments below, several were simply strings of upset emojis, but the rest were comments telling the troll to get a life, to crawl back into his cave, accusing him of ageism and misogyny.

Why hadn't Jenna hidden it? Sure, the comments were positive, but why would she let that sit there? She was so upset that this person was harassing her. She'd insisted he wasn't just an average troll. He was more sinister. He was a stalker, he was targeting her.

Then why let the comment sit there, attracting attention? She should have hidden it right away. Blocked him. After she took screen shots, of course, so she could report it.

If this was anyone else, Blythe would think they hadn't seen it. But Jenna always saw everything. It wasn't possible she hadn't noticed it this early in the evening. It was almost sick that she was allowing it to remain, gathering comments.

"Your turn," Garret said.

"Give me a minute."

"Blythe," he said.

"One minute."

She texted Jenna:

> Blythe: Don't know if you saw it, but the troll is back. His comment is getting a lot of activity. I thought you'd want to know so you can hide it ASAP.

When they finished the game, Blythe the winner, for the first time in a long while, she still hadn't heard back from Jenna.

CHAPTER 7

ANONYMOUS

*a*re we really all so needy? For attention, for affirmation? Social media came along and made us all addicts. Look at me. Look how good I look, look how much fun I'm having. Look how hot my husband, my wife, my girlfriend, my boyfriend is. Look at my gorgeous house, my cool car. Look at my adorable kids. Look at *me.*

What an amazing vacation I'm having! I'm traveling to Europe! Look at me in front of the Eiffel Tower, the Taj Mahal, the Sydney Opera House. Look at me backpacking, camping, eating out.

Oh, the eating out! The fabulous food, the elegant food. The sexy, seductive food. As if food is no longer meant to taste good, only to look stunning on a plate. Tiny morsels meant for a mouse, but so chic, the luscious colors, the breathtaking designs that rival Picasso's.

Look at the wine and the cocktails.

Look at my jewelry. My enormous diamond engagement ring sparkling in the sunlight.

I'm happy. I'm smart—see my graduation gown and my diploma from my elite school?

I'm not showing off! Not bragging. Not at all. I want you to share in my happiness. I'm just showing you the good times, sharing the joy. That's all. I want you to be happy for me. I'm happy for you. We're all so happy for each other.

See how many friends I have? See my beautiful family? We all adore each other.

This is our family reunion—forty-three of us at a fabulous house in the country, all dressed in blue. We're such a loving family. Look at the smiles on our faces, our arms around each other. We have it all!

We count our likes. So many likes, so many comments, so much positive feedback. Let me check again, and again, and *again*. Look at all my friends and family loving my happy life and telling me how happy they are for me. They love me so much, they like all the good things in my life. They laugh at my memes, they share my memes.

They cry with my sorrows and post their broken heart emojis.

It feels so, so good.

I didn't get as many likes as I thought I would.

Let me look again. A few more likes. It's late at night, I'll have more likes tomorrow. But now my post is buried. The algorithm moved on. Maybe someone will see it and like me more and then more people will see it and start liking it again. Maybe there's something else I can post. Another picture, more food, more memes, more happy times, more likes.

I'm not needy. It's fun. This is how I keep in touch with my friends and family. I can stay connected to that girl I met at the yoga retreat, reconnect with people who moved away. I can let people know about this thing I'm doing. If they're interested, they might want to buy this cool thing I made or listen to that podcast or attend this workshop or join this group. They might want to support this good cause. Maybe it will touch their heart like it did mine. Maybe they didn't see it, I'll just post it again. I'm just letting them know. It's a great way to spread the word.

But the algorithm didn't notice.

Wait, *this* time, it did! It noticed me. Everyone noticed me.

My pic went viral.

Her video became iconic.

What's the magic that makes it happen? There are classes and workshops in that. It's good to understand the human psyche. You never know when you're going to connect, hit a nerve, be in the right place at the right time.

Sometimes, it seems like we will stop at nothing to go viral.

CHAPTER 8

BLYTHE

*J*enna had never responded to Blythe's text. Since they were all meeting for lunch to celebrate Evie's forty-third birthday, maybe Blythe would hear more about the troll over the second glass of wine. Definitely she would hear more about it. Blythe and her friends never got together without discussing their entrepreneurial efforts. Part of that discussion always involved the constantly changing social media landscape and how to best keep up so they could use it to spotlight their business efforts.

Whenever Blythe thought about it, she was grateful for being alive at this time in history. It was exciting to be able to call your own shots with your career, to work for yourself, to take control and promote what you had to offer on a platform that allowed you to reach the entire world.

It was thrilling and challenging. Not that she could realistically get clients that were more than a twenty or thirty-minute drive from her home, but she was working on a plan for expanding virtually. Currently, she offered her services through in-person support at the gym and coaching sessions out of her home, but soon, she would be doing more through video calls and offering her availability in chat apps to provide constant encouragement. She was investigating whether she could join workout sessions through video without creating unnecessary liability.

The restaurant where they were meeting for Evie's lunch was so popular for the high-tech lunch crowd, Blythe had made the reservation three weeks ago. There was a small patio that had been set up for their group of five, separate from the main outdoor eating area. She'd stopped by earlier that morning to drop off a flower arrangement for the center of the table, and a single white rose to be placed on the napkin in front of each of her friends.

Her uncertainty around Lacey had faded. Sometimes, deciding how to view a situation was a choice. After the years of bullying she'd experienced as a child, she'd had nearly a year of therapy through the campus health center during her first year of college. It helped clean a lot of the bad stuff out of her head, and her heart.

One thing she'd learned was that bullying could set you up to interpret innocuous behavior as an attack because you were always on the lookout for it. Sometimes, other people's behavior wasn't about you. Much of the time, it wasn't about you. Everyone had issues.

They'd all been friends since their children were born, and they accepted each other as-is. That was the important thing to focus on. No one was sabotaging anyone.

Now, all five glasses were filled with pale white wine and they were raising them toward the center of the table. "Happy Birthday, Evie!"

Evie grinned. "You're the best. My perfect gifts."

They all took modest sips of wine and turned their attention to the menus.

After the food was ordered, and Evie had opened her gifts to *get that out of the way*, they ate sourdough bread and talked about their teenage children until their salads came.

"How is the podcast going?" Blythe asked.

"I'm blown away," Evie said. "I passed seven thousand listeners last week. It took almost fifteen years, but I feel pretty lucky." She grinned. "Seven thousand means one and one quarter new listeners every day for fifteen years. I wonder who all those quarter people are?" She put her finger on the side of her face and tapped it as if she were trying to picture what a quarter of a person looked like. "Do they even have one full ear?"

Blythe laughed. The others followed. She noticed that sometimes. They often followed her lead. She wasn't sure when that had started happening. It was a strange experience, feeling herself transformed from a child who was teased and shunned, to this. The kid who everyone made fun of to the woman everyone subtly glanced at to gauge her reaction.

Jenna complained about it all the time. *All* the time. She insisted Blythe needed to pay more attention to liking her posts immediately after they went up. *Everyone notices what you do. If you comment, if you post something serious or funny or heartfelt, they mimic you. Haven't you noticed? And that early boost gets things going so more people see it and interact with my content.*

Blythe hadn't noticed. Not until Jenna pointed it out. She honestly wasn't sure how she felt about it.

"It's a great podcast," Blythe said. "I follow your advice all the time."

"And you tell me that all the time," Evie said. "But thanks. I never get tired of hearing it."

"Me too," Lacey said. "I always wonder how you figured it out before us, since we all had our kids at the same time."

"I read a lot," Evie said. "And I talk to people. It's the interviews."

Their conversation veered back to kids for a while, as it often did. It didn't take much.

"How's Henry doing?" Evie asked Scarlett.

Scarlett's wide blue eyes grew teary for a moment. Her light, barely there freckles, darkened, then faded again. "He's good. I guess." She looked down at her plate. She picked up her water glass and took a large gulp. "It's one day at a time."

Henry was twelve, seven years younger than Cooper, Scarlett's son from her first short-lived marriage when she was barely twenty-one, and three years younger than Scarlett and Paul's daughter, Angela. Henry had had a violent rebellion at what everyone said was an extremely young age. First, abruptly refusing to play soccer anymore after an epic fit that seemed to erupt out of nowhere in the middle of a game.

This was followed by almost daily meltdowns over going to school. Scarlett and Paul investigated and hadn't been able to identify anything happening at school to cause his sudden hatred. Soon, he resisted leaving the house, viciously fighting against participating in family outings. He'd had a violent reaction when his father tried to photograph him with his step-brother on a family camping trip—attacking his father, tearing his shirt, pulling his hair, and finally, grabbing the phone and throwing it into the lake. He started refusing to visit his grandparents. One time, just as they were about to leave the house, he'd hidden in the hall closet and it was over half an hour before they found him.

They'd taken him to a child psychologist, but so far, they hadn't received any clear answers. The psychologist was baffled, which worried them further.

It probably wasn't the best way to fill the silence that settled over the table, but Blythe heard the words coming out of her mouth before she had time to consider how things might unfold. It was her first thought because it had been so close to the top of her mind, causing her to speak without thinking. "Did you get my text, Jenna? That troll was back and his comment on your last post was getting a lot of feedback."

Jenna said nothing.

Blythe looked up from her plate. Jenna was staring at her as if she had no idea what she was talking about. "Did you get—"

"I don't need a text to tell me someone is stalking me," Jenna said.

"Why didn't you hide it?"

"He keeps showing up under new names."

"That's why—"

"You have no idea how awful it feels." Jenna's voice trembled. "Why do you act like it's nothing?"

"Because it is. But you need to hide it."

"I had a troll," Scarlett said. "I took screen shots and reported it. They were able to—"

"I've done that and nothing changed," Jenna said.

"It takes a little while," Scarlett said. "Just be patient. And keep blocking."

Jenna blinked back tears. She picked up her wineglass and took a long swallow, emptying the glass. "Are we getting more wine, or what?"

"Since we're all driving ..." Evie glanced at her watch. "I'm ready for dessert." She flashed a grin at each one in turn and signaled their server for the dessert menus. "I feel like gelato."

"I'm on social media to promote my jewelry. Not get stalked!" Jenna said.

"We know," Lacey said. "We're all in this together."

"Don't get upset. It happens," Blythe said. "You can't let it get to you. But don't let the comment sit there and attract attention, unless that's what you want. It was boosting your post again."

"That's not what I want!" Jenna said. "I want people to buy my jewelry."

"But you did get attention, and that can lead to paying customers, right?" Blythe smiled.

Jenna picked up her wineglass and looked inside, appearing surprised it was empty, then upset that she couldn't find comfort there. She turned her head to the side and tucked her fine hair behind her ears, emphasizing her narrow face, making herself look vulnerable and almost childlike, her eyes wide and slightly panicked.

CHAPTER 9

*S*carlett's workout had gone well. She could now bench-press fifty pounds. Seeing the confident look on her face filled Blythe with satisfaction. This was the best part of her job—when a woman's desire to change the shape of her body slipped into second place, and then left her mind altogether, replaced by a sense of power that came from the knowledge that she was growing stronger, that she was capable and in control of herself.

When that happened, her clients spent less time glancing at the mirror and more time paying attention to the position of their hands to ensure they were maintaining the correct grip on the bars. They focused on proper form, their thoughts oriented toward the endorphin-infused thrill of working out rather than the results.

"You're quiet today," Blythe said.

Scarlett smiled but didn't meet her gaze. She picked up her towel and wiped down the bench.

"Everything okay?" Blythe asked.

Scarlett ran her finger along her hairline, then looked at her fingertip, checking for perspiration. As she opened her mouth to speak, Evie walked toward them, wrapping her waist-long blonde hair into a complicated knot as she moved closer.

"Not really," Scarlett said.

"Not really, what?" Evie said.

"Not really *okay*."

Evie glanced at Blythe and back at Scarlett, as if trying to decide whether she was welcome in the middle of a conversation already in progress.

"Henry?" Blythe asked.

"Paul." Scarlett let out a shrill laugh. "If it's not one of my boys, it's another, right? But it's not really funny."

Evie moved away from the bench press and began stretching. "What's wrong?"

"These dog pictures he's posting are getting out of control. He's posting like ten or fifteen a day." She looked like she wanted to cry.

"He's been doing that forever," Evie said. "What's wrong with it?"

"I know. But ... you don't think it's ... weird?"

Evie stretched her arms overhead, then leaned to the side. "No. Lacey posts more than once a day. So does Jenna."

"Ten or fifteen times?! It seems needy. Or something."

"He has twelve-thousand followers. I guess people like it," Evie said. "It's fun."

"Everyone loves dogs," Blythe said.

"But he's looking at it all the time, responding to comments, taking pictures, scoping out the neighborhood for dogs, fiddling with his phone."

"He's always posted lots of pictures on social media," Evie said. "I wouldn't worry about it. People love it. Remember when he used to post pictures of Cooper and Henry all the time? It was adorable."

"Until it wasn't because they got older," Scarlett said.

"So now he does the dogs. And who doesn't love dogs?" Evie laughed.

"We should get started," Blythe said.

"You don't think it's strange? What would you think if your husband was constantly posting pictures and always talking about what he was going to post next, organizing his pictures, watching for comments, figuring out what kind of shots get the most likes?"

"That's what we all do," Blythe said.

"But we're running a business," Scarlett said.

"It's *social* media," Evie said. "He's using it the right way." She laughed. "He's being social."

"They're not even our dogs!" Scarlett's voice was shrill. A woman using the free weights turned to look at them, then quickly turned away.

Blythe laughed. She hadn't meant to, but Scarlett sounded so deeply concerned, and yet also a little ridiculous, getting so upset about dogs.

"It feels ... I don't know. A little creepy? Stalker-ish?"

Evie laughed even louder. The woman at the dumbbell rack paused mid-curl, but didn't turn. Evie put her hand over her mouth. "Sorry. I shouldn't laugh. But it does sound funny. You can't stalk a dog. Can you?"

"Doesn't it seem invasive?" Scarlett asked. "Or wrong, somehow? Taking pictures of other people's dogs and posting them without permission?"

"Maybe," Blythe said. "Are you sure he doesn't have permission? Or maybe people are flattered."

"I don't know," Scarlett said. "Maybe he asks. I'm not sure, actually." She twisted her towel into a coil. "I should ... well ..."

Blythe patted her arm. "Try not to worry. It's fine. It makes him happy. People really do love it. Dogs are fun, and everyone likes seeing them. There's nothing strange about it."

Despite her reassuring words, she felt Scarlett was even more upset when she left. It seemed as if there might be something more that she hadn't said.

CHAPTER 10

FIFTEEN YEARS AGO: BLYTHE

Sitting on yoga mats in pre-natal class, all of them leaning against their husbands as they practiced breathing, Blythe had felt as if she'd made friends for life. Made friends, and re-captured an old friend.

Scarlett and Paul were so excited to have a child together. Scarlett had a seven-year-old son from her first marriage. An adorable little boy whom Paul doted on, posting photographs of him on social media non-stop. Cooper was a heart-throb. He had blonde hair that looked white in the sunlight and the most stunning blue eyes. There wasn't a single photograph in which that child didn't look like an absolute angel. He had a charming smile and always seemed to be looking directly into your eyes.

Paul's sister was a professional photographer, so some of the images were breathtaking. He was an outgoing kid, and Paul often added entertaining views of the world through a child's eyes.

Lacey and Miles lived only a few blocks from Garret and Blythe. They'd known each other since they'd bought the house. Blythe met Lacey at a coffee shop and they'd started talking. When they both got pregnant within weeks of each other, Lacey recommended the pre-natal class.

Blythe and Lacey connected right away with Scarlett, probably because she was the one who asked the most questions, and every question she posed was one Blythe and Lacey also had on their minds.

And then there were Evie and Isaac. To be honest, Blythe wondered if they were initially drawn to Evie because she was stunning—all that long blonde hair and a smile that made everyone feel as if she was in love with the whole world, and the best part of her day was seeing you. They kept staring at Evie, and to keep themselves from looking like stalker-ish freaks, they quickly introduced themselves. Soon, the four women were sitting near each other and talking as if they'd known each other for years, as pregnancy often does.

And Jenna. That had been like something out of a movie. Blythe wouldn't have believed it if she hadn't lived through it.

Jenna and Blythe had been friends in junior high and the early part of high school. Then Jenna vanished. She disappeared from Blythe's school and her life as if she'd never existed. Not a phone call or an email. Text messaging was still in its early days, and most teenagers didn't have phones.

It hurt so badly, it was part of what later drove Blythe into therapy.

Then, as if she was in a feel-good movie, one afternoon, she'd pulled a pair of maternity leggings off the rack. She held them up, turned, and nearly collided with a woman who also looked to be about six months pregnant, just as interested in the leggings as Blythe was.

The woman smiled, and Blythe realized, despite her slightly darker hair and eyes that consumed even more of her face than Blythe remembered, she was looking at her childhood friend. Jenna must have realized the same at the identical moment, because her lips parted and an inarticulate sound came out of her that somehow made absolute sense to Blythe.

Blythe flung the pants over the rack, and they wrapped their arms around each other. When they let go and stepped back to study each other's faces, their cheeks were wet with tears.

"What happened?" Blythe asked.

"It's a long story," Jenna said. "Very long."

They both bought two pairs of leggings—navy blue and dark green. They hurried out of the store and went to lunch, where they sat for three hours, drinking endless cups of herbal tea, talking about the years in-between. Jenna now lived with her husband, Oliver, about three miles from Blythe and Garret.

Blythe invited Jenna to the pre-natal class, and they became a group of five.

The men all seemed to get along. They recognized the inevitable. And they had plenty to talk about as well—the unknowns of first-time fatherhood. The thing that everyone tells you all about but you can't begin to comprehend the reality of until that child, or in Garret and Blythe's case, children, are placed on your belly for bonding and the world changes forever.

When all their babies were hurtling toward the six-month mark, most of their mothers getting a few solid hours of sleep every night, all of them proficient at infant care and opinionated about every aspect, discussing the details as if they were worthy of a G7 Summit, Evie announced she was starting a parenting podcast.

"You're an expert on parenting after five months?" Lacey asked.

"Absolutely not," Evie said. "That's the point. I'll talk about how I know almost nothing. I'll talk about how terrifying it is to be entrusted with the most important responsibility on the planet, then told to learn as I go." She chuckled and shifted Ben to her other hip, picked up her water bottle, and took a sip. "I think being honest about how scary it is, sharing my mistakes, and mixing it up with interviews with child psychologists, teachers, nutritionists, and other experts will be really interesting. And fun. And I'll learn more."

As she talked, the rest of them began to reveal secret dreams of wanting to do a bit more. All of them had been lucky enough to stay home and care for their infants, but none of them were in a position that an extra income wouldn't be useful. Besides, they wanted more. Something for themselves.

"We can get the word out on social media," Evie said. "It's free. It's an awesome way to share what we're doing."

"We'll have each other's backs," Lacey said.

"Always. Because we have each other's backs as moms," Scarlett said. "Social media is turning the entire planet into a community. It's connecting everyone. It's building stronger communities and bringing people closer together. People are finding old friends from childhood and high school, and family members they'd lost touch with. It's really amazing. And what a great way to share the things we want to do."

"Is it?" Lacey asked.

"Is it, what?" Scarlett asked.

"Is it making us closer? Making us a global community? Aren't human beings the same on social media as we are in real life? The same online as we are offline?"

"People share happy things. It brings out the best in us. They share fun pictures and good times. It makes us better."

"If you say so," Lacey said.

Blythe wanted to shiver. It was too awful to think about the horrors of the world being mirrored in social media. She avoided meeting anyone's gaze, but she didn't have to. There was a feeling in the room that suggested everyone was experiencing the same chill from Lacey's words, all of them holding their children closer, trying to get warm, to keep them safe.

CHAPTER 11

NOW: BLYTHE

*A*fter spending most of the day at the gym, eating a quinoa salad she'd packed, and meeting two more clients after Scarlett and Evie, Blythe wanted to be outdoors. She craved natural air and sunlight and whatever sounds the world wanted to throw her way, even if it wasn't simply the sound of the wind moving through trees and the chatter of birds, but the hum of traffic and the intermittent, grating intrusion of leaf blowers. No more high-energy music thumping through speakers and slightly too-cold forced air that made her hands so dry her rings spun around her fingers, riding over her knuckles.

It was cool enough to work in the garden, so she abandoned her dinner plans and placed an advanced order for Chinese food to be delivered at six-thirty.

She put on her gardening gloves, got her tools out of the garage, and went to work. It felt good to creep around in the dirt, pulling slender weeds before they became troublesome, plucking off dead leaves and blossoms, clipping the larger dead branches and vines, and clearing out the leaves that had fallen and blown in from nearby trees.

By the time she was finished, her shoulders and knees ached.

She went inside, drank a glass of water, then opened a bottle of white wine for dinner.

She took a shower and checked on Kelsey and Kate, who were playing games on their tablets. She preferred they would be outside on a spectacular summer afternoon, but neither one was overly addicted to their screens, so she tried not to make comments when they chose to shut out the world from time to time. They were significantly happier and more balanced than she'd been at their age.

In the living room, she curled up on the corner of the sofa and picked up her phone. She opened her social media accounts. Her bikini photo had a new comment. That was strange after all this time.

The moment she tapped on it, she felt as if someone had punched her hard in the chest, forcing the air out of her lungs.

Such a hot MILF. I'd like to give you a workout. What do you charge?

She dropped her phone onto the sofa and tried to breathe normally. Just as quickly, she grabbed the phone again. She tapped to hide the comment, but her hand was shaking. Instead, she hit the commenter's profile. The image was of a sports car. An obvious troll —following twenty-three accounts, no followers. She returned to her page, took a screenshot to file on her laptop, just in case, and hid the comment before blocking him.

For the first time ever, she hated the hiding feature. She wanted to delete each ugly word. She wanted to pluck the comment off the screen and tear it to shreds, flushing it down the toilet. She wasn't sure why she'd taken the screen shot and saved it. Just in case ... what? In case it happened again? In case it got worse? She shivered.

Her fingers shook as she returned to the main feed. She felt queasy. She was still having trouble breathing normally. Part of her wanted to hurl the phone at the bifold doors across from her, with a twisted desire to hear the resounding crack of glass. It was disgusting that people had nothing better to do with their lives than write horrible things on strangers' social media posts. What did they get out of it? Surely they knew they were instantly hidden and blocked. It hardly seemed worth the effort.

It was the same with the men who followed her, and her friends, claiming to be members of the *military* and *physicians, teachers* and *entrepreneurs*. All of them were *dog owners*. All of them *loved the outdoors*. Some of them claimed to be single dads, posting heart-warming pictures with their *children*, beside the pictures of them working out or sitting behind the wheel of a nice car. Many were more blatant, flaunting bare-chested photos. They all told Blythe and her friends they looked *nice*, they had *nice smiles*, did they want to be *friends?*

Why? Were there women who actually responded to those obvious fakes and trolls and worse? Maybe it was like playing the lottery or direct mail. Or roulette.

She let the screen of her phone go dark. She'd lost her desire to look at anything else.

Jenna's complaints about a stalker over the past few weeks flooded her mind. She felt guilty for the way she'd brushed it off, telling Jenna how to handle it as if the words themselves meant nothing. But Jenna hadn't mentioned any comments this degrading, had she? Blythe couldn't remember. She hadn't paid close enough attention.

She left her phone on the end table and went into the kitchen. She put out plates, napkins, and chopsticks. Garret would be home soon, dinner would be here. She poured a small glass of wine for herself. She needed it. She deserved it. When Garret heard about this, he would ... what would he say? The question was—would she tell him? She couldn't predict how he would react. He didn't care much for social media. He thought it was superficial. He didn't think she needed to use it as frequently as she did to promote her business.

Less is more, was his favorite mantra. He acted as if the algorithm, demanding—*Feed me or become invisible*—didn't exist.

She took a sip of wine. What she really wanted was to forget it had happened. She wanted those words to fade and evaporate into nothing. She wanted them out of her memory entirely. But because of that disgusting acronym, she had a feeling it was going to be a long time before she escaped the filthy sensation she had from reading it. The disgust and unwarranted sense of shame that made her feel as if she'd done something wrong.

She hated that creep, whoever he was. She'd done nothing wrong!

There was nothing sexy or provocative about that bathing suit or the photograph. She was an attractive woman who helped other women get into good physical condition, to feel comfortable with their bodies. She was strong and fit and she wanted to show, in the clearest way possible, that her approach worked.

Sure, she could have posed in a sports bra and spandex shorts. But she'd thought this would be a fun thing to do at the start of summer, something more casual and less about working out, more about enjoying life. It sickened her that someone had turned it into this. It wasn't fair!

She finished the glass of wine and followed it with a few sips of cold water. She stood by the window, gazing out at the backyard.

The wine had calmed her, slightly. She'd over-reacted. She was doing exactly what she'd advised Jenna not to do. It wasn't personal. He was a creep on the internet trying to get a reaction out of her. She needed to follow her own advice. And she had. She'd hidden the comment and blocked the troll, if he was even real. It was probably a bot, trying to get her to respond, to click on the profile, follow a link, and get caught in a phishing scam. Or a bored teenager, or a creep addicted to porn who hoped to find a woman to have a cyber-relationship with. She'd already given it far too much energy and space inside her head. Time to move on.

She finished the water.

A moment later, she heard the garage door open and Garret's car pull into his space. He didn't need to know about this. All he would do was connect it to Jenna and urge Blythe to be more sympathetic. And she certainly didn't want Kelsey and Kate thinking about things like this. It was likely her daughters knew more about this kind of garbage than she did. If so, she didn't want their suggestions. She was done with it.

She put wineglasses on the table, ran her fingers through her hair to lift it away from the sides of her face, and stretched her arms over her head.

When Garret walked into the kitchen, she felt better, as if it had never happened. A few minutes later, the doorbell rang. Their dinner was brought into the house on a wave of fabulous aromas, and they ate without anyone saying a word about social media.

At two o'clock in the morning, Blythe woke suddenly, feeling as if it were six o'clock and the sun was glowing around the edges of the bedroom blinds. The comment from the troll blazed across her mind like a neon sign, word-for-word, as if she'd read it only a moment ago. She heard the words as if someone were shouting them in her ears, a crude, growling voice delighting in her fear.

The worst part of running a home business was that strangers knew where she lived. She couldn't promote what she did without giving some indication of her location. They might not know the name of her street and the house number, but she'd freely mentioned the name of her city. She was trying to attract clients who lived locally. What else was she supposed to do? The name and location of her gym were public knowledge.

It was an easy Google search to find her home address.

Although she knew it was not the right thing for optimal sleep, and she usually tried very hard to avoid the practice, she got out of bed, went into the hallway, and took her phone off the charger on the shelf outside their bedroom. She sat on the bench that was positioned under a long, narrow window and unlocked the screen.

Notifications were silenced at night, so she had a chance to change her mind, to return, even now, to peaceful sleep, but she ignored the quiet nudge to put the phone back. She felt a sharp, stabbing pain in her stomach, so strong, she groaned softly and bent over.

There were fifty new comments on the bikini post. They were from three different user names. She didn't bother tapping the profiles. She knew they would have zero followers and the bios would be nonsense. All of them made rude comments about some aspect of her appearance—her body, her swimsuit, her age, her face. They made assumptions about her life and her behavior. Several asked her to post more bikini pics, suggesting she get a less conservative swimsuit.

She wanted to cry. She wanted to scream. Chinese food roiled and lurched in the pit of her stomach, rising like a threatening storm. It took her nearly fifteen minutes to take screen shots so she could report it, then hide and block all of them. Her thumbs shook as she fumbled with her phone, tears blinding her.

CHAPTER 12

*B*lythe had meant to tell Garret about the troll before they got out of bed, but because it had taken her until nearly four a.m. to fall back to sleep, he'd been up and showered before she'd woken. She hadn't felt consciousness creep over her until she heard the bedroom door, then opened her eyes to see him stepping into the hallway, closing the door softly behind him.

She got up quickly, brushed her teeth, and threw on her robe. She needed to talk to him before he left for work. She couldn't let this fester in the pit of her stomach all day, and she wasn't ready to talk to her friends about it. Although she knew it wasn't personal, it felt utterly personal. It felt as if someone had crept inside her house and was watching her pose beside her own swimming pool.

In the kitchen, Garret had already ground the beans and was pouring water into the coffeemaker. She got out two mugs, then moved up behind him. She leaned her head against his back, pressing the side of her face into his spine. It felt solid and calming, but still the nightmare, the waking horror of the early morning hours, churned inside her. The sour feeling in her stomach made her doubt she could endure more than a few sips of coffee, even though the aroma now filling the kitchen was inviting.

Garret turned and put his arms around her, kissed her forehead, then pulled away. "I need to get moving."

She had to talk fast. Once he was focused on starting his day, his mind was elsewhere and his answers would be quick and perfunctory.

"I got some trolling comments on that picture I posted of myself in my swimsuit."

"Not a surprise." He laughed and tapped her nose with his forefinger. He moved toward the fridge, his back toward her again.

"A *lot* of comments. And they were really ... crude. Some of them—"

"I thought people were pretty nice in the health coaching corner of social media." He pulled open the door and took out a carton of milk. He went to the cabinet for the granola.

"They're really upsetting. I feel—"

"What did they say?"

She filled both coffee mugs. Now that he'd asked, she didn't want to repeat any of them. She wasn't even sure she wanted to give him a sense of what they'd said. Although they remained lodged in her skull, every single word, she didn't feel she could speak them. It would make them more real, give them more power. It might make them more memorable.

And once Garret heard them, would they linger in his thoughts?

He sat at the bar and began eating his granola. She placed a mug of coffee in front of him.

"What kind of comments?" He asked.

"Just really crude and ugly stuff about my body and ... things."

"Are you going to tell me what they said or not?" he asked.

"What who said?"

Blythe turned. Kate and Kelsey stood in the doorway.

What were they doing up so early? It was summer. It was difficult to get them up on time when they had to get out the door for school. Now, it seemed as if they'd sensed a conversation they wanted to be part of, something they could offer opinions about.

Some drama to feed their summer days that were becoming too much the same.

"Nothing."

"I don't think so," Kelsey said. "When you say *nothing*, it's guaranteed to be something."

"A troll on your mom's social media," Garret said.

"I wasn't going to—"

"Oh, that," Kate said. "I saw that." She shuddered and made a face.

"Block the creeper. Report him," Kelsey said.

"I did."

Kate went to the fridge and grabbed individual bottles of OJ for herself and her sister. She handed one to Kelsey.

"Then what's the problem?" Kelsey asked.

"He keeps doing it. New profile names. At least I assume it's the same person. All the comments sound the same. I can't believe how many comments he manages in such a short time."

"They're fast." Kate pried off the cap and gulped her juice.

"It's a little scary, to be honest," Blythe said.

"That's how he wants you to feel," Kelsey said.

"Just delete the picture." Garret slid off the stool, took his bowl to the sink, and rinsed it.

"I don't want to delete it!" She hated that her voice was so shrill. She sounded unhinged. "Then he wins. It's my page. A random stranger shouldn't be controlling what I do and how I feel."

"Then don't let him," Kate said.

"But I—"

"Deleting it is the easiest thing," Garret said. "It doesn't mean he wins anything. Just get rid of it and move on. Maybe it was too provocative."

"It's not right." Her voice was even louder, but she couldn't control it. This wasn't how it was supposed to work. "There are a lot of great comments on there. Twenty or thirty clients who love what I've done for them wrote really good things about working with me, about how supportive I am, about how great they feel. I would lose all of that positive momentum."

"It's not the only place you have good reviews," Garret said.

"That's not the point. Besides, it's the most recent. Fresh comments matter."

Garret pressed his lips together, then spoke carefully. "Post something new. How about—"

"It's not the *point*!"

"Then just keep blocking and hiding," Kate said. "He'll give up."

"I gotta get going." Garret walked around the center island. He gulped the rest of his coffee and placed his mug on the counter. "Kiss?"

Blythe wasn't even sure what she wanted from him. She leaned into him, turning her head to the side so she could hear the thud of his heart. She wanted him to feel how violated she felt, but she didn't want to delete the post. She wanted his outrage to match her own, but she didn't want him telling her what to do, and she didn't like how he made it sound so easy. As if the solution was simple and had no impact.

She kissed him goodbye.

When he was gone, Kelsey and Kate seemed to think the drama of the conversation had ended. They wandered out of the room without offering any more advice. That was fine with her. She didn't want any more. She was not deleting the post.

It wasn't fair, and it wasn't right that a troll could bully her into taking down her photograph and destroying all those positive comments along with it. People had put time and effort into sharing their experiences. It was insulting to them as well.

Knowing her family, and their general lack of interest in the ups and downs of using social media to promote her business, they would forget about this conversation by evening. A few days from now, Garret might ask if she'd managed to rid herself of the troll, but that was it.

She would leave the picture and try to put it out of her mind. At the same time, she would have to remain vigilant in hiding any additional disgusting comments until, as Kate said, he gave up. Hopefully, that would happen soon. Maybe today.

CHAPTER 13

JENNA

*J*enna watched the pale brown sugar crystals slide from the tube into her coffee, mesmerized by the way they dissolved instantly, as if they'd never existed. That's how she felt with some of her social media posts. A beautiful thought she'd held in her mind, put out into the world, instantly obliterated by the heat of too much human activity. Or something like that.

She, Evie, and Blythe sat at a round table in the coffee shop they'd been going to for so long, they'd watched the owner's daughter grow from a baby kicking her feet in a carrier behind the counter to a young woman who was now working part-time as a barista in her mom's shop.

It made Jenna feel like there was continuity in the world, hope for the future. It was absurd to pin hope for the future on a child who had grown up inhaling the scent of coffee and now made espresso drinks after school and during the summer break, but for some reason she couldn't put her finger on, it made Jenna feel secure. Maybe she liked the obvious connection between the shop owner and her daughter, the sense that they were working as a team, that they loved each other, and the normal teenage fights didn't seem to interfere with their common goal to make the shop and its array of home-baked goods successful.

"Something horrible happened," Blythe said.

"Are the girls okay?" Evie's expression shifted from her usual breezy calm to one of worry.

"Yes, sorry. I shouldn't open with hysterics." Blythe gave a short laugh. "We're fine. There's a creep making rude comments on that picture I posted of myself by our pool."

"Aww. That was so cute," Evie said.

"It was nice," Jenna agreed. She felt her breath grow shallow, wondering what Blythe would say next, wondering if she'd be more sympathetic now, if she'd apologize for being so dismissive when Jenna had complained about being stalked.

"It's disgusting. Really rude comments. And so many." Blythe laughed bitterly. "It's not funny, not at all, but you can't imagine how many comments this creeper has made. I've almost lost count."

"More than ten?" Evie asked.

Blythe laughed so hard, coffee sloshed out of her cup onto the saucer a few inches below. She lowered the cup onto the saucer. "Closer to seventy-five or eighty."

Evie gasped. "Eighty? Did you report it?"

"Yes."

"What did they say?"

"You know how that goes. It takes time. They're *investigating*. I'm not that hopeful. I'm sure all the screen names will be long gone by the time they get around to checking."

"I'm so sorry," Evie said.

Jenna felt her throat tighten. Had Evie said she was sorry when Jenna was stalked? She didn't think so. Maybe she'd forgotten, she wasn't sure. She needed to be careful not to overreact. Everyone adored Blythe. She always got more attention. It wasn't good to read too much into it.

"They probably won't do anything," Blythe said.

"No, probably not." Evie took a bite of her scone.

"Garret thought I should delete the pic, but I feel like they win if I do that."

"Probably," Evie said.

They both looked at Jenna, as if this were an election and it was her role to cast the deciding vote.

"Who knows how someone like that thinks?" Jenna said. "It's like my stalker."

"I don't know if I'd call him a *stalker*," Blythe said. "That's more—"

"It feels like a stalker, when they're personally attacking you, and your business."

"That's true," Blythe agreed. "But I'm trying really hard not to overreact."

"That's good," Evie said. "You can't feed them, can't let him know he got to you. They want you to be scared, want you to be upset. The worst thing you can do is show that."

"How do you know what they want?" asked Jenna.

"That's who trolls are, at their core," Evie said.

She made it sound as if she were an authority on the subject, an expert who'd studied trolls extensively and was qualified to advise Blythe and Jenna on their psychological profiles.

"Are you an expert on internet bullies?" Jenna asked.

"All bullies are the same. Cowards."

"Everyone says that." Jenna picked up her cup and blew on her coffee. She could feel the heat coming off the surface. Still too hot. She held it in front of her, longing for it to cool so she could take a sip. "But I'm not sure anyone knows that for a fact. And it's really scary when a stranger attacks you on social media. You can't see their face, and even if you do, you don't know if it's their real face."

"That's because they're *cowards*," Evie said.

"I'd really like to believe that," Blythe said.

"Then do. Ignore it and don't let it get under your skin."

"You have to be careful," Jenna said. "Someone could really hurt you. Not taking it seriously is a mistake."

"I am taking it seriously," Blythe said. "That's why—"

"You didn't delete the post like Garret suggested," Jenna said.

"Because it's not fair that I should lose all those positive comments. I don't want him to win."

"I just hope it's not a mistake," Jenna said.

"I'm not going to live in fear. Social media is supposed to be fun."

"Good for you," Evie said.

"Don't you think a little healthy fear can be a good thing?" Jenna asked.

Neither one answered her question. After that, Evie deliberately changed the subject. It was so deliberate, it was almost embarrassing. It seemed as if they wanted to silence her. Evie certainly did. Why was it considered a flaw to be afraid of something scary? Blythe was right to be afraid of the comments. She should listen to Garret's advice. Why was she being so stubborn?

Later, at home, Jenna's feeling of anxiety increased. She spent three hours working on a series of beaded bracelets. The beads were so delicate, she needed a jeweler's loupe to see the holes to string them onto the fine cord. Each one had three sterling silver charms. It was part of what made the costs go up, but it also made them distinctive. When she was finished, she arranged them on an ash board that made the lightest pieces of jewelry stand out.

Often, she took her photographs on her own wrists, but sometimes she thought potential customers wanted to imagine the bracelets circling their own arms and she didn't want her skin tone or her bone structure or her hands interfering with their fantasies.

She posted the picture with a short comment about how bracelets could make you feel dressed up even if you were wearing jeans and a T-shirt. She waited five minutes, but there were no immediate reactions. That wasn't good. If the *likes* and *loves* and comments didn't appear right away, it meant the post would sink quickly in the non-stop flood of images.

She should have taken the time to set up her tripod and created a video. Or maybe done a rapid series of six or seven images to create a reel with music. She sighed and checked again. One like.

Why couldn't Blythe and her other friends do as they'd promised and have her back? Had their enthusiasm for supporting each other faded over the years, or was that her imagination? It wasn't that they didn't like her posts. They always did, eventually. She would have to dig deep to find one that any of them had missed. But sometimes they weren't as on top of it as she would like. Especially Blythe. If she liked it first, the others followed quickly. But too often, she took her sweet time about it.

When Jenna was finished cleaning up her workspace, she had ten likes, but nothing from Blythe. Scarlett had liked it and commented. It had now been twenty minutes. Where was Blythe? This was so frustrating. Sales were down.

Every night, as soon as Naomi left the dinner table, Oliver updated her on the uncertainty of his job. The evening before, he'd said he thought he had a forty percent chance of being caught in the layoffs that were coming soon.

"Did Ben *tell* you it was forty percent?"

"No."

"How can you say that?"

"It's my gut feeling."

His response twisted her stomach into a knot, making her wish she hadn't eaten dinner at all. When she refilled their wineglasses, Oliver had raised his eyebrows slightly, but he hadn't said anything.

Without thinking, knowing she was being too impulsive, fully aware she should walk away from her phone and distract herself with something else, she snapped a selfie. She surely looked as frightened as she felt. Still aware of what a mistake it was, she posted the photo and tapped in a caption—*Social media isn't always a friendly place. The trolls win more than they should. Why can't the good guys win?*

She immediately had three likes, which felt nice, but still nothing from Blythe and nothing from any of her other friends.

Leaving her phone on the worktable, promising herself she wouldn't look for the next thirty minutes, she walked down the hall to the kitchen, passing Naomi's closed bedroom door. Cooper was in there again. She heard music playing and the sound of their voices. All was good. In the kitchen, she poured a small glass of wine and took a sip. She removed the chicken breasts from the fridge and began pounding them for piccata.

When Oliver arrived home, she was on her second, small, glass of wine. He kissed her, took a rather large drink from her wineglass, and asked how her day had been.

She shrugged.

"I saw Cooper's truck out front."

She nodded.

He left the kitchen. A moment later, she heard him knocking on Naomi's bedroom door. She sighed when she heard Oliver's voice. It carried down the hallway, raised to be heard over the music and through the closed door. "We're about to have dinner, Coop. Time to head home."

Why couldn't he relax? If he thought he was being chill, he was not. The kids saw right through his forced friendliness, and the nickname for Cooper that no-one else used.

Dinner was quiet. Naomi was sour over the interruption to her afternoon, and Oliver was gloomy about whatever had happened at work. Jenna didn't even want to ask. Despite the wine, she was frustrated and more than a little annoyed with the results of her social media efforts. The bracelet post had received seventy-five likes and ten comments. The selfie about the trolls had over three hundred likes so far, forty-something comments, and crickets from Blythe.

After she and Oliver cleaned up the kitchen, she retreated to her workroom. She texted Blythe.

> Jenna: Are you mad at me? Why didn't you comment on my post about the trolls? I'm trying to support you now that you're being stalked too!

Blythe didn't respond until nine fifteen.

Blythe: Not mad. Busy. I honestly don't want to give attention to trolls. I'm not sure why you posted that. And I'm not being stalked. It's a troll.

Jenna felt like crying. Why was Blythe so cold to her sometimes? She didn't understand it.

CHAPTER 14

BLYTHE

*B*lythe had ignored Jenna's post about the trolls, because it honestly felt like Jenna was feeding the troll. She wasn't even sure if it was the same creep harassing Jenna who was now making disgusting comments on her photo. She hadn't bothered to look at the screen names. What did it matter? They kept changing the names. She wasn't even sure there was only one person harassing her. For all she knew, the disgusting comments attracted more creeps, and they started piling on.

Besides, she was tired of thinking about it.

She'd already been irritated with Jenna when they'd had coffee together. It had felt as if Jenna was trying to stir things up, as if she *wanted* Blythe to be afraid. Misery loves company. Jenna had been over-reacting for weeks, turning someone who was probably nothing more than a weird teenager who liked harassing adult women into someone more sinister by labeling him a stalker. And now she wanted Blythe fixated on it—a perverted way of bonding. Blythe refused to make a career out of worrying about the worst side of human nature.

She would have thought Jenna, of all people, would not give bullies more power than they deserved.

When she'd seen Jenna's comment about trolls winning, she'd

closed her apps and vowed not to look at social media for the rest of the evening. Then Jenna texted her. After replying to Jenna's text, she turned off her phone. It was all too much.

Even though it was a weeknight, she suggested a family movie night. It was summer, weeknights and weekends ran together for the twins. She made guacamole, opened a bag of tortilla chips, and the four of them sat on the sofa. They laughed and rolled their eyes through a comedy that was funny, if also a little ridiculous. It had been a perfect escape.

But now, she lay in bed, unable to sleep.

Maybe Garret was right. She was addicted to social media. She wasn't looking at it, but she couldn't stop thinking about it. The desire to know whether there were more comments scratched at her brain like rats scurrying around inside her skull. The image made her scalp itch. She turned on her side. She curled the pillow around her head, trying to make it stop.

She turned onto her back and placed her hands on her belly, taking a long slow breath, feeling the air enter her lungs, trying to focus on nothing but its movement in and out of her body like they taught in yoga. Ignoring her efforts, the thoughts continued to twist around inside her head. She wanted to scream.

After several more attempts at deep, slow breaths, she flipped onto her other side. She touched Garret's arm, stroking it softly. She ran her hand across his chest. She could wake him, start making love to him. That would calm her. But she could also imagine herself screaming silently inside her head, annoyed at the touch of his hands as her body continued refusing to relax and her thoughts kept their grip on what was happening inside her phone and out there on the internet—strangers clamoring for her attention.

She threw off the covers and climbed out of bed. She walked out of the room, closing the door softly behind her. She took her phone downstairs, got a glass of water, and curled up on the sofa.

This was a terrible mistake. It would make her night worse. Whatever she found here was going to destroy her sleep for hours, if not for the rest of the night. Everything she'd enjoyed about social media was now tainted with those disgusting comments. And so many of them. How did someone even think of that many horrible things to say? Even if there were no more comments from the troll, she was likely to find complaining text messages from Jenna.

She powered on her phone and waited.

Jenna hadn't sent any more texts, but her post about the troll had generated a lot of activity. Blythe hoped Jenna was happy about that, because she'd succeeded in burying her own photograph of her bracelets.

Her fingers trembled as she tapped her notifications. Twenty.

All of them were for the bikini photo.

Every single one was a disgusting comment about the photograph. There weren't any likes, just a long string of horrible comments from three different profile names that were nothing but a series of letters and numbers. She tried not to read every word of the comments as she made her way down the list, hiding each one. It had been a mistake to ignore it all evening because they'd been sitting there for hours.

Tears trickled down her cheeks as the words flickered past, asking for more thrilling photos, complaining she wasn't showing enough skin. How many people had seen these? She didn't want to think about it. Most people probably didn't read all the comments, so it didn't matter. Maybe no one had seen them. But she didn't know that, and it felt awful. She felt exposed and defeated. Suddenly, she no longer owned her profile or her photograph or anything about her online presence.

Garret was right. She should delete the photo. But that was so unfair. It was utterly and completely un-*fair*. Why couldn't these companies do anything to stop this?! They had all this technology, all this software, all these algorithms. Why was it so easy to set up new profiles with no other purpose than to harass innocent people? She shouldn't have to be dealing with this.

This was the public face of her business!

Sure, it was free. She had no right to complain about apps that were free to use. She'd been given the opportunity to promote her business for free. She'd taken advantage of that for years, so how could she complain? But it was still wrong. On some grand, cosmic scale of right and wrong, and how the world was supposed to work, it was wrong.

But of course, the world didn't work the way it was supposed to. It was filled with horrible things and bad people. And now one, or more, had latched onto her. Whether it was karma or chance or something else, she had no idea. But she still believed, despite all the things she'd lived through, that the best approach was ignoring it.

She was not deleting the picture.

There was no point telling Garret about it, and she was not breathing a word about this to Kelsey or Kate, who would both tell her she was being ridiculous. The success of her coaching business did not hang on the continuing presence of a single photograph of her in a swimsuit. But taking it down meant she was giving her power to a faceless stranger. She refused to do that.

To comfort herself further, she went into the kitchen and poured half a shot of vodka into a nice glass over two ice cubes. She cut two pieces of soft cheese and placed them on flatbread. She carried her snack to the living room and enjoyed it in the semi-darkness. She left her phone face down on the coffee table and didn't check it again before she returned to bed.

In the morning, she didn't get her phone as soon as she got out of bed, which was her usual habit. She took a long shower and dressed for the day. She went downstairs, grabbed her phone from the living room, and made a pot of coffee.

When she looked at her notifications, her heart began racing so fast, it felt as if the aroma of the coffee filling the kitchen had already infused her veins with three shots of espresso. She closed her eyes and put her hand on her heart as if it were possible to slow its furious beating. She wanted to scream. She was thankful Garret hadn't come down yet. At the same time, she wanted to collapse into his arms, sobbing.

She shoved the phone into her pocket and went outside, trying to think about what she was going to do, trying to decide how serious this was, even though she already knew. The troll ... or maybe Jenna was right—the stalker—had won.

Below the bikini picture, someone with a screen name she didn't recognize, maybe the same person, maybe not, had posted a photograph of Blythe outside her gym. She was smiling, happy, carefree. A woman who didn't know she was being harassed. And now, followed and photographed by a creep who knew where, and when, she went to the gym.

Did he also know where she lived? What else did this faceless stranger know about her?

CHAPTER 15

THIRTY YEARS AGO: BLYTHE

*B*lythe's mother told her it was important not to let other people define her. "You're not fat."

"Crystal said I am."

"Crystal is too thin. She looks unhealthy."

"Everyone says she looks amazing."

"Everyone is thirteen. They don't know anything."

It was her mother who didn't know anything. Was she blind? All she had to do was walk through any clothing store and look at the skimpy tops and short skirts, see the mannequins with their narrow hips and slender arms and legs. They were as cute and sleek as animated girls—long and smooth, their limbs like strands of pasta. Not that a few twirled strands of spaghetti ever touched their lips.

Crystal had said, "Pasta makes you fat". Morgan and Destiny had nodded in agreement, their heads large on their thin necks above their bony shoulders. Destiny was such a cool name. Why couldn't she have been named Destiny? Or Crystal? Blythe sounded like the name of an old lady.

The other girls never mentioned that, but the way they said her name, it sounded old, dragging out the *y*, ending it with a sharp laugh.

"Why can't I get that chocolate drink and have that for breakfast and lunch so I can lose weight? That's what Morgan did."

"It's extremely unhealthy," her mother said. "Girls your age should not be dieting. You shouldn't even think about the word. If you go outside a bit more, ride your bike, you'll slim down. You're still transitioning from childhood."

"I'm fat!" Blythe sobbed.

Her mother put her arms around her. She sat down on the armchair and pulled Blythe onto her lap.

Blythe pushed away from her, peeling her mother's arms off her waist where they pressed against her flesh. Her mother held on more tightly. Blythe cried out and struggled harder, losing her balance. She fell off her mother's lap, landing hard on the floor. She started crying.

"Oh, sweetheart. Come here." Her mother reached down.

"Leave me alone." Blythe pushed herself to her feet and ran down the hall to her room. She slammed the door and fell onto her bed. She pressed her face into her pillow, pushing harder until it was almost impossible to breathe. She didn't care. Maybe she would suffocate. She hated this. She was so, so fat. Everyone agreed.

Her mother would tell her it wasn't everyone. Just those three girls. Those emaciated girls who were dangerously thin, who made a career out of cruelty. Those were her mother's words. She wanted Blythe to ignore them. Her mother wanted Blythe to focus on kids who had better *values*.

Her mother acted as if ignoring them was so easy. As if they weren't everywhere all the time—standing by her locker when she was forced to bend over to open it. Whenever she had a chance, Crystal poked her in the butt. "So squishy! It's like two balloons. It feels exactly like I thought it would. Squish! Squish!"

Blythe didn't think her butt looked like balloons at all. She'd spent a lot of time in the dressing room when she was trying on bathing suits, so much time her mother had knocked on the door and asked in a very worried voice if she was okay. She'd been using the mirrors on three of the walls to turn slowly in every direction to see if her butt looked like balloons. Yes, it was bigger than it should have been, so much bigger than Crystal's, but it didn't look like balloons. Did it? She didn't think it did, but who could she ask? No one would give an honest opinion. Her mother would lie.

She didn't really have any friends. Not friends who could answer a question like that.

The two girls who had been her best friends in elementary school had moved away. She had no one. Kids in her classes talked to her. They were nice enough, especially if they wanted help with their homework. The kids who worked on the school newspaper with her were friendly, but they weren't friends. She couldn't ask their opinions about her butt.

When she was in the locker room, slinking back to her locker from the shower with the tiny white towel wrapped around her so tightly it was hard to breathe, Destiny and Morgan had appeared out of nowhere. Crystal had P.E. during a different period, but it seemed as if she'd given instructions to her loyal friends.

Blythe slid her underwear up under the towel, but she had to drop the towel to put on her bra. They were beside her immediately, as if they'd been beamed over like the characters on Star Trek.

Destiny poked the flesh around Blythe's waist. "It *is* like a donut! You need to lay off the donuts, Blyyyythe! You're growing an actual donut around your middle."

Then, the worst happened. Crystal and her friends signed up to work on the school newspaper. Blythe's one safe place was invaded by those slinky skinny tormenters. They were loud, and they acted as if all the best ideas belonged to them. They made friends with everyone, and Blythe felt as if she was often sitting in the corner, working on the least interesting stories, something for the third page, while the three of them literally grabbed the headlines.

In April, Crystal announced she was having a *massive* sleepover for all the girls on the newspaper staff. "We can use it to plan the final issue."

"That's not right," Blythe said. "The entire staff needs to plan it. Not just the girls."

67

Crystal heaved a dramatic sigh. She rolled her eyes and glanced at Destiny. "Fine. Even though I already ran it by Ms. Alvarez. We'll have a planning party at my house. The boys can leave after we eat pizza and do our planning. The girls can spend the night. Are you happy, Miss Rulebook?"

"It's not a rule. It just doesn't make sense to—"

"I said the boys can come. Why are you arguing?"

Blythe didn't say anything more.

The planning for the final issue was dictated by Crystal. If Blythe hadn't known better, she would have thought Crystal, Morgan, and Destiny had planned it all before any of the others even walked through the front door. But was Crystal that organized?

After the boys were gone, the evening turned into a typical slumber party. Not that Blythe had much experience. The parties she'd attended had all taken place when she was eight or nine years old. This was her first as a teenager, but she'd heard stories. There were lots of snacks, candy, and soda. There were stories of boys and breakups, kisses and who had let what boy go how far.

It seemed a little mysterious to Blythe. She wasn't sure she wanted to listen to all of it. She wanted to know, but she also felt left out. She felt like a little kid, someone who knew nothing about the world, nothing about boys.

Finally, the lights were turned out. Some of the girls went to sleep. Blythe saw Crystal, with her bright blonde hair, get out of her sleeping bag and tiptoe out of the room. Two shadowy figures followed. After that, Blythe drifted to sleep.

She was sure there was lots of tiptoeing around in the night, but Blythe was an extraordinarily deep sleeper. Her mother always commented on it. Her mother worried that if they had a fire or an earthquake, Blythe would sleep through it, and if something happened to prevent her parents or her sister from getting to her, Blythe would perish.

"You sleep like the dead," her mother said.

She hated hearing that. It sounded ominous. It was too scary, and she didn't like thinking about it.

The sun was fully up when Blythe woke the next morning.

She opened her eyes to see Crystal, Morgan, and Destiny sitting in a row on the sleeping bag beside her. They stared at her, tiny smiles on their faces, a look of anticipation in their eyes that said they were so eager for her to wake, they were considering shaking her until her eyes opened.

"Wish Bear is awake!" Crystal tapped Blythe's nose.

Blythe blinked rapidly. Her eyes watering from the assault of a finger on her nose.

"Hello, Wish Bear. Such a cute, pudgy bear. *Wishing* she was thin. But then she wouldn't be a cuddly, squishy, round little Care Bear!" Crystal's voice was a squeal, bordering on a shriek. "Good morning, Care Bear!"

"Want to see?" Destiny asked. She pulled a small mirror out of her pocket and held it up.

Blythe saw her face was smeared with turquoise paint. On her left cheek, mimicking the iconic stuffed bear that had risen to stardom in the eighties, was a yellow shooting star. She sat up, feeling the blood rush out of her head, leaving her slightly dizzy. "What did you do?"

"We made you look like the precious Care Bear you are," Destiny said. "Don't you just love it?"

Softly, far away, she heard her father's voice. *Never react. When you react, you give away your power.*

"I hate it." Her eyes filled with tears. They spilled over quickly, even though inside her mind she was screaming at herself—*Don't cry. Don't cry. Do not let them see you cry!* But she was crying.

"Aww. Don't cry, little Wish Bear!" Destiny dragged her long, sharp fingernail down Blythe's cheek. "Such a roly poly little bear you are. Wish for what you want. If you don't want to be a bowl of pudding, you can wish it away."

They poked at her stomach, bulging through the thin fabric of her nightgown. They pinched her cheek, telling her it was cute because it was so chubby. Finally, they let her wash her face. When her mother picked her up, a blue shadow lingered on Blythe's skin.

Her mother was not pleased. She called Crystal's mother and spoke to her for half an hour. Blythe couldn't hear what she said.

When the phone call ended, her mother said, "Things will be fine now. It's important to stay calm. I wanted to scream. I wanted to drive over there and rip that woman's eyes out, but it's important to remain calm."

After that, the girls left her alone. It didn't matter. Blythe still felt anxious the moment she walked through the main gate onto the school grounds every day. She felt slightly ill in her classes, always waiting for something to happen. And even though they never said a word, never even looked at her, she heard them inside her head. Blythe felt as if they lived there now, their voices louder than her own.

Toward the end of the school year, it was announced there would be a camp-out at a facility dedicated to family and group camping in the Sierra Foothills. It would be well-chaperoned. It would be a bonding and personal development experience for all the students.

Blythe insisted she was going. Her mother said, "Absolutely not."

"I want to go. *Everyone's* going!"

They argued about it for three weeks.

Her mother's last words on the subject were—"When will you learn, Blythe?"

CHAPTER 16

NOW: BLYTHE

Scarlett had brought her youngest son, Henry, over for a swim in Blythe's pool. He was supposed to bring a friend with him, but the friend had canceled at the last minute.

Sitting on the edge with their legs in the water, large floppy hats covering their faces, Scarlett leaned close so Blythe could hear her whisper. "I don't think his friend ever accepted the invite. I worry about him so much. When I see him after school, he's always alone. I'm not sure he has any friends, to be honest. More like classmates. Kids he says *hi* to, or works on projects with, but not actual friends."

Blythe moved her feet slowly through the water. "I know he's had a really hard time, but try not to let your anxiety take over. I know you know I was bullied when I was a kid. It was awful. And I realize that's not the issue for Henry, but I was pretty isolated, and I made my way through it. I don't mean to make it sound easy, or not painful—"

"But you're a girl."

"Yes."

"I just ..."

Blythe put her arm loosely around Scarlett's shoulders. "I'm just saying don't let your anxiety infect him. My mom did, and it doesn't help."

"I can't change how I feel."

Blythe squeezed her friend's shoulders, then let go. "I know. That's not what I'm saying. Just try to breathe. Maybe the stuff you feel is different from what he feels, so make sure he can say what he's feeling upset about instead of letting your feelings overtake his. That's all. His might be entirely different. Just as awful, but different."

"Yeah. That's actually something to think about, I guess."

Henry did a cannonball off the small diving board.

Scarlett and Blythe screeched as the water doused them.

Henry popped above the surface, laughing at the chaos he'd caused.

"Very funny," Scarlett said.

Henry laughed and dove under the water, kicking furiously, splashing them again.

"This was a good idea," Scarlett said. "Thanks."

"Any time."

"Did you see Lacey has a whole line of mugs now about body positivity?" Scarlett asked.

"I didn't."

"It seems a little ... not nice."

"Why? That's a good thing," Blythe said.

"They're offshoots from the mug she did after she posted about never achieving her coaching goals with you."

"Oh. I guess that's still ... okay. We all want to feel positive about ourselves, right?" Blythe said.

"Maybe body positivity was the wrong term. That's what Lacey calls them. But they have more attitude." Scarlett laughed. "Snark, actually."

"Like what?"

"Working out is still work and I already have a job."

"That doesn't seem too bad," Blythe said.

"Life is too short to eat five servings of veggies a day. Give me cheese."

Blythe moved her feet around in the water, wiggling her toes again. The statements Scarlett had repeated weren't terribly funny. Snark was a good word for it. But not funny snark. More whiney, in her opinion. But if it made people feel better when they had tea or coffee, what did it matter? In her experience, most gift mugs ended up making their way to the back of the cabinet, forgotten after a while, donated a few years later when people realized they had more mugs than they could ever hope to use.

Scarlett rattled off a few other not-very-clever sayings.

"I wonder how they'll do. They don't sound that funny, to be honest." Blythe leaned forward and cupped her hands in the water, splashing some onto her arms. It was getting hot. In about ten minutes, the sun would shift enough that they'd be shaded by the house, but right now, she was burning up. Or maybe, hearing about the mugs was making her uncomfortably warm.

"Whatever it is about her mugs and bags and stuff, people love them," Scarlett said. "If the comments on social media are anything to go by, people are going nuts over the new sayings."

"Interesting."

"There are a lot of comments about being sick of feeling like you have to look like a model all the time, that women's bodies are supposed to be soft and curvy, that working out is just one more thing women are expected to do in order to meet some media-created image of perfection."

"It's about being healthy."

"You say that, but ..." Scarlett paused.

"But, what?"

"Well, I don't think your bikini post gave that impression."

"Maybe not." Blythe did not want to think about that post, or anything that had happened because of it. She was willing to admit to herself it might have been a mistake, but everyone made mistakes. And she was not taking it down, if that was where Scarlett was headed with this.

"She wrote a long post about how painful it was working out, how she constantly felt like a failure. How she was always comparing herself."

"I'm really sorry she feels that way. I should talk to her," Blythe said.

"She mentioned how great you looked in that photo, and how she's sick of feeling shamed for not looking like a teenager in a swimsuit. That she's a mature woman who has had children, and she's proud of that. She wants people to know that about her. She said her body shows who she is and the life she's lived. Like the rings in a tree."

Blythe felt defensive. Why were they suddenly misinterpreting the purpose of her business? She felt as if no matter what she said, no one got it. "Most people want to be healthy. If you eat food that's good for you and gives you the energy you want, you're naturally going to lose some weight. In most cases, not always, obviously. But losing weight is not my focus. It really is not. It's about—"

"I don't think you give that impression, Blythe. Especially after the swimsuit picture. She's reacting to that. And people are really responding to her feelings."

Henry was now floating on the inflated mat, gazing up at the sky. Blythe wondered what he was thinking about. It was so hard to remember all of her thoughts and feelings at that age. Sometimes it seemed as if those feelings were still raw and right there on the surface. Other times, it seemed as if those things had happened so long ago, they'd happened to a different person.

She never intended her coaching to make anyone feel bad about themselves. She wanted to help. It made her want to cry, thinking that Lacey felt defeated and criticized. Why hadn't she said something to Blythe? How had she managed to make one of her closest friends feel so awful? But why was Lacey responding by creating an entire line of products that felt like a reproach for what she did? And why now?

Blythe had been a health coach for over ten years. Lacey had been her client for at least eight of those years. Had she been miserable the entire time? "I'm not going to let it ruin our friendship," Blythe said.

"That's good."

They were quiet for several minutes, both of them watching Henry drift across the surface of the pool, carried by the almost imperceptible movement of the water.

"You're a good person," Scarlett said.

"We all are. We try."

"The only thing is, what if the things she's selling damage your business?"

Blythe felt the shade finally move across the area where they were seated. Now, she was cold. Too cold. Why did Scarlett have to say that?

CHAPTER 17

*I*t was their wedding anniversary. This was not a milestone year—their seventeenth—but as he did every year, Garret had gone out of his way to plan something remarkable. He'd had a friend from work drop him off at the restaurant and scheduled an Uber to pick up Blythe. He'd also booked a hotel room for the night. That was all the information she'd been given. Both locations were a secret.

Blythe was busy creating seven new reels for her social media updates for the week. She'd decided the best way to deal with the troll, to bury the gnawing fear that he not only knew the name of her gym, he'd been watching her there without her having any awareness whatsoever, was to put it as far out of her mind as she possibly could. She'd also decided not to discuss it with anyone. Talking made the situation more real.

A troll was a troll. His objective was stirring up fear. That was the bottom line. He wanted her upset. He wanted her looking over her shoulder. Most of all, he wanted power over her. Nothing would delight him more than to see her removing her social media posts, canceling her gym membership and finding a new place to work out, dancing to his threats. She refused to do that. She was not giving in to fear.

He wasn't going to *do* anything. He just wanted her cowering and sick with worry. For all she knew, he'd downloaded that photo from a long-forgotten post of her own.

Editing the reels was giving her trouble. It often did. Her skills were in the gym and the kitchen, not with digital photography and technology. Even coming up with clever things to say was sometimes challenging. Day after day, every week, for years. She sometimes felt she was repeating herself. She worried the images she posted had a sameness to them. The food shots attracted a lot of positive reactions, and they were easy to do, but they still had a sameness to them. That had been the entire reason she'd done the selfie by the pool.

She shoved the thought out of her mind. She wasn't giving it any more attention. This was her wedding anniversary. All she needed to do was complete the last two reels.

It was five o'clock. She should be fine. Her makeup was done, her tiny purse filled with the essentials, except for her phone.

The doorbell rang. Hopefully, Kelsey would get it. Kate was out with a friend. She tapped the phone and held it, trying to trim the video. The bell rang again and her finger slipped. She sighed.

Clutching the phone, she hurried to the front door and yanked it open. A delivery guy stood on the front porch holding an arrangement of five yellow roses in a small vase. Her lucky number. She loved that Garret remembered things like that. Tiny little details that made her know he was always paying attention to her, that he loved the silly things about her as much as he loved the more meaningful aspects of her personality.

Smiling, she signed for the flowers and closed the door. She placed them on the table in the front hall and returned to the office.

When the bell rang again, she felt a surge of panic. It couldn't be five thirty. She wasn't dressed. The last reel wasn't finished. And although she'd foolishly saved it for last, it was the reel she wanted to post tomorrow. Gripping her phone, trying not to touch the screen, she raced to the door and flung it open.

"Ready?" The Uber driver was tall and muscular. Despite his build, he looked like he was fifteen years old.

"I ... almost. Do you mind waiting?"

"I'm not paid by the—"

"Two minutes."

He glared at her oversized T-shirt and workout pants. Also, despite his appearance, he seemed to have a sense that no woman who said she would be dressed for an elegant evening out in two minutes was telling the truth.

"Honest. Two minutes."

"I'll have to check with Mr. Farrell."

"Sure. Come in."

She felt a prick of fear the minute she made the offer, but it was safe. Wasn't it?

She left the door open and ran back to the office. She flopped on the small sofa and began fiddling with the reel. It wasn't cooperating and now that she was tense and conscious of the two minutes she'd promised, her fingers were shaking, making it more difficult. After several minutes, she realized she wasn't going to be able to fix it.

She heard him calling from the entryway. "Hello? Ms. Farrell? I need to—"

"I'm coming!" she called back. "Two more minutes. I promise." She turned off the light, left the office, and ran up the stairs.

She dropped her phone on the bed. Maybe she could get it to work during the ride to the restaurant. She had no idea how far it was, but surely she had at least ten or fifteen minutes. Was he taking her all the way to San Francisco? To the coast? Garret had said nothing about bringing a coat.

She pulled off her T-shirt and pants and lifted her dress off the bed where she'd placed it earlier.

When she was dressed, her hair combed, her makeup touched up, she sat on the bed. She was almost there, if she just took—

"Ms. Farrell?" The driver was calling for her again, his voice louder and filled with impatience. "I can't wait all evening. I need to get going. Are you taking the car or not?"

"I'll be right there." She stood. She was so close. She really needed this done. She was taking back her power. She would win this battle without removing her post. It was important to finish this.

Her phone pinged with a message from Garret.

> Garret: The Uber driver is upset. What's taking so long?

She ignored it. Almost there. Almost done.

Another message from Garret.

> Garret: Is something wrong? You can't keep him waiting like this. Are you okay?

If she took time to text back, it would slow her down.

Between the Uber driver calling up the stairs and the constant pinging from Garret, she had to give up. She couldn't finish. She would try in the car. She stepped into her shoes.

She walked down the stairs and followed the driver out to the waiting car. He didn't speak during the entire thirty five-minute trip to Palo Alto. He dropped her off at the restaurant without bothering to open the door for her. Not that Uber drivers usually did that, but this was a luxury car, and she was certain Garret had probably asked him to do that, might have even given him an up-front tip for that extra courtesy.

She had not been able to finish the reel in the car. He'd driven too fast, taken the turns with too much force, stopped abruptly at traffic lights. By the time they arrived, a small headache was forming in her left temple.

The restaurant was one of the most popular places in Palo Alto. She'd heard it took over a month to get a reservation. The host showed her to the table where Garret was waiting with a split of champagne in an ice bucket.

Garret looked at her with the saddest eyes she'd seen in a long while. He didn't say anything while she took her seat and the host placed the napkin across her lap.

After a few minutes of silence, Garret settled himself and gave her a forgiving smile. "The flowers came?"

"Thank you so much." She reached across the table and touched his hand. "They're absolutely perfect."

"Is everything okay?" He poured champagne into their glasses.

If she told him, he would be upset. But she couldn't lie. "It is now." She gave him the calmest, most loving smile she could manage. She needed to put the frustration behind her. A different reel would work for tomorrow. There were still six. She'd gotten too wrapped up in the rigid details of her plan. One day short was not a big deal. She could still accomplish her objective of overwhelming the troll. And the final reel could be—

"What happened?" Garret asked. "You don't look okay."

She took a sip of champagne. "I was trying to get all my social media reels for the week done, and one of them was—"

"You're bullshitting me, right?" He laughed. "You're late because you were floating in the pool sipping a glass of champagne, waiting for your surprise."

She giggled. "I wish."

"Seriously? You were late for our anniversary, you pissed off the driver who was supposed to give you a nice, comfortable ride to your surprise destination, just so you could screw around on social media?"

"I wasn't screwing around."

"You were. We have a date."

"And here we are."

He gulped his champagne and refilled his glass. He picked up the menu.

"Don't be angry."

Without looking up, he spoke in a low, hard voice. "I'm not angry, but I'm upset. You are addicted. Do you realize that?"

"I'm not. It's my job."

"Just keep telling yourself that. Your *job* is to be a health coach, not a social media influencer, or whatever the hell they call it, trying to get more attention than everyone else."

"That's not what I'm doing."

"Isn't it? We need to order."

After they'd made their selections and placed their order, they sipped the rest of the champagne, not speaking. When the champagne was gone and the appetizer had been presented, with great fanfare, and a bottle of wine opened, Garret seemed to relax. Slightly. He talked about his day. He asked about the sports camp plans for Kelsey and Kate.

He ate the last baby octopus and took a sip of wine. "You know, I really do think there's an addictive aspect to this social media thing. You honestly don't see that?"

"No. It's how I promote my coaching. You know that. We've talked about it a hundred—"

"I talked to Jenna the other day. She was almost crying because her sales are down. She was obsessing over social media and everyone else getting more attention than she does. I'm not telling you what to do, but maybe if you supported her more and weren't so focused on what you have to do for yourself, it would be more satisfying."

"That's really patronizing."

"It wasn't meant that way. I just thought that's how all of you started out—helping each other. It seems ... competitive now."

"I'm not competing with anyone."

"You talk about social media more than you talk about your work."

"It's demanding. It's always changing, and it's challenging to keep it fresh."

"Maybe it would help to back off. Maybe helping her would give you perspective."

"It's our anniversary." She gave him a weak smile. "Why don't we talk about us?" She raised her wineglass for a toast. "Seventeen years. It's almost impossible to remember my life without you."

He raised his glass toward hers. He was quiet for a moment, then spoke in a low voice. "I love you more than you'll ever know."

She let what he'd said soak into her. Putting love into words was impossible. And whose love was greater? Could they compare? Could they say that one loved the other more? Or could they find a way to ensure they loved each other equally? None of that could ever happen because you could never feel what the other person felt. But she liked hearing it. And she liked believing it. She loved the thrill, the romance of it all.

"I adore you," she said. "There hasn't been a single day that I haven't loved you."

"Are you trying to outdo me?"

"Maybe." She was glad they were done talking about Jenna. Hadn't she helped Jenna enough? She'd spent years repaying Jenna. When was it going to be enough? And why did she feel she had to repay her at all? Was that friendship?

CHAPTER 18

*A*t first, the response to her reels lifted Blythe's spirits. All the effort had been worth it. Garret's disappointment and the flicker of pain in his eyes had been a difficult price, but they'd moved past it. By the end of the meal, and after their night in a luxurious hotel room, a morning lounging around in a massive bed with an abundance of pillows, and soft white sheets, breakfast brought to their room, falling asleep again, then finally checking out, there hadn't been any lingering traces of upset.

Everything was good.

And the reels had drawn so much attention. The reaction was beyond what she'd hoped for. The comments and interest in her coaching filled her with enthusiasm. Expanding her business to offer online coaching was absolutely within reach. The troll was truly buried. She could move forward.

Lacey could sell thousands of mugs, and it would have no impact on Blythe's business. But burying the troll had been the important part. He was gone. Obliterated. It was true that ignoring bullies was the best response. They wanted attention, and she hadn't given it to him. He'd grown bored and gone somewhere else.

For a few days, she was blissfully happy. Proud of herself and brimming with confidence.

Then, as if he'd been gathering reinforcements, he was back.

By Thursday, she'd posted five reels. That was when he came barreling in with a vengeance.

Every single reel was hit with comments demanding more bikini pics, lewd comments, and taunting criticism. She stared at her phone, her knuckles growing white, like tiny blocks of ice. Her hand seemed molded to the phone, unable to even place it on the table or hide it in her pocket.

Comments slid relentlessly across the screen, an army of cockroaches devouring all the goodwill she'd created, turning everything dark and ugly.

She ran up the stairs to her bedroom, closing the door as softly as she could manage. She didn't want to alarm Kelsey and Kate. They were hypersensitive to her moods. If they sensed she was upset, they would either lecture her about not allowing social media control her mood, or they would get upset themselves, worried that the person they looked to as their rock and their weather vane was tilting off course, leaving them feeling uncertain about their own security in the world.

Why did teenagers today seem so much wiser than she'd been? She never would have lectured her mother about her emotional state. Neither had she ever seen her mother appear uncertain or knocked off course by anything as minor as this. Her mother always seemed to know what to do, always had an answer for everything.

Maybe social media had the answer to that as well—her kids possessed knowledge she hadn't acquired until she was in her twenties, thanks to social media, and the internet in general.

She shoved her phone under the mattress. It was a childish thing to do, and she wasn't sure what she hoped to accomplish by doing it, but she had to get it away from her. It was a better choice than hurling it at the window.

She collapsed onto the bed and curled up, hugging her knees to her chest. She closed her eyes and tried to think. It felt as if the public facing image of her coaching business was being pelted with rotten eggs. But if that were the case, she could get out a bucket and sponge, a bottle of cleanser, and clean it up. She could purchase new signage and make everything sparkling fresh.

With this, she had no idea how to fix it. She'd thought the reels were a perfect solution. But hours of work had been destroyed in the space of ten or fifteen minutes. Not only her own work, but all the positive responses from current and potential clients. Not only was she not making forward progress, she was slipping backwards, sliding down a steep hill with nothing to grab onto.

After lying in a pathetic ball of self-pity for nearly twenty minutes, she pulled herself together. Sort of. She sat up, ran her fingers through her hair, and stretched her arms over her head. She got up and went to the bathroom, splashed water on her face, and studied her reflection in the mirror. She looked haggard. Rather than a woman who ran a successful business who had spent the previous weekend enjoying a romantic dinner with her husband, a night in a five-star hotel having outstanding sex, with a couples' massage the following day, she looked like she'd just lost her job and had spent the last month trying to get a bank loan to save her family from financial ruin.

She put on lip gloss and returned to the bedroom. She slid her arm under the mattress and pulled out her phone.

Predictably, there were more messages from the troll and his buddies, or alter egos, whatever they were, demanding seductive photographs.

Without thinking, she deleted the original bikini photograph and all the reels she'd posted since her anniversary. It wasn't worth it.

He'd won after all.

But only this round. She was determined that would be true. It was only this round. She should have taken screen shots and reported it all, but what was the point? He would be long gone before they could uncover his identity. And what were the consequences? Closure of his accounts? He closed them himself, only to open new ones.

She laughed out loud and tossed her phone onto the bed.

A swim would clear her thoughts. She changed into a turquoise tank suit, braided her hair, and went out to the pool. She dove in off the springboard without testing the water. The surprise of cool water was always more pleasurable than a tentative dipping of her toes into the pool, getting a sense of what she could expect. The shock forced her into immediate movement. The pool was heated, but in hot weather, it still felt cold when her entire body plunged below the surface. She swam fast, kicking vigorously, taking smooth, deep breaths every few strokes.

Nine laps wiped all thoughts of her social media turmoil out of her mind. When she climbed the wide steps out of the shallow end and picked up her towel, she felt as if she was stepping into another dimension. Her skin was fresh and full of life, her head free of the weight she'd been carrying. She almost didn't care what was happening on her social media pages.

All she wanted to think about was making dinner.

She'd planned linguini with sautéed vegetables and a fruit salad. Both her girls were big fruit eaters. They would eat nothing else for dinner if she let them. She got to work peeling and scooping and cutting melon and strawberries, washing blueberries and raspberries. She turned on a playlist that made her feel like dancing, and began moving around the kitchen as if she were performing on a stage. It felt good, and soon she was smiling and thinking about her very full schedule for the following day.

The smile remained on her face until dinner was almost finished.

"Hey. Mama-Lama," said Kelsey. "I saw all your reels disappeared. You did a good job on them. What happened?"

Blythe shoved the last forkful of pasta into her mouth, bit down too hard, and managed to chomp on the inside of her bottom lip. She winced and let out a little cry of pain.

"Are you okay?" Garret asked.

"I bit my lip."

"So what's up with the disappeared reels?" Kelsey popped a

blueberry into her mouth, chewing it with her front teeth, like a mouse.

"They had the wrong feel."

"They were pretty good," Kate said.

"I'm thinking of a new angle."

"The algorithm doesn't like you if you take stuff down," Kelsey said.

"I know. But I risked it this time, because of what I'm planning."

"Sounds very secretive," Kelsey said. "What is it?"

"I can't say yet." She gave them a mysterious smile. At least she hoped that was the look she communicated. Her stomach was heaving and it was entirely possible her lips were quivering, as if she might be sick.

"Can't wait," Kelsey said.

"Don't you want our advice?" Kate asked.

"Maybe. But not yet." Blythe stood and began clearing the table. It was her daughters' job, but she needed to escape their scrutiny.

CHAPTER 19

FIFTEEN YEARS AGO: BLYTHE

This was the second potluck dinner the tightly knit group of pregnant friends and soon-to-be-dads had enjoyed together. It would probably be the last before the babies began to make their appearances. All five women were moving slowly, hands pressed into their lower backs when they stood, gently massaging their bellies while complaining that the sleepless nights with an infant couldn't possibly be worse than the sleeplessness they experienced now.

When they were finished eating, the men covered the casserole dishes so their wives could take it easy. Tea was made and ice cream was served. Chairs were pushed away from the table.

As if they'd agreed that everything that could be said about pregnancy had been said, and this might be their last opportunity to talk about something besides babies for a while, the conversation shifted, like a current changing direction, carrying them with it.

Blythe wasn't sure who started it. Her only thought was—*This is not what I want to be talking about when I have two babies coming in less than ten days.*

Guns.

There had been a home invasion in Menlo Park a month earlier. Only one of the two women who shared the apartment had been home. She owned a handgun. She didn't follow gun safety rules—keeping the ammunition locked in a separate location. She had the gun loaded, stored in the nightstand beside her bed.

Facing two men wearing ski masks, she'd backed into the bedroom, grabbed her gun, and shot one of them. She knew how to use her gun and had seriously injured him with one shot. The problem was, she was quickly overpowered by the second man, who then used her gun to kill her.

For the next forty-five minutes, Garret and the others rehashed all that had been covered in the news, all the opinions and analysis of gun laws, the history and statistics, especially those that reported how many people were killed by their own weapons kept on hand for self-defense.

Blythe was shocked by how much they could talk about a single incident, especially one they appeared to agree on. Maybe it was therapeutic. Her friends seemed to want to go over the details of what had happened, to review each horrible step that had led to that poor woman's death. They wanted to talk about home invasion, and how it could be prevented. They wanted to talk about gun safety and gun control laws.

"Can't we talk about something else?" Blythe's voice was soft. Too quiet, apparently, because no-one responded. Their voices grew louder, so maybe they had heard and they didn't want her dampening their enthusiasm for this subject they all wanted to carry on about, possibly for the rest of the evening.

Was it therapeutic? A way to work out their unspoken fears for the children who were about to enter their lives? These helpless human beings they were responsible for keeping safe and raising to healthy, adjusted, happy adulthood? How could you stop people from ringing your doorbell and barging into your home, tying you up while they robbed you, possibly killing you and your children? How did you keep these tiny creatures safe? Despite the complicated, well-engineered car seats and the endless flood of warnings about everything from swimming pools to internet safety, the responsibility was overwhelming.

"Even so," Lacey said, "I would never own a gun. Not ever. This demonstrates why."

Just as Blythe thought the conversation was winding down, losing energy, it took on a new life. Everyone echoed what Lacey had said.

Never.

It's too dangerous.

Especially with children in the house. Even if you lock up the bullets. Besides, if you do that, how can it keep you safe? It's too late.

I wouldn't even consider it.

Absolutely not. Never.

No way.

I'm not going to live in fear.

Not even for self-defense.

And on it went, repeating themselves, while Blythe continued to long for a new topic of conversation. Anything. Maybe they could discuss postpartum depression. It was more cheerful than this.

She stood slowly. She needed to pee. If she was lucky, by the time she returned, they would have moved on. Finally. She could hope. She would take her time. She would give herself a little tour of the parts of the house she hadn't seen.

The layout of the house accommodated her plan to take a tour. The main bathroom was all the way down the hall, past a small TV room, a home office, and the room outfitted for the new baby. Inside the bathroom, she leaned over the vanilla candle and inhaled its scent, then used the toilet. She washed her hands and dried them. She smoothed on some of the hand cream put out for guests.

Coming out of the bathroom, she turned right and took a quick peek into the master bedroom. Feeling guilty, she turned and hurried back past the bathroom. She went into the nursery even though she'd been shown it earlier. She took more time, looking at the precious ceramic bears on a small shelf, touching the soft cloths stacked on the changing table, and reading the framed poem above the gliding chair in the corner.

She went out and stepped into the office next door.

Soon Garret would start to worry about her. He always did these past few weeks, assuming she'd gone into labor if she was out of the room for more than ten minutes. She smiled at the thought.

She read the titles of the books on the shelf that ran from a work counter to just below the ceiling. She didn't go to the desk, that was too invasive. Instead, she crossed the room to another bookcase. Some shelf spaces were filled with books, others dedicated to art objects that had clearly been collected during trips overseas. This wasn't snooping. Everyone loved having their collections admired.

She looked at each one in turn. Then, as she moved closer to the wall where the desk sat, she looked down at a small table between the shelves and an armchair. The bottom of the table was a shelf, stuffed with stacks of books. The top was a drawer, which was partially opened. Inside, she saw what looked like the handle of a gun.

She felt a sudden intake of air.

It couldn't be. She'd sat there five minutes ago and listened to every single person insist they would never ever … Yet, she was sure that's what she was looking at.

Maybe it was a fancy cigar lighter. She pulled the drawer open. No. It was a gun, a very powerful-looking handgun. She closed the drawer quickly, jerking her head around to check the doorway.

She backed away from the table, her heart pounding so hard, she felt as if she'd heard someone fire the gun.

She left the room and went outside. The gathering was breaking up. Garret was standing near the end of the table, holding their salad bowl. "There you are. I was starting to worry. Any day now." He kissed the top of her head.

"It won't happen that fast."

He laughed. "Wouldn't that be nice if it did?"

Right now, she definitely did not want it happening. She didn't want to give birth to their child thinking about what she'd just seen.

CHAPTER 20

NOW: BLYTHE

Over the years, the bond of going through the births of their first children together had never frayed. It had grown stronger as their children became playmates, and the five women became a home business-owners' support group.

In addition to play dates and carpools, the couples shared summer barbecues and holiday parties. They'd organized camping trips and outings to baseball games.

Blythe loved the feeling of a solid group of friends who had managed to evolve through the years of cuddly babies and toddler-hood into the early teens. She was so grateful that she had the support of like-minded friends for her business. She was incredibly lucky. It made her smile with contentment when she sat across the patio and watched Garret talk to the other men, laughing and relaxed.

Tonight was their first barbecue of the summer. Oliver and Jenna were hosting. Naomi was having a sleepover with Kelsey and Kate.

They'd eaten grilled chicken and vegetables, potato salad, tossed green salad, and fruit. It had felt as if the food was in danger of sliding off Blythe's bright green plate as she'd carried it to the table. Now, she leaned back in her chair, enjoying the satisfied feeling as she sipped her wine and watched the sky fade to inky blue, the clouds like puffs of gray chalk dust.

The air was still warm on her bare shoulders, and the cool wine trailed down her throat like silk. As long as she didn't think about the mess that her social media presence had become, she didn't think her life could be any more perfect. She *wouldn't* think about it. Things would work themselves out. Eventually. Sitting here with her friends, her stomach filled with good food, and her thoughts drifting on a second glass of wine, she truly believed that.

The troll would give up on her now that the bikini picture was gone. Maybe she'd won after all. Yes, he'd ultimately forced her to take down the picture, but she remained the one in control, because at the same time, he couldn't post any more repulsive comments on it. She was slowly starving him.

She watched a few stars make their soft, quiet appearance, then turned her attention to Garret. He was sitting beside Paul, and just as she focused on them, it seemed as if everyone had chosen that moment to pause their conversations and follow her lead.

Paul was holding his phone, tilting it in Garret's direction.

"I post dog photos or videos a couple times a day. Even if they're not so-called dog people, everyone feels good when they see a dog. Especially the videos of them catching balls, or greeting their owner who's been gone for a long time. I'm doing what I can to bring positive energy to the world. To make people happier, even if it's only for a few seconds during the endless scroll."

"I know, dude," Garret said. "You tell me that every time I see you."

As if he hadn't heard Garret speak, Paul continued. "Dogs make people feel affection and love. It gives them a release of dopamine and all those endorphins."

"Yup," Garret said.

"It's more than a few times a day," Lacey said. "More like eight or ten."

"I like doing it. I'm an influencer. Creating content that's lifting people up instead of crushing their spirits."

"Good for you," Lacey said. "We need more of that."

"An influencer?" Jenna said.

"Eight or ten times a day seems a little ... needy," Garret said.

"Not at all," Paul said. "It's not about me. Dogs have greater emotional intelligence than people do. They sense moods. They're aware of danger even when we can't see it. People instinctively know that, so they feel safe when they see dogs. They know they can trust dogs, as long as they haven't been abused, and they're well cared for by their owners."

Oliver laughed. "They get all that from a picture of a Shih Tzu with hair over its eyes?"

"That's where the content creation comes in," Paul said. "I take photographs that convey some kind of canine emotion. Or shows them responding to human emotion."

"That's a lot to get from a dog. Especially one that's not yours," Scarlett said.

Garret looked pointedly at Scarlett. "You're not thrilled with his social media gig?"

She shrugged. "It's just a hobby."

Paul looked hurt. Although, if it wasn't a hobby, what was it? Blythe felt as if the conversation was headed somewhere uncomfortable. She wanted to direct it onto a different course, but nothing came to mind. Social media was not her favorite topic of conversation right now. And she didn't want Jenna to start going on about being stalked.

With his attention still fixed on Scarlett, Garret said, "Are you worried that ninety percent of the comments on the dog pics are from women?"

"That's not true," Paul said. "But it makes me wonder, what are you doing? Spying on me, counting my comments? That's a little needy yourself. Or obsessive might be a better way to describe it."

"Just something I noticed. I do like the dogs," Garret said. "You're one hundred percent correct on that front. But while they were parading by, I couldn't help noticing all the hearts and flowers from women."

"I haven't noticed," Paul said.

Garret laughed. "Your responses to each and every one say otherwise."

"I have to reply to everyone, to keep my posts noticed by the algorithm."

"Oh, the great algorithm," Garret said. "The god of the twenty-first century whom we must feed with hourly sacrifices of our time and mental stability."

Everyone laughed.

Blythe smiled.

"But seriously," Garret said. "All those women." He gave Scarlett a teasing smile. "No wonder he posts fifteen a day."

"Ten," Paul said. "Sometimes not even that many."

"How do you find time to work, if you're always out stalking strange dogs?" Oliver asked.

"Why is everyone piling on?" Blythe asked. "Everyone loves the dog pics. You can't control who comments on your posts." She regretted it the moment she said it.

She felt a cold, hard stare from Jenna. Luckily for Blythe, Lacey saved her. Although in the end, what she said might have been worse. "You should probably be more careful," Lacey said, her tone stern. "Some women might take all those posts, and the personal responses, especially with the hearts and flowers, as a signal of availability."

"They don't," Paul said.

"You'd be surprised how people misinterpret things," Lacey said. "Especially online. You know the truism—eighty percent of communication is non-verbal. Emojis are worse. They're so open to misinterpretation."

"No one thinks I'm available," Paul said. "My profile says I'm married to the love of my life."

Miles put his arm around Lacey, pulling her close. "Most people don't look at your profile," he said.

"I look at everyone's profiles," Paul said.

"You're an outlier." Miles took a swallow of beer, setting the bottle on the table with a thump, as if that were the final word on the matter.

"I'm just saying, people can assume things, depending on how you present yourself," Lacey said.

"I'm *presenting* myself as a dog lover."

"It's back to the nonverbal thing." Lacey was not going to back down. She never did. "You don't know for certain how you're coming across. People assume things. You have to be extra-careful in how you present yourself. It's one place where you *should* constantly second-guess yourself."

Blythe sipped her wine. Was Lacey talking to Paul, or was she trying to make a veiled comment to Blythe? Was the new line of body positive mugs more aggressively targeting Blythe's business than she'd realized? What was going on with her?

Blythe couldn't figure out if Lacey was being hostile, or if everything was looking dark and off center because the troll was distorting everything around her. She wanted to ask the question. She wanted to confront Lacey right now. Her cheeks were getting hot, as if they were all staring at her, thinking about that bikini picture. It had felt so natural and innocent when she'd come up with the idea. She'd never expected it to turn into something so awful.

How could an idea that came out of excitement and enthusiasm for her desire to help people achieve their goals, to improve their health, to feel good, turn into something so hideous? It was so unfair. And she felt like somehow, it was all her fault for being naïve, or lying to herself. Was she lying to herself? She really didn't think so, but she wasn't even sure about that anymore.

CHAPTER 21

*T*heir disagreement started as soon as the car doors closed. Blythe hadn't meant to start an argument. She'd thought Garret would admit he'd been out of line and maybe even volunteer to text an apology to Paul. Instead, he doubled down.

"That was mean, what you said to Paul," she said.

"What did I say?"

"That he was needy. And implying that he posts dog pictures so women will pay attention to him."

"I don't think that's what I said."

"You definitely said he was needy."

"Ten posts a day is needy. Begging people to notice you, to like you, to pay attention to you."

"No, it's not. There's a lot of negative stuff on social media. Like he said, his posts make people happy. I think it's great that he's trying to make people feel good."

"Well, I think he's addicted to the dopamine."

"I know you're not into social media, but that doesn't mean other people don't enjoy it. You can't go around calling it an addiction just because you don't like it. Maybe you're jealous."

Garret laughed. "I'm not jealous."

"I could call watching sports and following the team standings an addiction. Why is that such a big part of your life?"

"Okay. Fair enough," Garret said.

Things deflated slightly after that. But then, neither of them could quite let it go.

"It was still mean," Blythe said. "He's not doing it to connect with women he doesn't know. It felt like you were trying to wind up Scarlett."

"I wasn't. I just think it's all a bit much. And it's a little weird that he's spending so much time having these micro interactions with hundreds, maybe thousands, of women he doesn't know."

"You don't think you have an obsession of your own, since you took the time to check out the profiles of his followers? That must have taken a lot of time."

"I didn't check them out. But it didn't take more than a quick glance to notice his following is extremely skewed toward women. That's all."

"You're reading too much into it," she said.

"I don't think I am."

At home, they hardly spoke beyond the necessities, kissing each other goodnight in the briefest way possible. Blythe wasn't sure if there was a chill between them, or they were both simply tired and the disagreement had run its course. It was no secret that Garret believed social media played too big a role in her life, in her business, in the lives of their friends. He was bothered by Kate and Kelsey's enjoyment of TikTok. Whenever one of them wanted to show him something on the app, his impatience and irritation were palpable, at least to Blythe. She was never sure whether the girls picked up on it.

This wasn't the time to be thinking about it. By morning, they would have forgotten. Maybe. Lacey's comments still bothered her as well, but she was exhausted. It had been a long evening, a little too much wine, and she was still burned out from the emotional upheaval caused by the troll.

The moment the lights were out though, it was a different story.

Her eyelids were no longer thick, drifting down over her eyes. Her mind no longer felt soft and ready to let go of her thoughts. A jolt of energy seemed to course through her body. She wanted to think about the details of their evening, replay the conversations. More than that, she wanted to look at Paul's feed herself. She wanted to find out if Garret's impression was correct, or if he'd overreacted.

The moment she heard Garret's breathing reach a deeper, evenly paced state, she slid out of bed. She took her phone off the charger and went downstairs. She got a glass of water and curled up at the end of the sofa, leaving the lights off so that all she saw was the rectangular glow of the screen.

Paul did indeed post reels and photographs of dogs eight, ten, sometimes twelve times a day. It was madness. She wondered how he did his job. He must have a library full of photographs and videos. She was aware that he took their golden lab on long walks every evening, but now she wondered if poor Jasper got any exercise at all, if his owner was constantly stopping to snap photos and clips of the other pets they encountered. Looking at his feed, it was easy to get the impression there were more dogs than people in their suburban neighborhood.

She suppressed a laugh at the thought.

It was tedious work, tapping each image and scrolling through the comments. There were a lot. More than she wanted to bother counting. And if she planned to scope out the gender of each one, she would have to click on each tiny profile picture. Even that wasn't always enough. Some people used their own pets as profile pictures. Others used their children, grandchildren, flowers, vacation spots, sports team logos.

How on earth had Garret determined that most of the commenters were women? He would have had to spend an awful lot of time analyzing the activity. It did seem to be pushing toward obsession. Unless he'd made sexist assumptions—everyone who used a flower or the photo of a couple or children was automatically female? Everyone who included a heart in their comments, or used exclusively emojis, including hearts, was female? Maybe that was it.

What she couldn't understand was—why had he been looking at all? Garret was so disinterested in social media. He hardly paid attention to what she posted. Occasionally, he would let her know he'd seen something. A few times a year he posted a photograph from a vacation or shared a meme to his own profile, but that was about it.

Looking with such focused interest and at such a deep level of detail at the comments on Paul's dog photographs was out of character for him. Was he looking for something specific, or was he concerned about their friend's mental health? Maybe his comment about Paul's constant posts being needy had been carefully worded, covering up what he truly thought.

It was also possible he was trying to protect her. It wouldn't be surprising if he'd gone scrolling through everyone's feeds, trying to find evidence of the troll who was harassing her. He'd only commented on Paul's because he was bothered by the excessive number of posts and wondered what drove Paul to be overly involved with so many strangers.

As she continued her search through Paul's photographs, she tried to recall some of the screen names the troll had used. The first one, and a few others, were burned into her brain. Most of the rest, she'd forgotten because there'd been so many comments, she'd focused on hiding them as quickly as possible, not wanting the horrible words to cling to her memory. Sometimes, it was almost impossible to tell the difference between real people and bots and trolls without looking at their profiles. Regular people often added numbers to their names, so that wasn't always a telling detail.

It was exhausting. She felt utterly depleted, longing to sink into her pillow, but at the same time, wildly alert and aware that if she returned to bed, sleep would remain elusive, leaving her twisting around in the sheets for hours, growing more and more agitated.

She wanted it all to stop.

And Lacey had almost flat-out blamed her for what had happened. That comment about how people *presented* themselves. What was that supposed to mean? Blythe wasn't sure if she was reading into it or not. Lacey had been looking at Paul when she'd said it. She seemed to be directing her comments to him, suggesting his hearts and flowers and attention were hinting to all his female followers that he might be interested in longer chats, that he might be lonely, available, and, possibly, looking for companionship.

Or had that little speech been meant for Blythe? It could absolutely be taken that way. Lacey might have been warning Blythe and Paul both.

But neither one of them had done anything wrong! They were simply posting pieces of their lives, things they cared about. Paul and his love for dogs and the joy they evoked. Blythe and her enthusiasm for pursuing a healthy lifestyle!

There was nothing wrong with the way either of them *presented* themselves. So what was Lacey trying to say? Did she suspect she knew the identity of Blythe's troll? Was the person trolling Blythe the same person bothering Jenna? Lacey hadn't directed her disapproving tone to Jenna at all.

Trying to figure it out made her even more tired and anxious. She scrolled through Paul's feed for another hour before she was so exhausted she put her phone away. She went to bed, falling into a light sleep that was punctuated by the flashing light of a phone screen, filled with blurred messages she couldn't read.

CHAPTER 22

THIRTY YEARS AGO: BLYTHE

*B*lythe's mother fought against her going to the end of the school year camping trip, but Blythe refused to back down.

If she didn't go, she would feel like every kid in her class was out having fun but her.

She would never fit in. She would never find friends.

This time would be different.

Maybe they were tired of making fun of her. They'd used the Care Bear jokes so many times, and they weren't even that funny.

"Why do you want to put yourself in a position where they can hurt you?" her mother asked. "I don't understand."

"They might not."

"They will. That's who they are. They absolutely will," her mother said.

"You don't know that for sure."

Her mother hugged her, pulling Blythe's head close to her chest, pressing her skull against her breastbone until it ached.

"It makes my heart hurt to see you hurt when they do those things," her mother said.

Blythe pulled away. "It's not about your heart. It's my life. And I want to go camping."

Her mother shoved her hand through her hair, gripping it at the roots. She looked tired. "I just hope ..."

A bus took them to the campground. There was one teacher or parent chaperone for every eight kids. It made Blythe feel safer, knowing the constant presence of adults would make it harder for the three girls to torment her. An adult would always be within earshot, always watching. An adult would be lying close to each cluster of kids burrowed inside their sleeping bags. She was safe.

It turned out the adults liked to hang out with other adults. They sat at the picnic tables, sipping coffee out of travel cups, talking, occasionally popping their heads up like gophers to check what was going on around them, to ensure the rules of staying within the identified boundaries were being followed.

Some adults were assigned to lifeguard duty at the side of the small mountain lake, but they were laser-focused on their life-preserving responsibilities, clocking headcount at all times. Teenage drama was not on their duty list.

And so it began, with small whispers, standing in the shallow water of the lake.

Blythe wore shorts and a T-shirt. She hadn't even brought her swimsuit. Her mother had laid it out on the bed, placing it on top of her beach towel with her cover-up top beside it. When her mother left the room, Blythe had packed the towel in her duffel bag, then shoved the swimsuit and cover-up into her bottom dresser drawer beneath her hoodies and sweatshirts.

"Aren't you going swimming?" Crystal purred. "It's so hot." She wiped her hand across her brow, then jutted her left hip out where the thin strap of her bikini hugged her exposed bone.

"I like wading," Blythe said.

"You're sweating like a pig."

Blythe turned slightly. The water was cooling her down, but the back of her neck was plastered with damp hairs that hadn't been caught in her ponytail. She couldn't wipe it now. She would prove Crystal right.

Morgan bent over, cupped some water in her hands, and flung it at Blythe.

Blythe let out an involuntary squeal.

"Re-*lax*. You sound like a little piggy too. I was just trying to cool you down. We don't want you to get heatstroke," Morgan said.

"Such a plump little piggy," Crystal said. "She looks so hot."

As if her words had been a secret command to the others, they all began splashing her. Blythe stumbled out of the water and across the sandy beach to the grassy area. She picked up her towel and patted the water off her face. It was so hot. Now she couldn't even go wading. She didn't want her mother to be right. Why did they always have to find her? And when they did, the other kids seemed to evaporate, as if no one wanted to be around these three either, so they left Blythe alone. No one stopped them. No one seemed to even notice what they were doing.

Right now, most of the kids were in the water, tossing beach balls, or swimming out to the three wood rafts anchored near the edge of the roped off swimming section. She wadded her towel into a ball and began walking back to the area where they'd set up tents and sleeping bags around the clusters of picnic tables.

There was one table with coolers where they could take snacks whenever they wanted—granola bars or fruit, as well as packets of spreadable cheese with crackers. The coolers filled with ice offered bottled water and juice drinks. She grabbed an orange-flavored drink with a tiny straw attached and two packages of crackers and cheese. She took them with her to a grove of trees she'd found when they first arrived. Settled with her back against a redwood tree, knees bent, she peeled back the plastic seal on the crackers and cheese.

She'd finished the first packet when she heard Crystal's shrill laugh. She shoved the empty packet into the pocket of her shorts, unwrapped the straw and stabbed it into the drink. She took a few sips. A moment later, the three girls were standing in a semi-circle, staring down at her. Sometimes she felt as if they'd hidden a tracking device inside every pair of shoes she owned because they always seemed to be able to find her, no matter how elusive she thought she was.

"Eating again? We just had lunch, like twenty minutes ago."

"It was almost three hours," Blythe said.

"You eat all the time. No wonder you're so plump." Crystal sat beside her, leaning against the tree. She grabbed the unopened cheese and tossed it to Morgan. "You don't need this."

"Give it back to me." She'd already eaten the other snack, but having this one taken away had the odd effect of making her feel as if she hadn't eaten all day. Her stomach growled, craving the salty snack.

"Oh, my goodness! Someone's tummy sounds so upset." Crystal stabbed her finger into Blythe's stomach.

"Ouch." Blythe wriggled away from her. Twigs and pebbles snagged the skin on the back of her legs. A stick caught on the edge of her shorts and gouged the soft flesh of her inner thigh. Tears filled her eyes, but she bit her tongue to keep herself from crying out again.

"You are so fat. I think you're fatter than ever." Crystal grabbed her lower leg and dragged Blythe back toward her, causing Blythe to lose her balance. She fell to the side, losing the support of the tree. She landed hard on her elbow. A sharp pain shot through her arm all the way to her neck. This time, she couldn't help it. She cried out. She tried to push herself to her feet, but the heels of her hands skidded on the tiny rocks.

"Don't run away. We're trying to help you." Crystal yanked harder on her leg.

Blythe fell backwards, smacking her head on the ground. She grunted and rolled to the side, trying to escape.

"What is that!?"

She felt Crystal launch herself across her legs, landing hard, then groping around her hips.

"Another snack? You already ate one! And now you're hiding more? What's wrong with you?"

"Give it back to me." Blythe scrabbled away like a crab, stones digging into her palms, her wrists aching as she tried to pull against the grip Crystal still had on her leg.

"There are wild animals out here," Destiny said. "Coyotes. Mountain lions. Do you know that?"

Blythe felt herself starting to cry. She collapsed onto her tailbone, no longer able to hold herself up. She sat her juice drink on the ground, the liquid slowly seeping out into the dirt.

"You're basically fattening yourself up for them!" Destiny squealed.

All three girls cackled like crones around a boiling cauldron, into which they planned to toss a human sacrifice.

Blythe was sobbing now. Why wouldn't they leave her alone? Didn't they want to go swimming with the other kids? It was so hot. They were still in their swimsuits. They should be in the lake, showing off for the boys, splashing around, swimming to the raft or sunning themselves on the sand. Why was it so much fun to torture her? She didn't understand.

"You're the fattest one here. The mountain lions will sniff the air and come straight to your sleeping bag," Destiny said.

"The coyotes will howl," Morgan said.

"They'll smell all that juicy fat," Destiny said.

"And lick their lips," Morgan said.

Crystal giggled. "Coyotes don't have lips. But they'll salivate for sure. And they'll be howling and their howls will be saying, *Which one is the fattest?* And the fattest by a long shot is the girl right there. The one with the reddish hair. So easy to pick out. Such white, white skin, glowing in the moonlight."

"They will so, *so* find you. And they'll do a mountain lion and coyote dance of joy!" said Morgan.

"And then," Destiny licked her lips with a loud smack. "They will eat you. Because you have so much juicy, delicious fat."

All three shrieked with laughter. Crystal stood, still laughing, as if she'd never heard anything so hysterically funny in her entire life. She picked up Blythe's orange drink and squeezed it until the container was empty. She dropped it into the goopy puddle she'd created. She peeled off the cover on the crackers. She spread cheese on the first cracker and handed it to Destiny. She did the same with the other two, handing one to Morgan, and eating the last one herself.

"That was delish!" Crystal said. "Maybe we saved you from becoming a midnight snack. Try not to eat so much now. We'll be watching." She wiggled her index finger at Blythe as if chastising her.

They turned and sauntered back toward the lake.

Blythe stood and picked up the trash they'd tossed around before leaving. She took it to the trashcan, dumped it, and walked away from the camping area, following a short trail, looking for another cluster of trees where she wouldn't be found. A place where she could cry without being heard, without being seen.

That evening, she was famished, but only ate two tablespoons of the baked beans, and three bites of her hotdog. She could feel the eyes of the three girls boring into her, even though they were seated far away. After a volleyball game at dusk, followed by a campfire with songs and some ghost stories read by the seventh grade English teacher, they all used the restroom facilities to wash and brush before getting into their sleeping bags.

No one was tired. Bedtime had been dictated by the sun and the lack of anything to do, since they were without TV and without adequate light for any further group activities. There was a lot of whispering and sneaking around. People brought snacks into their sleeping bags despite the dire warnings about wild animals, although more likely to be raccoons and possums. Still mountain lions, coyotes, and even bears weren't unheard of.

Every half hour, the adults made the rounds of the tents, issuing threats about making sure there was *absolutely no food* in the tent, and going to sleep, and mostly checking to make sure there were no boys in any girls' tents and vice versa.

Blythe was in a tent with five girls she didn't know well. Her sleeping bag was by the zippered opening, which she liked because she thought she would feel claustrophobic near the back of the tent.

She liked the idea of being able to easily escape, although she couldn't explain to herself why she might need to. She also liked knowing she could get up the moment it grew light and slip outside to spend some time alone by the lake, drinking in the quiet.

Finally, most of the tents were quiet, with only the occasional whisper or giggle puncturing the night air. Blythe drifted to sleep, feeling more alone than she ever had in her life. Her mother had been absolutely right. She shouldn't have come. Even the other girls in her tent mostly ignored her.

She woke to the sound of the zipper beside her, the flap opening. She opened her eyes into the beam of a flashlight, the glow catching the edge of Crystal's narrow face, her eyes fierce, filled with determination, and a certain amount of malice.

"Okay, little piggy. You thought it was so important to fatten yourself up. The mountain lions are waiting." Crystal grabbed the end of Blythe's sleeping bag and pulled her through the opening. "And don't you dare make a sound, or things will get really bad for you."

Destiny was beside her, and she quickly grabbed the other corner of the sleeping bag. Together, they began pulling Blythe out of the tent and across the campsite toward the woods.

Blythe struggled, twisting wildly inside her bag, trying to creep out the opening, but they were moving too fast. Destiny had lifted her slightly off the ground so her head was bumping against Destiny's knees.

"Please," she whimpered. "Please don't do this. Take me back."

"You fattened yourself up. It's your own fault," Destiny said.

"You are *so* heavy. This is hard work," Crystal said.

Blythe began sobbing. A moment later, a thick piece of fabric, maybe a sock, was stuffed into her mouth. She coughed and gagged. She tried pulling it out, but they twisted the bag so it was folded tightly around her, turning it into a cocoon that prevented her from moving any of her limbs more than a few inches from her sides.

After what seemed like half an hour, but was probably only a few minutes, they dropped her onto the ground. The flashlight went out. They sank into total darkness except for the faraway stars and a thin sliver of the moon. It was impossible to even see Crystal in the darkness.

"You'll make a yummy midnight snack," Crystal said. "Sweet dreams. And I don't recommend trying to find your way back. You'll get lost in the dark and you might never be found. Better to wait for daylight."

The flashlight came on, but it quickly grew dim, then disappeared as the girls ran back the way they'd come.

Blythe curled up, hugging her knees. She cried so hard her chest ached.

After a long time, she stopped, too tired to cry anymore. She poked her head out of her sleeping bag and saw nothing but darkness and the even darker forms of trees and large boulders. She scooted deeper into her bag, folded the excess fabric over her head, and tried not to think about what might happen.

After a long while, she fell asleep.

The sound of something running, followed by a screech, woke her. As if her body had already felt fear before she'd woken, her heart was pounding the moment she was conscious. Her breath came in short gasps. She tried to soften it, hoping the creature didn't hear her panicked sounds.

When it faded into the night, she lay in the silence, then slowly inched toward the top of her sleeping bag. She poked her face out, hoping for some sign of morning light. It was still completely dark.

Another sound—the crunch of someone walking? She pinched the bag around her face, trying to make the exposed part of her as small as possible. Then, without warning, a bright light shone in her face. She blinked, squinted, then closed her eyes for a moment.

She opened them again in narrow slits. A girl she'd seen before, but had never spoken to, a girl who was new at her school this year, stared down at her. She held the flashlight, staring into Blythe's eyes.

Blythe wondered what horrible punishment would be delivered now.

CHAPTER 23

NOW: BLYTHE

It was a risk to show up at Lacey's house uninvited and unannounced, but one Blythe had decided she needed to take. Normally, she and her friends texted or called before they stopped by. But if she did that, Lacey would ask about the purpose of her visit, and Blythe felt completely helpless to explain that.

Instead, she'd made a quick trip to her favorite gift store. She'd bought Lacey a vanilla scented candle, a bottle of milk body lotion, and a decorative stone heart. Explaining the gift would also be a challenge. She would see how things unfolded. Hopefully, it wouldn't feel awkward. Hopefully, she wouldn't look like she was trying to buy her way back into Lacey's affection.

Couldn't a friend bring a gift for no reason? That would be her explanation.

The purpose of her visit was to find out why Lacey had cancelled her last three workout sessions. She had a pretty good idea, but Lacey needed to tell her. And if Lacey was giving up altogether, she needed to tell her that, too. Lacey couldn't keep cancelling each week. It was stressful not knowing until the last minute whether or not she was coming. And it was hard on Blythe's schedule because she couldn't plan anything else. It was unfair and it would damage their friendship if it went on like this.

Besides, she wanted to clear the air. She wanted to know what was going on.

She rang the bell.

Lacey opened the door. She didn't look surprised. She must have checked the security camera before she answered. "This is a surprise."

"I have something for you." Blythe held out the white box with its wide, white silk ribbon.

"My birthday's not until September."

"It's just for fun."

"Thank you. I ..." Lacey laughed. "I'm not sure what to say."

"You already said it. Do you have time to talk?"

Lacey laughed again, with a harder edge this time. "So, it's not just for fun. It's to get you in the door when I wasn't expecting you."

"Don't be like that. Please. We really need to talk. Don't you think?"

Lacey relaxed her posture and brushed her hair away from her face. "Okay." She stepped away from the door, opening it wider.

Blythe entered the house and followed Lacey to the kitchen. Lacey placed the box on the counter. "Coffee?"

"Sure."

Lacey poured grounds into the coffeemaker, filled it with water, and turned it on. She got two mugs out of the cabinet and turned her attention to the gift. "Should I open it?"

"Yes."

Lacey untied the bow and removed the gifts. "Thank you. You're so sweet."

Blythe smiled. "You're welcome."

"I still don't understand why."

"Maybe because I've missed your workouts."

"That's a bit much for a few workouts. Is this a guilt trip?"

"Not at all."

Lacey poured coffee into the mugs and placed them on the table. They sat across from each other. A warm breeze came through the open window behind Blythe. "You keep cancelling. I'm not sure if you're quitting or something else is going on."

"Do you make personal visits and bring gifts to all your clients who cancel a few sessions?"

"This is different. We're friends. If something's wrong, I want to know."

Lacey was quiet for a few seconds. She picked up her mug and blew on the coffee. She took a tentative sip. "It's just all a little much. I'm tired of feeling shitty about myself. I've decided to focus on self-acceptance." She gave Blythe a smile that bordered on grim.

"You can work on your health and accept yourself at the same time. I never meant to give the impression that—"

"But you do give that *impression*." Lacey made air quotes with her free hand. "It's always about doing more. Adding another pound to the weight machine, pushing harder, replacing a cookie with a carrot."

Blythe laughed. "I don't think I ever suggested you should replace a cookie with a carrot."

"You know what I'm talking about. It's never enough. It's like there's always something wrong with me. Something wrong with how much I can lift, how much cardio I'm doing, what I'm eating. And underneath it all—how my body looks, how much I weigh."

"You chose your weight goal. You wanted to—"

"You're right. I did. But now I've decided my weight goal is the weight I am. In fact, I'm not going to weigh myself at all anymore. It's kind of sick. Always measuring yourself. Always thinking you need to be different than you are."

"I never said you need to be different. I'm really sorry if it came across that way." Blythe took a sip of coffee. It was delicious. She took another soothing taste. It made her feel warm and comforted. Until the caffeine kicked in, it was calming. "Is that what all the mugs are about—accepting?"

"Absolutely. You put a lot of things on your social pages that make people feel they aren't quite what they should be."

"I don't think I do that."

"It's subtle, but it's there. I want to add an alternative viewpoint."

"I wish you wouldn't tag me. It ... well, I don't want it to hurt my business."

Lacey let out a staccato laugh. "I doubt that. There are plenty of women who want to get into shape. Who think they aren't good enough, who believe they need to sculpt themselves into something perfect."

"That's not what I do. You're not being fair."

"Maybe not, but I want people to accept themselves. To feel happy in their own skin, to be at home in the bodies they were born with, not always trying to be someone else."

"I'm not trying to push people to be anyone else," Blythe said.

"To be honest, I think your approach is more damaging than you realize. Maybe others feel that too. People don't always see the reality of their own situations as clearly as others do."

Blythe sipped more coffee. If she spoke, she might start crying. She wanted to help people focus on their *health*. What Lacey was saying was entirely unfair. She'd never once suggested that anyone wasn't good enough or that they shouldn't accept themselves as they were. She should know that better than anyone. She *did* know that. She'd lived it. And she was always, *always* hyper-aware of that when she was working with her clients.

"It sounds like you don't have a very good opinion of what I post on social media," Blythe said. "Or my work overall."

Lacey looked serious, but said nothing.

"Is there another reason you don't want health coaching anymore?"

"No." Lacey had barely touched her coffee. Now she pushed the mug away from her. She glanced at her watch.

Blythe decided to ignore the obvious signal. She would never get this settled if she left now. "Are you sure? I feel like something isn't right with us."

"Really?"

"All of that about Paul's social media ... at the barbecue. You said he needed to be careful about how he presented himself," Blythe said.

"Everyone loves dogs. Right?"

"So, was that directed at me?"

"It wasn't *directed* at anyone," Lacey said. "I was talking about social media in general. People should be careful. Don't you think? You never know who you're talking to, when it's not someone you know personally. Paul, all of us."

"So do you think I'm presenting a message that implies people aren't okay, that they need to fix themselves, or something like that? Or are you talking about trolls? Like Jenna's and—"

Lacey burst out laughing. "I barely remember the conversation. If you feel you need to take it to heart, then you should. If you think there's something wrong with what you're doing, you're the one who needs to decide that. It's not my business to tell you what to post or what to say, or how to interact with clients or strangers or anyone."

Blythe took another sip of coffee. It was starting to make her stomach feel tense. She wasn't used to drinking a second cup in the middle of the morning. When she did, she usually had something to eat with it. She put the mug down. This wasn't how she'd thought things would go, but she had no idea how to get their friendship back on a smoother path. It sounded like their coaching relationship was over, which was probably for the best.

But Lacey was a close friend, and she suddenly seemed almost hostile. Blythe still wasn't entirely sure what she'd done. Everything Lacey had said sounded like a deliberate twisting of Blythe's words and intentions.

"I'm really sorry if I ever made you feel you had to change who you are, or that I don't accept you, if that's it. And I don't ..." This was too hard. Why was she doing this? She didn't have to apologize for how she *presented* herself, whatever that meant. All she was doing was trying to be herself. Just like Lacey was. If they started picking apart and analyzing every little thing, every photograph, every comment, every reaction, they would drive themselves insane.

Lacey stood. "I have some things I need to take care of."

Blythe pushed her chair away from the table. "Thanks for the coffee."

"Any time."

Blythe stood, and Lacey gave her a hug.

It felt warm and almost ... forgiving.

Was she misinterpreting everything? Maybe she was the one who had made it uncomfortable by bringing a gift, by not simply accepting that Lacey didn't want to get coaching anymore, by grilling her and challenging her reasons for quitting. It wasn't that complicated after all.

At the same time, she still felt there was something Lacey wasn't saying.

CHAPTER 24

*W*hen Blythe arrived home, she had forty minutes to kill before her client arrived for a coaching session on meal planning. There wasn't enough time to work on new content for social media, and it only took a few minutes to respond to the comments that had appeared while she'd been at Lacey's. She was too edgy to read, and she wasn't in the mood to put the time to good use with a dust cloth or a sponge.

She sat on the sofa and stared out at the backyard through the bifold doors. A hummingbird swooped up to the hanging fuchsia, darting from blossom to blossom. Normally, she loved watching the exquisite, delicate creatures with their shimmering feathers and nearly invisible wings that fluttered like she imagined fairy wings might. But now, she found its frantic movements mirrored her feelings—anxious and unable to settle.

Picking up her phone, she spent the remaining time scrolling through social media, adding likes and comments to others' posts. She took extra care to make a thoughtful comment on Lacey's most recent update.

The meeting with her client helped her regain her footing. Hannah was eager to learn how she could change her cooking style without sending her family into fits of complaining. She sat beside

Blythe, looking at the large computer display on the desk, her eyes wide with interest, snapping screen shots, even though Blythe kept reminding her she would be emailing a summary of everything they talked about, complete with links.

When they were finished, Hannah thanked her, gushing that she was so grateful. Part of the reason for her interest was that her daughter's doctor had said she was low on iron. Hannah was excited that her whole family could start getting healthier. She couldn't wait to feel like she had more energy. She laughed. "I'm tired of being tired."

When Hannah was gone, Blythe closed the browser windows and documents on her computer. Whatever was bothering Lacey, maybe it had more to do with Lacey. If she felt Blythe was trying to make her change, that Blythe made her feel as if she couldn't accept herself, that was something inside Lacey. It had nothing to do with Blythe's coaching.

The thought calmed her, although the throbbing sense of anxiety lingered, refusing to leave her alone.

She picked up her phone. Five texts from Jenna. One from Kate. She read Kate's first.

> Kate: Sleeping over at Mira's. OK? Her mom will bring me by later to pick up my stuff.

Blythe smiled that her daughter asked permission by tossing an *OK?* in the middle of informing Blythe of her plans. She was pleased with Kate's confidence, then wondered if Kate should be a little more ... something ... at her age. No, she was pleased. She smiled and texted back, telling Kate to have a good time.

Jenna's texts were panicked requests for Blythe to call her as soon as possible. Why Jenna hadn't called her instead of texting requests that, by the final message, sounded like demands? She tapped Jenna's number.

After a single ring, Jenna answered. "What took so long?"

"I had a client."

"You always have a client."

"I don't, but what's the emergency?"

Jenna's voice sounded teary. "My sales are tanking. I don't get it. For the past week, they've been half of what's typical."

"That's terrible," Blythe said. "I'm really sorry. Do you have any idea what's going on?"

"No! And I ... we could ... I feel like I'm letting Oliver down. We rely on my income. I've been working at this for years. I put so much into this. Everything. And my work is so beautiful. I know it is. People love it. I just don't understand why ..." She broke off, crying softly.

"I'm really sorry ..." Blythe did not know what to say. Was Jenna asking for suggestions? After her conversation with Lacey, she was still feeling wobbly. She was in no position to give advice about self-promotion, if that's what Jenna was looking for. And she certainly didn't have any insight into why there'd been a sudden downturn in sales. She knew nothing about jewelry. She knew nothing at all about selling a physical product.

"I was thinking I should have a massive sale," Jenna said.

"Massive?"

"Huge discounts—sixty percent, maybe."

"Won't that cut into—"

"I'd still make a profit. But if I can triple the quantity or more, then—"

"It sounds risky. But if you think it would work."

"I don't *know* what will work. I'm desperate! Why do you think it's not selling?"

"I don't know. Everyone has different tastes." She couldn't point out it was expensive. She'd hinted at it before, and every time she did, Jenna flipped out. Surely she knew that. Selling things online was tricky. There was the trust issue ... and taste was part of it. The bracelets and necklaces Jenna made were often impulse buys at art fairs. Online sales were more difficult.

"Are you listening?" Jenna asked.

"Yes."

"Why are you so distracted?"

"I'm ... I have a lot on my mind. I was talking to Lacey. She implied I'm presenting myself wrong on social media. That Paul is too, I guess. It feels like she's hinting that I *invited* this troll."

"That's not true. Does she think I invited the creeper who's stalking *me*!?"

"She didn't say, but maybe."

"It's traumatizing, you know? Accusing someone of asking for that, or doing anything to cause a bully or stalker to pick on you. It's the worst. You know that."

Blythe didn't say anything. It *was* traumatizing. She hated Lacey's implication that she'd invited the disgusting, degrading comments on her posts. Had Lacey read all of them? Telling Blythe it was her fault that those things had been said to her, and about her, was almost as painful as the comments themselves.

It felt as if Lacey had been trying to get their friends to believe they were all attracting unwanted attention—that Paul was enticing women to comment on his photographs, getting some thrill out of all their gushing words. Lacey acted as if he was putting himself out there trying to get women to come on to him, to contact him in his DMs.

Lacey hadn't said any of that, but the way she spoke ... her tone was so harsh and critical. Blythe couldn't get the words out of her mind—*You have to be careful about how you present yourself.*

"I don't think she was talking about you," Blythe said.

"But the same thing happened to me. She might as well have."

Blythe moved the phone away from her ear. She tapped it to put it on speakerphone.

"I'm upset that she said—"

"Yes." Blythe felt tired and confused. She didn't know what to think. "I should get going."

"But we didn't finish talking about my sales. I'm losing my mind. I don't know how I'm going to fix this. You have to help me."

"I don't have any ideas."

"Do you think I should have a massive sale or not?"

"I don't know. Maybe?"

"I need more support. Our group was supposed to have each other's backs. Remember? It feels like that's starting to crumble," Jenna said.

"Maybe we're all moving into a new phase."

Jenna made a sound that was like the pained cry of an animal. A few minutes later, they said their goodbyes. It was clear Jenna was wounded, but Blythe felt helpless. She had no idea how to boost Jenna's business. What they were offering was too different. It was one thing to support each other with social media likes and breezy comments, but she couldn't be giving strategic advice. It wasn't fair of Jenna to ask.

She checked her feeds to see what had happened while she was talking. Not much. She responded to a few comments, stuck the phone in her pocket, and walked down the hall toward the kitchen, completely uninspired about making dinner.

When she checked her phone again, ten minutes later, her first instinct was to stuff it into the garbage disposal, turn on the water, and flip the switch. She imagined listening to the metal teeth grind the plastic and glass, chewing through until it reached the chips and wires inside. Then it would all be gone. Except it wouldn't. It would live on in cyberspace.

Another comment from the troll. Front and center on the blandest post she could have imagined.

She'd posted a photograph of a rack of colorful dumbbells, set in a pyramid formation. She'd altered the photo to black and white, then added neon color to the weights, giving it a dramatic, retro look. She loved it, and she didn't think there was anything whatsoever that could attract a nasty comment. But there it was.

You know your fans like to see your bod in a bikini. What happened to you? Stop holding back—why aren't you putting yourself out there?!

Something about the tone felt different from the previous trolling comments. She stared at it, knowing she should make it disappear as fast as she could, but she was unable to stop staring.

Maybe it was the use of the word *bod*. Maybe it was the insistence she should stop holding back. But she felt it echoed her conversation with Lacey.

It was impossible to put her finger on why she thought that. Paranoia? The way the words were arranged? The deepening unsettled feeling in her chest that had become more pervasive since she'd left Lacey's, rather than dissolving with that hug that had seemed so forgiving?

It had to be paranoia. There was no way a woman who had been her friend for fifteen years, who had raised her children alongside Blythe, who had been a client and a huge supporter of Blythe's wellness career, would do something so underhanded. So downright cruel. Lacey would *never* set up an anonymous account to harass her.

But why couldn't Blythe stop thinking that something in those words echoed her conversation with Lacey?

CHAPTER 25

*T*hat evening, Kelsey also ended up going out to spend the night with a friend.

Blythe opened a bottle of wine, knowing Garret would think it was because they were having a romantic dinner for two, but the truth was, she needed it to calm the flashes of anxiety pulsing through her body every time she saw a notification appear on her phone.

After dinner, they took the bottle and their glasses outside to the patio. They sat in the Adirondack chairs, gazing at the darkening water of the pool and the lush plants surrounding it. The night air was warm and quiet except for the voices of children kicking a soccer ball three houses a way.

After clearing the notifications, Blythe placed her phone on the small table between their chairs. None of them looked alarming, and she didn't want to interrupt the good mood by paying attention to social media when she should be enjoying her husband's company. She probably should have left the phone in the house, but Garret's phone was also on the table.

If he was honest, he was as handcuffed to it as she was, waiting for a late arriving email he was expecting from a colleague, checking the news or a sports update, and his constant interest in the weather.

She took a sip of wine. She let out a deep sigh as she placed her glass on the table.

"Tired?" Garret asked.

"A little. Stressful day."

"What's going on?"

"Jenna's worried that sales are down. Lacey said I make her feel like she can't accept herself for who she is, or something like that. So she's finished with coaching."

"Hm."

He sounded disinterested, possibly only distracted. She wondered if she should tell him the rest. She picked up her glass and took another sip. As she turned to put it down, a notification flashed across the screen. The patio was dark except for the strings of lights across the area where they sat. The notification appeared like a beacon, the light hitting the glass, making the wine glow.

It was from a strange screen name—a series of numbers and letters, including two X's and a Z. Not a good sign. She felt the garlic from dinner rise in her esophagus. She grabbed the stem of her glass and took a large gulp.

"Are you okay?" Garret looked at her with concern.

She nodded, unable to speak. She picked up the bottle and poured a small amount of wine into her glass.

"Slow down," Garret said.

She took another swallow and placed her glass and the bottle on the table.

"What's happening?" he asked.

She grabbed her phone, opened it, and began hiding the comments without reading. She blocked the account.

"I thought we weren't doing phones," Garret said.

"It's the troll. I can't let the comments sit there. The things they write are so ..." She shuddered. She stared at her phone, expecting more to pop up any minute.

"Why do you even need the damn accounts? It hardly seems worth it if you're stressed all the time."

"I'm not."

"You are. Every time I look at you, I see panic on your face. You're hunched over your phone like a gargoyle, stabbing your finger at it, scowling and muttering to yourself."

She laughed. She didn't want to because she felt sick and anxious and angry, but she couldn't help herself. She laughed. It felt nice.

"It's good you can still laugh," he said. "Seriously, why do you need it? You have a full slate of clients."

"But they come and go. Lacey quit, right?"

"Can't you get new clients the old-fashioned way? Word of mouth? Flyers at the gym or something?"

"No one looks at all those tacky papers hanging at the gym."

"Do a nice one. Pay someone to put it together so it has a pro feel to it."

"I have to be on social media. It keeps the momentum. My current clients use it to communicate with each other, and with me."

He took a sip of wine. He turned his face toward the three small queen palms to his right.

Silence fell over them. The kids playing soccer had gone inside. It was so quiet she wondered if she should talk, simply to fill the space with sound, pushing away the sensation that he was waiting for her to admit social media was turning her into a gargoyle. There should be a better explanation for why social media was critical to her business, but right now, she couldn't seem to think of what it might be. She just knew that everyone was on there, and disappearing would make it look like her business wasn't thriving. If she didn't exist on social media, most of her clients would form the impression she didn't exist at all.

In some ways, she wondered if that was true of human beings as well as businesses. It was how people found you. It was how they communicated. Social media was the reflection of your existence, *proof* of your existence. Wasn't it? But Garret's presence there was thin, almost invisible, and his life was full and complete. He was centered and calm. He was content with his life. Despite his demanding position with a high-tech company, he experienced less stress than she did most of the time.

Garret picked up the wine bottle and refilled both their glasses. He placed the now-empty bottle on the ground. "The thing that's bothering me, since you've had this trolling issue, is that half the activity on social media appears to be scammers, bots, trolls, or people with even darker intentions."

"It's not half."

"Based on your reactions lately, I think it is. And I'm concerned about Kelsey and Kate."

"What do they have to do with it?"

"I'm starting to worry about how your social media activity affects their safety."

"Why?"

"Because you're right, the things this creep, or creeps, whichever it is, has said are really disgusting. And even though it's just words, you don't know if it's going to escalate."

"I still don't see what that has to do with Kelsey and Kate."

"You've posted pictures of them in the past. What's to keep this freak from doing something to hurt them? Even if it's virtual, it would be devastating. And what if it's worse?"

CHAPTER 26

*B*lythe downed the remainder of her wine in three gulps. She stood and went into the house without speaking another word to Garret. The pain in her heart was so sharp, if she were older, she'd be certain she was having a heart attack.

After all the grace and tenderness and forgiveness she'd shown to Garret over the years, all the acceptance of his flaws and mistakes, she'd thought he also saw the best in her. She'd thought he looked at her always through loving eyes, knowing she had the best intentions, even when she screwed up. Most of all, she'd thought he knew, she'd *believed* he knew with every cell in his brain, that she loved their daughters more than her own life. She would *never* do anything to hurt them, to expose them to even the slightest chance of harm. She would jump in front of a speeding car, shoving them out of the way, not giving a moment's thought to what might happen to her own body, as long as every single bone in their bodies remained solid and whole.

Her social media wasn't about Kelsey and Kate. It was built around her coaching business. As far as she could recall, she rarely mentioned her family, and never by name. She sometimes made comments about Garret and had occasionally posted pictures of the two of them, but she'd always asked him first.

She had no memory of posting photographs of her daughters. The thought filled her with dread. And guilt.

Had she posted photographs of them on her public account?

Was her rage at Garret misplaced?

He was still on the patio, sipping his wine. He looked calm and relaxed, unbothered that he'd accused her of not caring about Kelsey and Kate's safety. Was that what he'd said? Now, she wasn't quite sure exactly what he'd said. Lately, I couldn't seem to remember anything clearly.

When would she have posted pictures of her daughters? She couldn't think of a reason why that would have seemed a good fit. Often, she asked, and received permission, to post pictures and stories of the women she coached. Photographs of herself with happy, glowing clients. Pictures of them sharing smoothies after a workout, or photographs they sent of themselves or their families eating meals from recipes she'd helped develop for their meal planning.

There were hundreds, thousands of pictures over the years. And plenty of those had been her own meals, smoothies, selfies, photographs of her workout clothes, gym equipment, videos of her feet running, videos of her curling dumbbells, videos of her athletic shoe-clad feet doing steps ...

She could hardly remember all the things she'd posted.

But Kelsey and Kate?

She never posted vacation photos. She was absolutely sure she'd never mentioned their names. She wasn't even sure she'd said anything about having twins, or noted their ages specifically. She'd probably made comments about having daughters, about mothering toddlers and then school-aged kids, about the transition into the pre-teen years. But it was all generic.

On her private accounts, she shared family pictures, but never on her public page. Never.

Now, she felt an overwhelming panic that she'd either made a mistake at some point, or that she'd been so naïve in the early years, she hadn't thought about it. Maybe when they were younger, before the darker aspects of social media revealed themselves, she'd been less cautious?

Glancing outside, she saw Garret still sipping wine. Still unconcerned with how he'd attacked her in the most tender area of her heart. What had he said, exactly? She didn't know anymore. But she did know one thing. She needed to comb through years of posts, thousands of photographs, to see whether Garret was misremembering.

She grabbed a bottle of sparkling lemon water from the fridge, took her phone into the office, and curled up on the sofa.

She opened her accounts and began the tedious, hand-cramping task of scrolling back through the timeline of her business's online history. It should have been an uplifting and satisfying journey, seeing all the really quite beautiful and enticing photographs and videos, the thousands of likes, hundreds of comments on many posts. Instead, it made her eyes bleary. Her fingers grew stiff. The back of her hand and her wrist ached as she swept her finger across her phone. Every so often, she changed hands.

After twenty or thirty minutes, Garret knocked and opened the door. "Seriously? You left me alone out there? You had to sneak away to feed your addiction?"

She couldn't put her phone down. She would lose her place and be forced to start over. She balanced it carefully as she looked up at him. "I'm not feeding my *addiction*, Garret. I'm checking to see if there are any pictures of our daughters! You seem to think I'm endangering them, as if it's my fault that some creep is harassing *me*. So I'm going through every damn photograph I've posted for the past ten years to make sure I'm not mistaken. Because I'm pretty sure I never posted their pictures! But now, I'm *not* sure. So I have to check. Thanks for that. And thanks for assuming I'm not careful about looking out for their safety." She looked down at her phone.

He stepped into the office. She could feel him moving closer. She shrank into the sofa and started scrolling, more slowly this time.

"That's not what I said."

"Yes, it is."

"I didn't mean—"

"Whatever you meant, you put doubt in my mind. So now, I have to check."

"Can I help? I'm sorry."

"No. You can't *help*."

"I didn't mean to say you would do anything to hurt them. I just think you spend so much time on social media. And you're always upset about it. The whole thing seems so ... unhealthy."

"It's life. Sometimes life is unhealthy." She ran her finger slowly across the screen. She'd covered two years now.

"Do you want to watch a movie?"

"I can't. I'm not doing anything until I look at every single picture. I don't want to expose them to this creep because he won't go away and I don't know what he wants. So I'm not stopping until I've checked the whole thing."

"That could take the rest of the evening."

"It might."

"I thought we—"

"I'm not going to stop and have to start all over tomorrow. And to be honest, you scared me. So I want to be sure there's absolutely nothing that puts them in danger. As you said."

"I don't think I said—"

"You did."

"I'm sorry. It's possible I misremembered. Or confused it with your personal account."

"I'll know before I go to bed." She lifted her face slightly and gave him a determined grimace.

"I hope you'll be done before—"

"I'll be done when I'm done."

He left without saying anything further.

She continued scrolling, losing track of time. She'd now reached the point in her life when the twins would have been eight or nine years old. It was probably far enough. No troll was going to put in this much effort, was he? She didn't think so. It seemed absurd. But when she thought about the work he'd already put into harassing her, scaring her, making her squirm with shame and discomfort, she wasn't sure.

When she was finally finished, she was more upset with Garret than ever. There hadn't been a single photograph of their daughters. She'd wasted a perfect, relaxing evening because of Garret's irrational dislike of social media. Clearly, he'd confused her personal accounts with her business accounts. Or, he hadn't confused anything at all. He'd assumed, because he hadn't looked at what she posted often enough to have a good sense of what her brand looked like.

She tossed the phone onto the sofa beside her, leaned her head back, and pressed her hands over her face. She was tired, but too wound up for sleep. She had a slight headache, despite her constant sipping from the sparkling water. The bottle was empty, but she felt too drained to walk to the kitchen for another. She was craving sugar, but was too tired even to go searching for a cookie or a piece of candy.

Lowering her hands, she picked up her phone. A notification. It never stopped.

Where are those pics? I keep asking and asking. Hotties need to show UP.

It was posted on her photograph of the weights. Unbelievable. Now, it didn't matter what she posted. Everything was provocative to this freak. She hid the message, her eyes blurred with tears of exhaustion and frustration.

Another comment popped up before she could block the profile.

Wear the black one. You'll burn it all down in that one. Even now.

Her face was so hot, she felt drops of perspiration around her hairline. Her heart raced as she hid the comment and blocked the name. She powered down her phone.

Was this real? She never wore black. She always wore beachy earth tones—sage and sand and pale gray-blue. She didn't recall ever owning a black swimsuit. And if she had, did this mean this person knew her? Had known her? Was this one of the girls who had bullied her? Did she own a black swimsuit then? She didn't remember ever wearing a swimsuit when those horrible girls were around.

Or was it all just a mind trip to drive her insane? She wasn't sure if someone was watching her, someone who knew her, who knew her life. Or was he simply trying to terrify her? If that was the case, it was working. One hundred percent, it was working.

CHAPTER 27

JENNA

*E*very night, Oliver told her more ominous-sounding stories about the atmosphere at work. Many were simply rumors he'd heard from co-workers. Some were conclusions drawn from noticing which people were invited to meetings and who was excluded. A few of his concerns swirled around projects that had been put on hold, or that appeared to be canceled, but for which no one in authority would give a straight answer. All of this added up to the appearance of an increasing belief that his job was at risk.

Nothing definite had been said. No percentage of employees to be cut had been mentioned. The organizations that might be affected hadn't been named. It was all speculation mixed with far too much gossip and worry.

"You should focus on doing great work. Showing them how valuable you are," Jenna said.

"I don't think you understand the dynamic." Oliver cut off a large piece of chicken and shoved it into his mouth. He chewed vigorously, as if he were chewing a large, slightly stale piece of gum.

"Do you like the chicken?" she asked.

"Yeah. Yeah, it's fine."

"Fine? Or do you like it?"

"I like it."

"So, it's good?"

"Yes."

"If they see you focused on work instead of gossiping, if they notice you're—"

"You don't get it, Jenna."

"I'm trying to be positive."

"And I appreciate that." He smiled.

She glanced toward the entryway at the sound of the front door opening. Naomi had gone to an amusement park for the day. She'd agreed to be home by ten o'clock, so hearing the door this early was startling.

The door remained closed. "Did you hear that?" Jenna asked.

"Hm."

"The door. Was someone at the front door?"

"I don't think so," he said.

She resumed eating. She was proud of herself. She hadn't allowed concerns about Oliver's job to trouble her all day. She'd focused on creating reels and several series of still photos to post on social media.

It was so easy to let her fears start eating away at the back of her mind. Slowly, they crept forward, worming their way through every part of her brain, until she was consumed, unable to accomplish the simplest task. She couldn't take a photograph or add the hook to a bracelet, much less work on writing exciting words that would make people stop their mindless scrolling to click on her photos, look through the images, and finally, click the button to make the jump to her online store.

From there, she had to further entice them to fall in love with her jewelry through beautifully shot photographs, without chasing them away with prices that were too high. She had to persuade them to trust her so they would select a few pieces, enter their address and phone number, and finally, their credit card information, or select the button for a payment service app. There were a lot of hurdles.

After putting in hours of work, everything was ready for the big sale she'd planned. This evening, she would call Blythe and ask her to look at the staging pages on her website. She would send her the posts planned for social media to get her input. Hopefully, Blythe would be less self-absorbed than she'd been the last time Jenna tried talking to her.

She asked Oliver for an update on the rumors, asked him what percentage he thought his odds were today. He loved answering that question. She only half-listened to his answers. She wanted to get back to her project. She was eager for it to be finished. She couldn't wait to send it live and watch the sales accelerate. She couldn't wait to present Oliver with a big fat check, to see the worry disappear from his eyes, if only for a short time.

After dinner, they loaded the dishwasher. "I'll finish washing up," he said.

She knew he would settle in watching the news when he was done. She grabbed her phone and went into her workroom. She texted Blythe, asking if she had time for a quick call.

It was ten minutes before Blythe responded.

Blythe: What's up?

Jenna: I wanted to show you the web pages and stuff for my sale. It will only take five minutes.

Blythe: Are you sure it won't take longer?

Jenna felt her jaw tighten until it ached. Yes, she was sure. And was it really that awful if it took six minutes? Or seven? She added a thumbs up and hit Blythe's number.

"It's for my blowout sale," she said when Blythe answered.

"What blowout sale?" Blythe's voice sounded far away.

"Hello?" Jenna said. "I can't hear you very well."

"I'm here." Blythe's voice was marginally louder.

"That sale I asked you about. To get things turned around. To get more attention."

"Right."

"Don't you remember? We talked about it. How can you not remember?"

Blythe was quiet. There were some background noises, then silence.

"Do you remember talking about it?"

"Yes. Are you going to show me the pages? I only have a few minutes."

Jenna felt like crying. Why was Blythe being so cold? It felt like she didn't care. This was important. It felt like a matter of life and death. If Oliver lost his job ... but she didn't want to talk about that right now. Garret knew, she'd mentioned Oliver's job instability to him, but Blythe was so ... prickly. Like she was too busy.

She didn't understand why *none* of her friends seemed to support her as much anymore.

She tapped her laptop message app to send the link. "Did you get it?"

"Yes."

"What do you think?"

"Give me a second."

Jenna waited, trying to breathe slowly. This was making her more nervous about the sale. If Blythe didn't think it was a good idea, maybe it wasn't. If she ended up not selling much, it was possible she could lose money after all. Maybe the whole thing was a ridiculous dream. No matter how hard she worked, how well she did, there was no way she could make up for Oliver's income if he lost his job.

She absolutely couldn't make enough to cover the loss of their medical insurance. What was she thinking?

"It looks great," Blythe said.

"You think so?"

"Yes."

"Can I send you the images and stuff for my socials? Do you have time to look?"

"I'm ..." Blythe paused. "Sure."

"I'm sorry if I'm bothering you," Jenna said.

"I'm just having a hard time right now. Something awful happened. That creep. He's getting worse. I can't get him to go away. I keep ignoring him and he won't leave me alone. He's—"

"I know exactly how you feel," Jenna said. "I couldn't think about anything else when that stalker was after me."

"This is different."

"How?"

"It's more personal. He seems to know things about me. Or acts like he does. I don't know. It's scary."

"Well, mine stopped, so I'm sure—"

"I'm sorry. I don't have time to look at your social stuff right now. I really am sorry. I'm sure it's great. Your pages look great. I hope the sale kills it."

"I hope so too," Jenna said.

"I need to go."

"Sure, okay. Bye."

Blythe ended the call. Jenna had hoped Blythe would look at all the things she'd put together. She wanted to be sure it was cohesive. She'd hoped for a cold eye on any mistakes or pieces that didn't fit. She wanted to know if it was enticing, if it would be interesting to Blythe, if it would make her click through to buy.

Now she had none of those answers. She could call the others, but she definitely wasn't calling Lacey. Selling mugs and T-shirts was entirely different. Anything Lacey had to offer would be completely useless. She hardly had to sell at all. She just put up pictures and people bought stuff. It was sickening.

Evie and Scarlett would probably have good insights, but she felt completely deflated after listening to Blythe. She didn't think she could generate enough enthusiasm to ask them in a way that didn't seem needy and panicked. If they even hinted at something negative, she would take it personally. She wanted Blythe's encouragement first.

She slammed her laptop closed.

When Jenna had complained about having a stalker, Blythe acted as if it were a minor annoyance. Now that Blythe was experiencing the same thing, it was suddenly a crisis of epic proportions.

CHAPTER 28

BLYTHE

*A*fter letting her dinner settle, Blythe grabbed her athletic bag and told Garret and the girls she was going to the gym. "Why so late?" Garret asked.

"I haven't done strength training for three days. My muscles are getting twitchy." She smiled and kissed the side of his mouth. "I won't be too long."

He grabbed her hand and held it to his cheek. She slid it from his grasp and left.

It was a lie that she hadn't lifted weights for three days. It was not a lie that her muscles felt twitchy, but lately, they felt that way all the time. She couldn't sit still.

As she worked her way through the weight machines, her promise that she wouldn't be gone too long faded to the back of her mind. She hadn't mentioned a specific time. Garret wouldn't notice if she lingered a bit. She took longer with each set, deliberately slowing her pace, pushing her muscles to exhaustion. After finishing the weights, she spent another fifteen minutes stretching.

By the time she left the gym, it was dark. It was almost nine twenty. She walked to her car, keys in hand. The lot was much emptier than it had been when she'd arrived. She'd had to park around the side of the wing that housed the indoor pool.

As she headed in that direction, moving farther away from the building, she heard footsteps behind her. They were loud, not the soft tap of athletic shoes. They almost sounded as if the person wanted her to know there was someone following. She didn't want to turn, but it sounded as if the footsteps were moving faster, closing the distance between them.

Despite her instinct, she turned.

The moment she did, the person moved quickly toward the building so she couldn't see anything of what they were wearing, or even determine whether it was a man or woman. She continued walking, faster now. She only had to round the swimming pool wing and walk halfway down the row of empty parking spaces to where her white compact SUV sat alone, glowing under dim lights.

Again, she heard the footsteps.

Once she passed the corner of the building, no one inside the gym would be able to see her. There were no windows on that side of the pool building. She was probably over-reacting, but she felt edgy. The person had acted so strangely, moving to where they couldn't be seen the moment she'd turned.

She made a sharp left, headed away from the building, still hearing the footsteps behind her. She walked toward the main parking area where there were more cars, then turned again, hurrying back toward the gym entrance. Inside the doors, she turned. The person was nowhere to be seen. She stood there for a moment, feeling slightly foolish but still unsettled.

After a moment, she went to the check-in desk.

A guy in his mid-thirties was seated behind the computer.

"Is there someone who can walk me to my car?" Blythe asked.

He stared at her as if she'd asked if there was someone who could weave her hair into French braids.

"Someone was following me. I'm parked on the other side of the pool building. My car is the only one out there. I just feel a little ..." She shrugged and gave him a tiny smile.

"Oh. Sure. No problem." He picked up his phone off the desk

and sent a text. "Can't be too careful." He smiled. "One of the trainers will be here in a sec."

"Thanks."

A moment later, a woman who taught some of the yoga classes Blythe had taken appeared near the end of the counter. She gave Blythe a warm smile. "I'll walk out with you."

"You don't feel uncomfortable walking back alone?" Blythe asked.

The woman held up her hand. In her palm was a small canister of pepper spray.

Blythe laughed, then regretted it, because it didn't seem like the correct response. They went out the doors and walked quickly around the side of the building. The woman waited while Blythe opened the door and climbed into her car. The person she'd seen earlier was nowhere around.

Blythe thanked her escort, closed the door, and locked it. The woman walked back toward the gym and Blythe started the car. Her hands were shaking.

Was this a random stranger following women who came out of the gym alone, or could it be the social media troll? It seemed far-fetched to think it was the same person, but the comment about the bathing suit and the photograph of her coming out of the gym made her think it wasn't out of the question.

She pulled out of the parking lot, drove slowly down the narrow street, and turned left. She stopped at the traffic light and glanced in the rearview mirror, still feeling jittery.

When the light changed, there was a car behind her, following too closely for her taste, but that wasn't unheard of. It was more unsettling at night when the headlights consumed her rearview mirror, glaring into her eyes, almost blinding her. She adjusted the mirror. It wasn't the correct angle, but at least it minimized the effect of the headlights.

She increased her speed. The car behind her did the same.

Those lights! She couldn't even see what type of car it was, following that closely. It seemed to have its high beams on, obliterating the entire vehicle. No wonder the lights were so glaring in her mirror. She adjusted the mirror again. Now, it was almost useless.

She stopped at a light. At the next traffic light, she would turn, taking a different route home. She was less than a mile away now, and once she made that turn, she'd be rid of them. The light changed. She hit the accelerator too hard, leaping into the intersection. She eased off and drove through.

As she approached the next intersection, she signaled, although she hated doing it with this person right on her tail, as if they intended to continue following her.

Could it be the same person from the gym? The online creep? Every logical part of her mind told her she was losing her grip if she considered either of those possibilities for even half a second, but she couldn't stop thinking about both things. She felt it, as if a warning signal was going off, an animal instinct shouting at her that she was in danger. This was what they meant when they said listen to your gut, follow your intuition.

The light was green. She ignored a lifetime of good driving habits and turned without signaling. The car with its too-bright headlights made a sharp turn the moment the driver realized Blythe was turning.

He *was* following her. But why would he do that? Nothing could happen. She was safe. She shouldn't be worrying, giving into panic. Garret was waiting for her. A locked, perfectly secured house was waiting for her.

But she was leading him directly to her home. Once he knew where she lived, she couldn't take back that information. She'd heard of people driving to police stations in these situations. Sitting outside and leaning on the horn. Did those stories come from the scary urban legends told around kids' campfires, or were they bona fide safety suggestions provided by law enforcement? She wasn't sure.

As she slowed, leaving the main thoroughfare to enter the neighborhood surrounding her home, the car was so close it felt as if she was towing it behind her on a short, heavy chain. The blinding lights continued to obliterate the color and model of the car. She couldn't even tell if it was a sedan, a small truck, or an SUV.

It seemed like a mistake to lead it all the way to her driveway, but she had no idea where else she could go. It wasn't as if she had the driving skills to shake it loose, to drive in such an expert and erratic fashion that she could slip out of sight, leaving it far behind.

Her phone sat in the cup holder beside her. Maybe she should call Garret. Warn him. But what would she say? If Garret came outside to wait for her, what would that accomplish? She could dial 911, but imagining herself explaining the situation made her feel she might be overreacting. Paranoid.

Maybe this person was simply a bad driver who happened to live nearby, who happened to be driving home at the same time she was. The moment she turned into her driveway, he or she would disappear into the night.

She turned onto her street and slowed further as she came to her driveway. She pulled in.

The moment she turned, wanting to get a good look, to try to determine the type of car, it accelerated, racing away at a speed that was wildly unsafe for their quiet, narrow street. It moved so quickly, all its identifying details were obscured by the even darker shadows of the trees whose branches covered the sidewalks and extended partially into the street.

Blythe pushed the remote to open the garage door, pulled slowly inside, and turned off the engine. She pressed the remote again to close the door. Then she crossed her arms on the steering wheel, rested her forehead on her wrists, and began softly crying.

CHAPTER 29

*O*nce her sobs subsided, Blythe wiped the tears off her face and blew her nose. She turned on the overhead light and patted away the makeup smudged beneath her eyes. She opened her water bottle and splashed some cold water onto a clean tissue, pressing it to her face to remove the redness.

She wasn't going to tell Garret about this. Not yet. Now that she was locked inside her garage, the car that had followed her long gone, almost an illusion, she felt safe. More or less. It could have been anything. The list of possibilities ran from the paranoid to the petty. She wasn't sure where Garret would land on that scale. If he believed there was a chance that the troll had emerged from the internet into her physical life, he would likely want her to delete all her social media accounts. If he believed it was simply someone following too closely, he would think she was coming unglued.

Neither outcome was something she wanted to face. She wished she could tell him and he would acknowledge the fear she'd felt in the moment, her wildly vacillating thoughts, and the natural uncertainty women felt in situations like those, the knee-jerk leap to the worst-case scenario that men often couldn't get their heads around, at least not at a visceral level.

Maybe later. Maybe tomorrow. Or maybe the whole thing

would dissolve into nothing. Besides, the edginess she'd been experiencing from the trolling might have made her react with more intensity.

She got out of the car and went inside.

Garret was waiting in the kitchen. "What took so long?"

"I did a longer workout than I'd planned. I should have texted."

"I meant in the garage. I heard the door five or six minutes ago."

"Oh." She laughed. "I was checking my phone. You know me. Addicted." She went to where he stood by the sink, kissed his lips tenderly, then stepped away. "I need a shower." She left the room before he could say any more.

After taking a longer than usual hot shower, drying her hair, and changing into her favorite soft cotton shorts and tank top for bed, she went downstairs. Garret was scrolling through the endless list of shows from their various streaming services.

"Can't decide what to watch?" She cuddled beside him, placing her phone on the end table.

"What are you in the mood for?" he asked.

They finally decided on a documentary.

Twenty minutes into it, she felt Garret's breathing shift. She moved away and saw his head had fallen forward slightly. She smiled. She nudged his body and tucked a pillow behind his shoulders, moving his head. Hopefully, it would keep him from getting a stiff neck. She paused the documentary and picked up her phone.

A group text from Lacey had arrived just after they'd started watching the show.

> Lacey: Hi everyone! I don't want to sound all braggy, but I have amazing news. My latest line of mugs has blown up. I made almost $23,000 in the past two weeks. Can you believe it?! To celebrate, I want to have a fabulous party. I'm thinking a limo trip and spa day in Calistoga. My treat for the best girls in the whole world! I would never have had all this success without YOU!!!

The others had already replied multiple times. There were messages back and forth congratulating Lacey and expressing pleased shock at her incredible success. Lacey had gushed further about how her off-the-chart sales proved that being herself, accepting her body and her life as it was, putting herself out there, had released some karmic magic that caused her business to explode in ways she couldn't have imagined.

There were messages discussing the importance of finding your niche, messages about how this had been their purpose all along, to support each other in finding the right fit for their skills.

Evie asked why they hadn't heard from Blythe.

Jenna asked if she'd picked a date yet. Lacey told everyone to send her their available dates in email because the text thread was getting messy.

Blythe added her congratulations, letting them know she'd been away from her phone.

The texting went on as her friends continued to repeat themselves, still expressing shock that so much money could be made selling mugs and bags, thrilled that Lacey had managed to strike a chord with her existing customers and, obviously, find so many new ones.

> Lacey: Letting go of my fitness obsession was the best thing I ever did.

> Jenna: Maybe not the BEST, LOL, but good for you!

> Lacey: It's a real lesson in not trying too hard. In going with the flow.

> Scarlett: I keep learning that lesson and forgetting it. LOL.

> Evie: Maybe that should be on a mug!

Lacey: Excellent idea! I'll credit you.

Blythe sent a few more messages to show her support for the group's mood, but she felt herself getting tired.

It was all too much. The hint that someone had seen her in a swimsuit she couldn't recall. Being followed, the adrenaline overload from the intense fear. Whether it had been warranted or not, the feelings were real. And now this. She was genuinely happy for Lacey. The limo ride and spa day with her friends would be fabulous. She couldn't wait. It had been a long time since they'd done something fun for an entire day without their husbands. It would bring them closer. Maybe it would smooth out some of the rough spots that seemed to be developing.

But she couldn't help seeing the continued smugness, or whatever it was, in Lacey's constant reference to self-acceptance. How did Lacey manage to make something so positive sound like an attack on Blythe? Every time she spoke about it, she made it sound as if Blythe's entire reason for existing, the express purpose of her coaching business, was to undermine how women felt about their bodies.

That couldn't be further from the truth. She'd never said or suggested anything like that. She didn't understand how Lacey had managed to twist it around so badly. Knowing Lacey believed those things hurt, and she couldn't seem to make it stop.

She sent the group a yawning emoji followed by a message telling them she was heading to bed. She woke Garret and followed him up the stairs. She put her phone on *do not disturb,* and climbed the stairs, placing her phone on the charger in the hallway beside Garret's. She washed her face, brushed and flossed her teeth, and put on lotion.

After leaving the bathroom, she stood at the foot of the bed, looking at the outline of Garret's body. He was breathing quietly and evenly. Already asleep again. He didn't move or shift his head to see why she was studying him instead of getting into bed.

She walked out of the bedroom and went to the window in the

hallway that faced the front of the house. She looked down on the street, partially blocked by trees. She glanced to the left. A car sat in front of the house across the street, three houses down from theirs. Like the other cars parked on the street, it was mostly obscured by the overhanging branches, but the headlights were on, sending a sharp sting of fear through her heart.

Her whole body tensed. Even her toes curled slightly. She had no idea if it was the same car. Like before, the thought seemed born of paranoia, but because of the trolling that wouldn't stop, she couldn't avoid thinking there was a connection.

She folded her arms across her chest to keep from shivering and rubbed her arms. She wanted it to leave. She didn't want to go to bed until it disappeared, but she couldn't stand here all night watching it. Neither was it a good idea to go out and confront the driver.

She wondered if the police would come if she reported it. Wasn't that illegal, to sit in a car watching someone's house? If it wasn't, it definitely should be.

She wasn't sure how long she stood there. Maybe five minutes, maybe twenty. Finally, the car made a sudden turn and drove away. Again, too quickly, and too shrouded by trees for her to determine anything about its make or color.

Frustrated, she went into the bedroom and slid into bed.

"Where were you?" Garret's voice was clear, without any suggestion of having woken just that moment.

"Looking out the hall window. For some reason, I'm not very tired. I forgot I feel this way when I go to the gym at night. I shouldn't do that."

"Mmm." He didn't sound convinced.

CHAPTER 30

ANONYMOUS

*S*ocial media is surreal.

There's far too much posting. There's too much emoting and there are *way* too many opinions.

Does anyone really need or want to hear the opinions of hundreds, maybe thousands, of people day in and day out, year after year after year? And I'm not only talking about political opinions. There are opinions about *everything*—how pets should behave, which pets are superior, which breeds are the finest, what people should do with their landscaping, what kind of clothing is the best, where everyone should shop, or not. There are opinions about music and films and books. Restaurants and how people drive and sports and vacation spots and even the *kind* of vacation that's the most rewarding or relaxing. There are opinions about work-life balance and child-rearing. *Child-rearing!* Parenting choices drive wedges into communities that last lifetimes. And people get *hot* about their opinions. As if the fate of the world hangs on whether soccer or basketball is more thrilling, this team or that more worthy of the season title.

It's insanity.

No wonder everyone is so pissed off all the time.

Their brains are infested with the opinions of their family and friends and neighbors and absolute total strangers.

People will fight to the death over whether a movie or a book or a music group is the greatest thing ever or the worst piece of trash. They'll argue about what kind of coffee drink you should wait all year for, and post long, passionate opinions about why that coffee drink is something they cannot live without, or, if you can't live without it, there's something permanently broken inside your soul.

If you go to a party, you don't get all wound up and start screaming at everyone that they have to eat the guacamole and if they don't like the guacamole, they're an ignorant, unrefined cretin. No one would ever do that. At parties, people talk in normal voices, and they keep the majority of their thoughts to themselves. They take turns talking, most of the time. Sure, sometimes voices are raised, there are interruptions and disagreements. Yeah, big parties with lots of alcohol can get out of control. But most of the time, it's not like that.

But online it's not a non-stop flood of shouting. No one is listening. There's constant jabbering and shoving opinions down everyone's throats.

On social media, people seem to forget that everyone can *see* what they're posting. Everyone!

Don't they think about that for one single minute?

Again, real-life parties. Because even though it's virtual, it's still real life! If you're at a party with fifty people and you're talking to the three people you came with, telling them something personal, and some suddenly turns off the music and the whole room goes silent, do you keep shouting about something really personal that happened to you?

I don't think so.

But that's what a lot of people do on social media. A *lot* of people.

On and on, talking about medical problems and asking about their children and giving out the details of their divorce or the horrible thing that happened at work or the bar. They'll say anything.

Do they forget everyone is listening? Potentially, the entire *world* is listening? And there it is, forever. Anyone can take a screen shot and keep it and you won't even know. They can take a piece of your life, capture it and save it and bring it back and shove your face in it a year later or five or ten or twenty years later. When you least expect it.

So you hand over all these photographs of yourself and all the things in your head and all the stuff that happened in your life, all the things that hurt you and pissed you off, and even the good stuff, maybe things that should just be remembered by you and the people you were with, and you throw them out there for the whole world to mess around with.

It's kind of creepy and strange and a little disturbing, if you think about it.

CHAPTER 31

THIRTY YEARS AGO: BLYTHE

*W*ith the new girl's flashlight shining in her eyes, Blythe felt them filling with tears. She blinked. She pulled her arm out of her bag and pushed the flashlight away from her face.

Lying there waiting for a mountain lion or coyote to tear her to shreds had been the most terrifying experience of her life. She didn't care what this girl had been sent to do to her. Nothing could be as bad as what she'd just lived through. She didn't care if the girl got angry that Blythe had batted her flashlight out of the way.

"Why are you sleeping way out here?" the girl asked. "It's really unsafe."

Blythe stared at the girl's face, only parts of it visible in the light that was now close to her waist instead of being held directly in front of her as it had been a moment earlier.

"Duh," Blythe said. "They dragged me out here and I don't have a light. There's no way to get back until the sun comes up."

"Who?"

"Crystal. Her friend."

"Why did they bring you out here?"

"They hate me."

"Why?" The girl sat on the sleeping bag, landing directly on Blythe's ankles.

"Ouch!"

"Move your legs. Why do they hate you?"

"I'm fat."

"Let's see." The girl grabbed the edge of the sleeping bag.

"No." Blythe sat up. "I want to go back."

"Do you have shoes?"

"No. I don't care. I don't want to stay out here. It's scary."

"You can use my socks. I'll wear my shoes. What's your name?"

"Blythe."

"I'm Jenna."

After Blythe had crawled out of her sleeping bag and Jenna had seen her body, she didn't make a comment. Whether or not she agreed with Crystal's assessment that Blythe was fat, she didn't say. Not then or ever.

They walked back to the campsite. Blythe carried her badly rolled up sleeping bag. Jenna carried the flashlight, pointing out rocks so Blythe could avoid them, her feet mostly unprotected by Jenna's thin socks. They talked about Crystal and her friends. Jenna said she'd moved to a new apartment because her parents split up. She lived with her mom. Her dad had vanished, but he sent money.

After that, they became friends.

Jenna was like a magic potion. Being her friend brought other kids into Blythe's life. It seemed as if they now saw Blythe through Jenna's eyes. Because Jenna liked her, she must be worth hanging out with. Blythe tried not to think too much about what that meant. She tried not to think about why she wasn't likable on her own, why she needed the new girl's stamp of approval.

Most of the kids were crazy about Jenna, for the simple reason that Jenna was a little crazy. She made everything fun and exciting because there was almost nothing she wouldn't do.

Jenna was the one who got everyone in their English class to stay home sick one day, even though they were all given detention as a result. She brought two bags of lemons she'd stolen off a tree on her way to school and convinced everyone to eat an entire lemon with their lunch.

She walked up to the smartest boy in their year when he was sitting in the library researching a paper, sat on the table in front of him, leaned forward, and gave him a long, deep kiss. At least it was long until he stopped her, pushing her to the side with such force on the well-polished table she slid onto the floor and got kicked out of the library for shrieking.

During their Sophomore year in high school, she jumped onto the hood of the football quarterback's car when he was backing out of a parking spot. He lowered his window and told her to get off. She refused. He started driving. She grabbed onto the edge of the window frame. As he increased the speed, she screamed at him to go faster.

Blythe mostly stood on the sidelines, watching. Jenna made her feel alive, in the center of a whirlwind. She liked never knowing what Jenna might do. She loved going to school every day, knowing that something surprising would happen.

Blythe loved knowing she was Jenna's best friend. Jenna told her everything. Everyone talked to Jenna, so she knew a lot of secrets and she shared all of them with Blythe. She told Blythe how badly she felt about her dad leaving, that he didn't want to be around her anymore.

"Why did he leave?" Blythe couldn't imagine her father not living with her. The thought of him moving out of their house, never seeing him again, except for a visit during the summer, made her feel like someone was squeezing her heart. She could hardly sit up straight, could hardly breathe, thinking about it.

"Issues. With my mom."

"What kind of issues?"

"Sex, you dipshit."

"Oh," Blythe wasn't sure she understood any more than she had before Jenna told her. She still wanted to ask, *What kind of issues? How was sex an issue?* "I don't really—"

"He was fucking other women," Jenna said.

"Oh."

"My mom was not having that."

It sounded complicated and confusing. Blythe wasn't sure why Jenna knew anything about it. Had her mother told her? Did her father sit her down and say, *I'm leaving because ...?* She couldn't even finish the thought because she wasn't sure how that conversation would even go.

Still, it made Blythe feel special that Jenna could tell her things like that. It made her feel important that she knew about adult issues. And she was absolutely sure, even though Jenna acted tough, and pretended it didn't hurt, that Jenna was hurting ... a lot. So she was glad Jenna trusted her enough to tell her. That meant she was definitely Jenna's *best* friend. She'd never had a friend like this.

When they were in their Junior year, Jenna outdid herself in attracting attention and making a name for herself. She even got a mention in the yearbook for it, although it was written cryptically because the yearbook supervisor would have banned it if they'd known. And it didn't have a photo to go with it. Just a brief note about Jenna being— *The first girl into the lake, the last one out.*

A group of kids had driven to a small lake in the foothills to hang out on a hot summer evening. When the sun started to go down, instead of cooling off, the air stayed just as hot. The guys said they were fed up with wading around and skipping stones. They stripped off their shirts and went swimming in their shorts. The hot air would dry them fast enough when they got out.

As the sun dipped behind the foothills, Jenna stood, stripped off all her clothes and ran into the lake. Laughing and shrieking, she swam naked while everyone watched, mostly the boys. When she was done, she walked out with an absolute lack of concern, picked up her clothes and dressed again.

Blythe was stunned. She never asked her why she did it. She admired Jenna's confidence. She was proud to have such a confident friend, a friend who didn't care what anyone thought of her thin, almost bony body.

Sometimes, Jenna scared her a little bit. But that was part of the fun. They'd vowed to be best friends for life, and life itself could be scary, so being scared by your best friend once in a while was okay, wasn't it?

CHAPTER 32

NOW: BLYTHE

The girls' trip to the spa was still three weeks away, but Blythe and Evie were wandering around the shopping center looking for summer dresses.

"I feel like showing up to lunch in a sundress," Evie had said. "I'll wear leggings in the limo, obviously. But I want to look fabulous for lunch. High-heeled sandals and an exotic dress."

"Isn't Calistoga casual?" Blythe asked.

"So what?"

So, here they were, drifting from store to store, trying on dresses. Blythe had decided she would do the same, although she was not sure she needed more than the two pairs of high-heeled sandals she already owned. She couldn't imagine when she would wear them again, unless a wedding invite came their way, and there wasn't anyone she could think of who might be headed in that direction any time in the next four or five years.

It had been two hours, they'd hit half the stores. Evie had two dresses on hold. Blythe had one.

"Let's grab a smoothie," Evie said. "I need a break."

They walked back the way they'd come toward the wing where a few cafes opened onto a garden area with a glass ceiling above. They ordered smoothies and found a booth.

As they sipped their drinks, they checked their phones, sweeping away text messages to be answered later, checking their social media feeds.

"Any more slime from the troll?" Evie asked.

"Some, but not as often."

"Yuck." Evie sucked on her straw, drawing the dark red slushy mixture into her mouth.

"It feels like it's never going to stop," Blythe said. "It's driving me insane. And it's made social media not very much fun. Part of the reason I'm not getting as much from him is because I'm not posting as often."

Evie sipped her drink, nodding. "I thought it seemed like you were doing less."

"I hate it. I feel like he's controlling my life. But I don't know how to make it stop. I've reported it over and over, but they're *investigating*. I think he puts up and takes down user names so fast, they can't connect it to an email address, so they can't figure out his identity."

"Makes sense," Evie said.

"I've wondered if it's not a guy."

"It's always a guy," Evie said.

"I assumed that, because it was all about my body and sex. But what if it's not?"

"That seems unlikely."

"Do you think ... I feel terrible saying this, but I have to. It's been bothering me for a while now. Can you keep it to yourself?"

"Always," Evie said. "You know that."

"Promise? I really need to tell someone, and I trust you. I know you keep things to yourself when I ask, but this is really bad."

Evie held her gaze.

Blythe knew she would, she didn't need to say more. Still. "Really bad." She laughed.

"Okay. I get it. Say it, or don't."

"Do you think ..." Blythe leaned over the table, lowering her voice. "Do you think Lacey would do something like that? Because she was so upset with me?"

Evie recoiled slightly. "I … I can't imagine her doing something so … disgusting."

"I know. I'm sorry. I said it was bad. But …"

"Why do you think that?"

"She seemed … she still seems really upset that I somehow made her feel like she couldn't be happy with who she is. That I was making her feel bad about herself. I can't even … I don't get it. I coached her for *years*. I don't know what happened. I tried talking to her about it, but I didn't get anywhere. She shut me down."

"But she's so excited about the mugs. It seems like she worked out all her feelings, whatever they were," Evie said.

Blythe twirled the straw around inside the cup, watching the thick mixture move sluggishly around the sides. She wasn't sure why she thought Lacey would do something so awful to her. They'd been friends for so many years. And Lacey was the most fun-loving, easy-going of all her friends. There'd never been anything to suggest she had a vindictive or even a petty streak.

But something about that troll telling her to *put herself out there* had made her think of Lacey's remarks about people being more careful about how they presented themselves. As if the troll was mocking her? Telling her the opposite? Taunting her to do what Lacey had said she shouldn't? Blythe couldn't put her finger on it, but she couldn't get that phrase out of her mind.

Watching Evie trying to hide her concern, attempting to keep a neutral, supportive expression on her face, made Blythe feel as if she sounded like the paranoid lunatic she felt she was becoming. So which was it? Had her friend turned into an internet troll, so furious at something Blythe had inadvertently communicated in her coaching that she started an entire line of self-affirming merchandise to subtly diss Blythe's business? And then tried her hand at anonymous trolling? Or had the trolling turned Blythe into a gargoyle after all, peering over her shoulder and looking at someone she loved with suspicion?

"It doesn't seem like something she would do," Evie said softly.

"No. Probably not." Blythe took a sip of her drink. "The constant harassment, the ugliness ... it really gets under my skin. I try not to let it, but it does. It eats at me all the time."

"I can't imagine."

"I try not to read what he, or she, writes. But I see it, and the words stick in my head. And they keep coming back. Like a song lyric that gets stuck on a loop."

"It must be awful."

"I feel like I'm losing my mind. I can't make it stop. I don't know if I should turn off comments for a while."

"That might be a good idea."

"But I worry what it will do to engagement with my posts."

Evie nodded.

Blythe felt as if a palpable gloom had settled over them. The smoothie tasted sour. Evie looked uncomfortable, anxious to leave. They were supposed to be having a good time, getting ready for a day of pampering and fun, and Blythe was spoiling it. A day that would be hosted by the person she was accusing of doing something despicable. She felt ill.

"I don't know why I'm saying this," Blythe said. "Why I'm even thinking it. I shouldn't have ... I ..." She picked up her drink and put the straw between her lips, afraid that speaking any more words would make it worse.

Evie reached across the table and touched Blythe's forearm with her fingertips. "It's understandable. The mugs are a little ..." She laughed, then rolled her eyes to the side. "I can see why it would feel personal. And the stress of what that troll has done to you. I don't understand why he's targeting you. Or what he's getting out of it. You've been really good about not reacting."

"You've seen the comments?"

Evie nodded. "A few."

"I try to delete them right away." Her voice caught. "It's worse, knowing other people are seeing them."

"It's hard to stay on top of bots, if that's what it is. They go so fast. You can't compete."

Blythe nodded. "I don't think it's a bot. It's too specific. Too personal."

"Should we get going?" Evie asked.

Blythe wished Evie would say something that would give her a flash of insight, something encouraging that would make her feel she wasn't stuck on this hamster wheel indefinitely. It was childish to depend on another person, instead of your own inner resources, to lift your mood. At the same time, wasn't that part of what made friendship meaningful? She needed support. She wanted ... something. Even just a different perspective. She supposed she'd been given that, but it hadn't done much to change her feelings. She was still trapped. Her social media was still held captive by a faceless monster.

They both ended up buying dresses they loved. Evie bought two pairs of high-heeled sandals. "Now that my kids are older, I plan to enjoy a more glamorous life."

"I should aspire to that," Blythe said.

"You should! Do you want to try on a pair?"

"Next time."

"I'll bring both pairs to Calistoga, and you can see if you want to give them a trial run."

Blythe laughed. "Okay."

When they said goodbye, she felt better. By the time she was home, she would have described her mood as content.

Because it was hot out, Garret barbecued chicken. She served the potato salad she'd made that morning and the fruit Kate had cut up while she was shopping.

The girls splashed around in the pool while she and Garret watched, sipping sparkling water and not complaining when drops of pool water landed on their steamy skin.

She was woken at four in the morning by her phone, the sound of a call warbling from the hallway. She threw off the covers and got out of bed. Only her friends, her parents, and a few of her daughters' friends' parents had access to override her do not disturb setting. A lump of panic formed in her throat as she hurried to the phone and grabbed it.

Evie.

"Oh my God, Blythe. It's so awful." Evie's tone was rushed, trembling. "You aren't going to ... I can't ... are you sitting down? Sit down. I ..." Her voice was raw. "Miles called. Lacey ... she ... are you sitting?"

Blythe sat down hard on the carpeted floor. "What's wrong?"

"She's dead! Lacey's dead!" Evie's voice broke. "Murdered. Someone murdered her!" She began sobbing. She gasped and continued. "They were on the back patio, celebrating her success. Lacey and Miles. Drinking ... they were ... drinking champagne. On the patio ... and ... and ...." She started crying again.

Blythe felt the air stop in her lungs, then she let out a painful sob. A wave of grief, followed by crushing guilt, washed over her. This couldn't be right. "Murdered? Dead?"

"Drinking champagne. Miles went to bed. He was asleep ... he woke up, and she wasn't there. He went to look for her ... she's dead! Someone killed her! She—"

"How? Why?"

"I don't know!" Evie wailed. "She wasn't breathing. And there was ... there was ..." Evie began sobbing so loudly, Blythe moved the phone away from her ear.

After several minutes, Evie spoke, her voice reduced to a rough whisper. "A plastic bag. There was a plastic bag over her head." Evie was crying more softly now.

Blythe pressed the phone to her head, letting the edge dig into her skull, welcoming the pain. She was crying, huge sobs tearing through her chest. Lacey couldn't be dead. And instead of feeling the loss of her friend, all she could feel was this horrible, crushing guilt. Why was she dead? Why would someone—

"What's wrong?"

She looked up at Garret. His eyes were filled with fear. He

squatted in front of her, taking hold of her wrist. "What happened?"

"Lacey's dead."

He rocked back, losing his balance. He landed, sitting with his knees splayed. "Dead?"

"Murdered!"

"I need to call the others," Evie said, her voice hoarse.

"Okay. Yes. I'll—"

"Talk soon," Evie said.

The call ended.

Blythe put the phone on the floor and crept toward Garret. He put his arms around her and together they lowered themselves down until they were lying on the floor, holding each other. Blythe continued crying, grateful that Garret didn't ask her to tell him anything more just yet.

CHAPTER 33

*E*ventually, Blythe and Garret got up off the floor and returned to bed.

She didn't sleep. She lay on her side, her back to Garret, crying softly, on and off, until her body wore itself out and the tears seemed to evaporate and there was no moisture left inside. It was almost worse. When the tears stopped, the pain grew more intense.

At six fifteen, she gave up and climbed out of bed. She showered and went down to make coffee. A few minutes later, Garret was in the kitchen with her. She told him the rest of the details that she hadn't been able to speak earlier. They drank coffee, staring at each other across the table, occasionally asking—*Why?* and *Who?*

Her phone was blowing up with text messages from Jenna and Scarlett. She responded with emojis, unable to find any words. Despite all the tears that had poured out of her, she felt as if her brain were swimming in a bowl of thick mucous. She wasn't sure she could write a coherent sentence.

After they ate buttered toast, which was all she could manage, Garret left for work, telling her to call as soon as she knew more.

Blythe poured another cup of coffee, went into the living room, and called Evie. She was closest to Lacey and Miles, partially because she'd interviewed them so many times for her podcast. They loved talking about their parenting journey, and both of them were personable. Miles could be outrageously funny. They were great guests. Blythe wondered if Miles would ever say something funny again.

"Have you heard anything more?" Blythe asked.

"Miles said the police are still there—going through the house and all over the patio. They'll be talking to her friends. Their neighbors."

"Why are they talking to her friends?"

"To get information. Because they'll be looking for the person who killed her."

"What would her friends know?"

"I have no idea. That's just how it's done. You've seen cop shows ... they talk to everyone."

"We're not on TV," Blythe said.

"I know that. This is so awful, it's so ... I'm just telling you what Miles told me. I didn't ask him why. That poor man. I didn't ask him anything. All I do is listen. I'm arranging meals. What days do you want to sign up for?"

Blythe walked to the other room while they talked about Miles's and Lacey's daughter, Violet, and about the unreality of everything. She opened her tablet and texted a few dates to Evie. "But slot me in wherever you have openings. Okay?"

When Kelsey and Kate woke, she told them what had happened, advising them to wait a few hours before texting Violet.

"That's not right," Kate said. "It's not like there's some politeness rule. This is so messed up. Why would we wait?" She left the kitchen. Kelsey followed.

They were right. It wasn't a time to think about some false idea of propriety. Violet needed to know everyone was thinking about her. Giving her space was a ridiculous concept.

Blythe thumbed through her one-pot cookbook, looking for meals she could bring to the Abbott family, or what was left of it.

She had two clients that afternoon, but nothing to fill her morning. She ended up spending the entire time on the phone, talking first to Jenna, then Scarlett. Both had the same stunned tone to their voices. They spoke in the same disbelieving way, one minute unable to comprehend Lacey was even gone, the next moment filled with shock and outrage, and a large dose of fear over the fact that she'd been murdered in her own backyard, while her husband and daughter were sleeping right inside the house.

It was the most horrific crime that had ever happened in their city, as far as they were aware. It was impossible to get their minds around it. And the circumstances were so horrible—smothered by a plastic bag?

"How could that happen? Wouldn't she fight them off? Claw the bag away from her face? I don't understand," Scarlett said, echoing what each of them had already said multiple times.

Blythe didn't know. Evie hadn't said. She would have mentioned it, wouldn't she? But didn't the police usually keep some pieces of information to themselves? Another fact that seemed solid because it was repeated so often on TV shows. What did any of them know?

It was difficult to focus on her clients. She was sure she was doing them a disservice. She should have canceled, but once they were seated in her office, it was too late. She smiled and talked, hearing her voice as if she were standing at the end of a tunnel, listening to herself, unable to comprehend the words. But they must have made sense, because her clients nodded, took notes, asked questions, which she also seemed to answer coherently. No one gave her a puzzled look or asked her to repeat anything.

When she was finished, she collapsed on the sofa and closed her eyes. Part of the exhaustion came from her lack of sleep, but the rest was from trying to settle her thoughts. She was working overtime to tell herself she didn't need to feel guilty. She hadn't done anything wrong. Lacey had been acting strangely and someone had been unmercifully harassing Blythe. It didn't make her a terrible human being to speculate in her own thoughts, and to mention her mild paranoia to one of her closest friends. She hadn't accused Lacey. She hadn't assumed and gossiped and passed unsubstantiated rumors. She'd simply wondered.

Hopefully, as the shock wore off, as she worked her way through her loss, the guilt would dissolve. For now, she was determined to focus on all the wonderful memories she had of Lacey and their fifteen-year friendship. Not that single regrettable moment.

Garret had been home for exactly four minutes when the doorbell rang. She saw on the security camera it was a woman and man who looked like stock figures auditioning to be police detectives. It almost seemed as if they'd been watching to see when he arrived home before walking to the door.

She was mildly curious to hear what they would ask. She also wondered if she would learn more about the strange and sickening circumstances of what had happened to Lacey. And beneath those two thoughts was a slender thread of anxiety. Maybe because she wasn't used to talking to the police. Maybe because the very thought of someone in authority like that made you feel nervous about being perfectly accurate with the truth. Maybe because a stranger asking questions risked them asking something about your life you didn't want to talk about.

She went to the door with Garret just behind her.

"Blythe and Garret Farrell?" the woman asked.

"Yes."

"I'm Detective Banner, and this is Detective Madeira. We understand you're close friends with Lacey Abbott."

"Yes. I—"

"You're aware that she was murdered last night?"

Blythe nodded.

"We'd like to ask you a few questions."

"Sure." Garret's voice behind her was too loud in her ear. He sounded almost eager. For some reason, it irritated her, and she found herself feeling more cautious about talking to them. What were they going to ask? She and Garret couldn't possibly have any information. If the detectives had questions about their lives or about Lacey and Miles, she wasn't keen about sharing it with them.

They needed to find a killer, not spend time talking to friends. It was probably just a time-filler while they figured out what they were going to do.

She and Garret ushered the detectives into the living room. Both took seats on the sofa. Blythe sat on the loveseat and Garret settled into the armchair, looking comfortable and prepared for a lengthy, friendly conversation.

They began with perfunctory questions about how long Blythe and Garret had known the Abbotts. They asked what their relationship was like and how often they saw them.

"Do they have a good marriage?" Detective Banner asked.

"Yes," Blythe said.

"Of course, you only know what you see on the surface," Garret said.

Blythe forced herself to keep her attention on the detectives. She didn't want to make it worse by glaring at her husband, but she had no idea why he would say something like that. He made it sound as if there was something wrong. Of course, you only knew what you saw on the surface, but he didn't have to highlight that. Everyone knew that.

"So, no problems, you know of?" Banner asked.

"No problems at all. We're very close, Lacey and I," Blythe said. "I think I would have a hint if there was anything seriously wrong."

Detective Madeira made a note in his phone.

"What about their daughter? Violet. Any problems there?" Detective Banner asked.

"What does that have to do with Lacey being murdered?" Blythe asked.

"We're trying to get a sense of the family. In the case of their daughter, we'll be looking into her friends to determine if there were any kids with issues, that kind of thing."

"Violet's an amazing girl," Blythe said.

Detective Banner looked pointedly at Garret.

"Yes," Garret said. "She's a great kid. Does well in school. No problems. Just typical teenage stuff."

"What's typical? Drugs?"

"No, nothing like that. Just ... typical. Fighting about clothes, curfews," Garret said.

"Anything in their lives we should know about?"

"Why do you need to know about their lives?" Blythe asked. "What does that mean?"

"Financial problems? Drug use? Gambling issues? Legal problems?"

"No." And before Garret could chime in with any commentary, Blythe added, "Absolutely not. As I said, I'm ... I *was* very close friends with Lacey. She was also a client for my health coaching business, so I saw her on a regular basis for that as well as our social lives, as couples, and with a group of women I know. We've been in their home a hundred times, vacationed together. We're all open books to each other."

"Is that right?" Detective Madeira asked. "That's unusual."

"Is it?" Garret asked.

"Then you would know if they had any enemies?"

Blythe laughed. "Of course not. Normal people don't have enemies."

"You'd be surprised," Detective Madeira said. "Even so-called normal people, living nice suburban lives, can have some fairly explosive conflicts."

"The Abbots don't," Blythe said.

"You seem very sure," Detective Banner said.

"I am."

"And you?" Both detectives looked at Garret.

"Not that I'm aware of," Garret said.

Blythe sighed. Would she be considered an enemy? Had Lacey viewed her that way? She'd seemed almost hostile when Blythe stopped by with her gift. And the pithy sayings on the mugs, tagging Blythe's page ... that too could be seen as somewhat ... hostile.

If these detectives knew about that, would they characterize her as an enemy? She thought of enemies as people who were in the drug business or the mob, gangsters. It was a concept that was foreign to her world.

She was not an enemy. And, of course, she hadn't killed Lacey. She would never kill someone. As upset as she'd been, even in her fleeting thoughts about Lacey being the troll, she would never, ever wish her dead.

The detectives stood. "Thank you for your time. As the investigation progresses, we may want to ask more questions."

Blythe stood. Detective Banner handed her two cards. "Call us if you think of anything that might be relevant."

"There was no evidence of a struggle or violence of any kind," Detective Madeira said. "We think she passed out from drinking too much and the bag was placed over her head. The toxicology report may give us more insight, but we think she was likely murdered by someone she knew."

CHAPTER 34

SCARLETT

*T*he memorial service for Lacey Abbott would be held at the Community Center. The Center offered a spacious room with a wall of windows that faced a large pond surrounded by clusters of palm trees and flowering plants. Over five hundred people were expected to attend. The room capacity was three-hundred-fifty, but accommodations were being made to open all the back and side doors, with chairs and speakers set up on the outside patio so people could listen from there.

Scarlett was wearing a pink floral dress. She felt uncomfortable as she looked in the mirror. It seemed wrong, somehow. She couldn't believe the idea of black for a memorial service was so deeply ingrained in her psyche. It must come from a lifetime of TV shows and films because she'd never attended a memorial service, or even her grandparent's funerals, where people dressed exclusively in black. It was just that pink floral seemed a step too far.

But the instructions from Evie had been clear. She'd been told by Miles—there was no doubt it was what Lacey would have wanted. Lacey loved wearing white. She loved bright colors. The decor of her home was a splash of color from one room to the next. Every time they saw her, the polish on her fingernails and toenails was a different, brilliant color.

No black. Instead, the brightest colors they could find in their closets.

"That's ... bright," Paul said.

Scarlett raised her eyes and looked at his reflection behind her. He wore khaki slacks and a navy blue shirt. "I know. I feel like I should sit in the flower garden instead of the front row." She giggled, then started crying. It was like that every day. When would it stop?

"You look great." He crossed the room, placed his hand gently on the back of her neck, and kissed her.

"Thanks. It is bright, though."

"I'm sure the others will be equally flamboyant," he said.

"Flamboyant doesn't seem like the right mood for a memorial service."

"Or it could be exactly the right tone. It's supposed to be a celebration of her life, right?" he asked.

Scarlett's eyes filled with tears again. Logically, she knew that, but her heart wasn't in it. Maybe once she was seated with her family, her friends and their families gathered around her, the music that Lacey loved filling the room, everyone telling stories that brought her to life again, the gloom would lift. For an hour or two.

"There's a problem," Paul said.

"What's that?" Scarlett walked into the bathroom and grabbed a tissue.

"Henry doesn't want to go. Too many people staring at him."

"No one will be staring at him. No one will be looking at him at all. Didn't you tell him that?"

"I did, but—"

"Why are you telling me? You should have told him he's going. I know it's hard for him, but this isn't something we're debating. This is—"

"I know. But he ... you know what he does."

Scarlett felt something deeper than the tears that had been seeping out for Lacey press against her throat, twisting her heart, filling her lungs with wet cement. She started coughing uncontrollably.

Paul came into the bathroom. "Are you okay?"

She shook her head. She put her hand on the counter to steady herself. Paul placed his arm around her shoulders, pulling her close, then wrapped his other arm around her. She wanted to lean into him, but she couldn't. Why hadn't he fixed this? If Henry was already in his room, already hiding under the bed, things were only going to get worse. Why hadn't Paul managed it before it got to this point?

"Please go fix it," she said.

"He wants you."

"Oh, God." She pulled away from him, the tears flowing again. She couldn't do this. They were leaving in forty-five minutes. Both boys needed to be dressed. Paul was supposed to manage the situation. She'd spent several days calmly talking to Henry about it. He'd been so much better lately. Why was this happening? It wasn't fair.

"Can Angela help?" she asked.

"She's in the shower."

"Where's Cooper?"

"He said he'd stay here with Henry."

"No."

"It might be for the—"

"No!" Her voice echoed off the tiled walls. "We're all going. She ... all of them, are friends of our whole family. She wasn't just my friend. We need to support Miles. And Violet. This is unacceptable." She pushed past her husband and walked out of the bedroom.

She went to Cooper's room first. The door was closed. She knocked. His door was always closed. He might be inside, he might not. She knocked again, then opened the door. Empty. Walking toward the living room, she called his name. Shouted might be a better description. She needed to calm down. The grief and her constant worry over Henry were boiling up. She needed to breathe. Losing control wasn't going to make this go any better.

Focus on getting everyone to the memorial. That was all she

needed to think about. Staying calm. Detaching. Choosing the right words.

"Cooper!" She stood at the entrance to the family room. He was playing a video game. "Please turn that off and get dressed."

"Not going."

"You are. This isn't about Henry. Or you. Or any of us. The only people we should be thinking about are Violet and Miles. Please."

"What about Lacey?"

She walked across the room and stood in front of the screen. "She's gone. Violet and Miles are broken into a thousand pieces. They need us. Go get dressed." She was slightly surprised when he put down the game controller.

She left the room and went to Henry's room. She lay on the floor by the bed. Predictably, she saw her son looking out at her, eyes wide, his expression unreadable.

"Henry. Remember when Violet showed you where those tiny tree frogs lived? When we went camping?"

Henry blinked.

"Do you remember?"

"Yeah."

"You looked at that picture of Violet holding one on her palm every day for the rest of the summer. Remember?"

He blinked, then nodded.

She felt a flicker of hope. "Her mom is gone."

A tear oozed out of his right eye. Scarlett reached out and gently wiped it away. "I know you don't want to think about that. It's too awful to think about. And that will never happen to me."

"You don't know that."

"I don't. But things like this ... they're really shocking and scary because they don't happen very often. Hardly ever. Once in your whole life. I've never known anyone who was murdered. But the thing is, Violet needs all her friends."

"Cooper said there'll be hundreds of people."

"Yes, but every single one will make Violet feel a little better. For a while."

"I don't like people looking at me."

"They won't be looking at you."

"They will. 'Cuz we'll be in front."

"They'll only see the back of us."

"No!"

She shouldn't have said that. But she also had to temper her words with the truth. She reached out her hand and wrapped her fingers around his wrist. "Violet's feelings are more important than ours. Besides, everyone will be looking at the people who are standing up talking. And they'll be looking at Violet and Miles, even though that's really hard for her. Some people will look out the windows at the trees and the sky. Because they'll be thinking about Lacey."

"I don't want—"

"Sometimes, we have to think about other people. Not how we feel. This is one of those times. I need you to get dressed. Cooper is getting dressed."

"What if they—"

"No one is thinking about you, Henry. *No one*. And Violet really, really needs you."

She let go of his wrist and sat up. A moment later, she stood, and as she did, he wriggled out from under the bed. She went out of his room and leaned against the wall, pressing her head against it, feeling the relief wash through her. The therapy seemed to be helping, but it was taking so long. It felt like it was killing her, one day at a time, instead of in the space of three minutes, like that plastic bag had killed Lacey. She shuddered and went to finish getting ready.

☆ ☆ ☆

The memorial made her laugh and cry. It filled her with good memories. Jenna was seated to Scarlett's right, and she held her hand for the last twenty minutes, not wanting to let go when the final song was played.

They mingled with their friends and other acquaintances outside, everyone nibbling small sandwiches and crackers with cheese that had been set up in the kitchen area behind the event room. Scarlett separated herself from the crowd and took a few photographs of the flower arrangements on the tables placed around the patio area where the overflow chairs had been earlier. She turned to find herself face-to-face with Violet. Although they'd spoken earlier, Scarlett put her arms around Violet, holding her close. Violet leaned into her, resting her head on Scarlett's shoulder.

Finally, she moved away. "Thanks. That felt nice." She smiled, her eyes blurry, but her expression calm. She'd always been a girl who didn't hide her feelings, who wasn't afraid to cry or tell people how she felt, good or bad. She didn't shy away from offering gushing compliments and heartfelt praise.

"Will you take a picture of me and my dad?" Violet asked.

"I ... okay. I ... do you think it's ...?"

Violet laughed. "People act like a memorial has to be all serious and not like real life. This is our life now. Without my mom." The tears spilled over and ran down her cheeks. "But I want to remember it. Because it's such a beautiful day. And all these people." She turned around, then back to face Scarlett. "I don't want to forget all these people who showed up to let us know they cared about her. Take lots of pictures? Okay? Please?"

Scarlett followed Violet to where her father stood gazing at the pond. Paul was beside him. His lips were parted as if he felt he needed to say something immediately, but nothing was coming out of his mouth.

"Hey, Dad. Photo op." Violet wove her arm around her father's waist and turned him gently toward Scarlett.

Scarlett snapped two photos. Violet nudged her father closer to Paul. "Another."

Scarlett took two more.

Violet reached out her hand. "Let me have your phone so I can get you three."

For the next forty minutes, Violet led Scarlett around, instructing her to take photos, most of them with Violet and the guests. After the first ten or so, Scarlett relaxed. It was clear that Violet was feeling she could remove herself from all the expressions of sorrow and condolences by involving herself in photographs. It was familiar and safe. And maybe she was right. Once the day was over, she probably wouldn't remember a single moment, but she could re-live it through the pictures.

That evening, Scarlett sat on the sofa, curled into the corner, scrolling through the photographs. She texted them to Violet in groups of five, receiving a steady flow of hearts in response. Beside her was a glass of wine. Her third, but she wanted it. She felt an almost ecstatic sense of satisfaction for how the day had gone—an overwhelming sense of relief that Henry had cooperated, climbed out of his self-made cave, and seemed to manage the entire event with ease.

Oddly, she felt a certain amount of the often-touted closure that they'd said goodbye to Lacey. She knew the road of grief would be long and rocky, but it felt as if they'd all taken the first step together.

When she'd finished sending the pictures, she clicked over to social media. Violet had posted the photo of herself and Miles, as well as a few older pictures of her mother and their family. She'd written a long, heartfelt message about her mom and the depth of her loss.

Scarlett selected a picture of herself, Jenna, Blythe, and Evie. She found an older picture of the four of them with Lacey and posted both. She wrote a short comment about their friendship and loss. She tapped to post it before she could second-guess herself.

Within half an hour, her post had blown up. Over four hundred likes and more than two hundred comments that she was having trouble keeping up with. She put her phone down, pushing it away so she wouldn't be tempted to grab it. She turned so she wouldn't see the constantly flashing notifications.

Picking up her wineglass, she took a long, soothing sip. She closed her eyes and let the images and memories of the day pass through her thoughts, disjointed and filled with intense, overwhelming emotions. She felt tears bubbling behind her eyelids, but let them stay there. She took another sip of wine.

When the glass was empty, she placed it on the table and picked up her phone. Her post was exploding like a wildfire, spreading outside her circle of friends, outside her customers for her handpainted greeting cards. The words of comfort were so encouraging. She couldn't stop reading them. Her *thankyous* were genuine.

She scrolled back to the top. Several people had shared her post. That was strange. Aside from Evie, Blythe, and Jenna, it didn't seem like something that would be shared. She clicked to see.

Paul. She gasped softly. With nearly thirteen thousand followers now, he had over three thousand likes. It was horrible. Ghoulish. He'd added a comment when he shared it, highlighting how young Lacey was, that she was murdered! She scrolled through the comments. Many were asking questions, wanting details. It was sickening. Disgusting.

Why? Why would he do that? These people were total strangers. And now they were making comments about the murder of one of her closest friends! Speculating about Lacey's life and her family and how she'd died, and why and what her body might have—

Scarlett dropped her phone onto the sofa. She covered her face with her hands. What was wrong with him? And now she felt horrible. What kind of person was she? Why had *she* posted about it? Why had she felt such a satisfying warmth, seeing how many likes and comments she got in the wake of her friend's death?

For a few minutes, it felt beautiful. Now, it felt ugly.

CHAPTER 35

ANONYMOUS

Oh, the humanity!

Such an iconic saying. Mocked because of ... I'm not sure why it's become kind of a joke because when it was uttered, it was a horrific tragedy. The Hindenburg was disintegrating before their eyes, human beings burned alive. The newscaster was crying out with helpless despair. Why has it turned into something that's repeated with such cynical, almost disdainful ridicule now?

Surely that says something about humanity. Doesn't it?

Maybe all it says is that we can't cope with the worst horrors, so we minimize them, or trivialize them. We run from them, hide from them, bury them.

But oh the humanity on social media after Lacey Abbott's memorial—her celebration of life.

On social media, it felt like a celebration of her death. A celebration of death, period.

So many people wanting to share how they felt about her being so young—too young, so beautiful. Death was so *wrong*. This wasn't how things were *supposed* to be. All true statements, but all so .... Who can even say? It felt like a show. A great big, ugly show about death. But maybe it was that lurking terror, needing to say something to keep it from roaring so loudly it drowned out everything else.

They had to say how shocked they were, how sad they felt. They needed to write out their feelings for their closest friends and total strangers.

Everyone wanted to know the details. The people who were close to her tiptoed carefully up to the subject. Strangers barged right in as if they were doing research for true crime podcasts.

When did it happen? Who found her? How long was she out there alone? That sounds terrible, to be lying in the dark on a lounge chair —dead! Alone!

Sad face emoji. Crying face emoji.

How could this happen? It seems like a safe neighborhood. Nothing like this has happened before.

Do they know who did it?

Was it someone she knew?

Did she fight them off?

And all the pictures. Everyone smiling, wearing their nicest clothes. Grinning with their arms around each other. Most of them wore dark glasses as the sun splashed across their faces. It was surreal. If the captions didn't say it was a memorial, it could have been a family reunion, a wedding reception, a summer afternoon barbecue for which everyone got more dressed up than usual.

A few people asked how Violet was doing. As if she wouldn't see all the posts. As if it never crossed their minds that this was all out in public and she should be discussed by a bunch of adults, analyzed and picked apart, her life a project for them to work on in their little comments, deciding what kind of help she needed.

Was it a good idea for Violet to be left alone?

Did she need a surrogate mother?

What about therapy?

Someone should absolutely talk to her father about getting her into therapy. Sooner rather than later.

Her father needed to keep a close eye on her schoolwork. That would be the first sign of a problem—that she wasn't handling her grief well.

Depression. She needed to be watched closely for signs of depression.

And what about Miles?

How did he feel about his dead wife and his daughter being discussed, investigated, and analyzed in public? How did he feel about the smiling faces as people stood around saying goodbye to the woman he'd loved, including his own forced grin? It was possible he hadn't seen any of it, and equally possible he'd seen every stinging word, every thoughtless, pathetic, careless, heartfelt emoji.

Maybe he liked it. Maybe he wanted to burn it all down. Maybe he was too busy trying to figure out who had murdered his wife so he could exact revenge.

CHAPTER 36

BLYTHE

Since the night Blythe had received that horrible phone call from Evie, there hadn't been a single trolling comment on her social media. When she finally emerged from the tension of the police detectives sitting in her living room, and the emotional devastation of the memorial, Blythe had found herself scrolling through her older posts, checking to see if she'd missed a comment.

There was nothing.

As the hours passed and the notifications on her screen continued to be those she looked forward to, those that lifted her mood and made her feel connected to her clients and friends, to interested strangers, a guilty, disloyal thought crept forward from the back of her mind. It blossomed into something that knocked the breath out of her each time it appeared—Lacey had been the troll, after all.

It was too much of a coincidence that her death had brought a sudden end to the degrading comments. They'd been constant and overwhelming. Rarely had she gone more than twenty-four hours without something popping up to fill her with disgust. Words that made her feel as if she never wanted to leave her house again. Words that made her terrified for the world her daughters would be living in.

And now, nothing.

Since the night of Lacey's murder, she hadn't received a single comment.

Had she? She didn't want to go back and start un-hiding horrible comments to double-check that she was remembering correctly, reviewing the dates on the words she'd worked so hard to wipe out of her head. She was almost certain she was right.

She closed her eyes and thought back over each day since that devastating night. She remembered texting with her friends. She hadn't posted to social media at all for several days after Lacey was murdered. That first day, she hadn't even responded to comments made on her previous posts, but she'd noticed them come across the screen and there'd been nothing from the troll. She was sure she'd remember. It would have pushed her over the edge. And she would have taken the time to hide and block. It was the rhythm of her life —hide and block.

There was no explanation for the ending of the comments except that Lacey had been the one posting them. With that thought, came an immediate release of the guilt that had weighed her down. She hadn't realized how much she'd hated herself for the past two weeks. She hadn't realized how she'd pulled into herself, hardly noticing her daughters, only half-listening because she was consumed with guilty feelings. When she spoke to her friends, she felt as if she answered from a script, disconnected and far away. All because of that persistent guilt about what a horrible person she was for thinking Lacey was the troll.

But now, all of that was gone. She wasn't making unfair, malicious accusations. It was the truth. There was no other explanation for a merciless troll who had tormented her for a month, stopping the moment Lacey Abbott took her last breath.

A new ache replaced the guilt she'd felt. Along with the loss of her friend, she felt she'd lost years of her life. Had their friendship been something that existed only inside her head? And for how long? Since the very beginning, or had it changed at some point?

She would never know the answer. The endlessness of that, the absolute finality, was crushing. She would never know why Lacey had tried to destroy her business. And worse, why she'd written such cruel, hurtful things to her. Lacey must have hated her with a passion deeper than anything Blythe had ever experienced.

Blythe had known betrayal that had dropped her to her knees. She'd known hurt and rage. But she'd never hated anyone enough to do something like that. She'd never had the impulse to take revenge.

Now, she would have to live the rest of her life with unanswered questions and the memories of a friendship that was nothing but shards of glass she couldn't begin to piece together.

That evening, Blythe and Garret took Kelsey and Kate out for pizza and then to play miniature golf. As Blythe tapped her bright yellow ball around the small course, over arched bridges, through opening and closing doors, and into the open mouths of oversized animals, she drifted in a haze of confusion. It felt as if the experience of all her friendships was distorted. She wondered which parts had been real, and which parts imagined. Had Lacey lied about who she was to all of them, or only to Blythe?

Was their entire group based on a lie? Were others hiding their feelings? She felt as if someone had covered the surface of her life with grease, tilted it at an impossible angle, and everything she knew was sliding rapidly toward an abyss. Nothing was real. Her friend was dead. Never in a million years had she imagined someone her age, someone in their group of friends dying. They were healthy. They were young. Death had seemed decades away. Murder was something that happened to people they didn't know, people who lived somewhere else.

Were they truly friends? Was anything real?

She watched her daughters teasing and competing, laughing and arguing. She loved how close they were to each other. Would it always be that way? She wanted that more than almost anything in the world, but there wasn't a single thing she could do about it.

She'd thought she and her friends would remain close through old age, to the very end. Now she wondered if they were close at all. And she wondered why she'd believed that when she knew she was guilty of her own pretense and lies.

Her phone vibrated in her pocket.

This was supposed to be family time. She put her hand on it.

"Your turn, Mom," Kate said.

She put her hand back on her putter, lined up the club, and tapped the ball. It raced past the hole and hit the side. She walked over to where it sat and tapped again. Another tap, and finally, it was in the cup with a satisfying clunk. She waited while the others finished, her hand on her pocket, feeling her phone with the promise of a message.

They'd said no phones. Promised no one would look. She and Garret only brought their phones with them because it was the safe thing to do. Just in case. You never knew when there might be an emergency situation.

As the others walked to the next hole, Kate stopping at the little stand to write down their scores, Blythe held back. She pulled out her phone and looked at the screen.

I gave you time to show every angle. What's taking so looooong?

She shoved the phone into her pocket. She had to block him. But then Garret and the girls would know she'd checked her phone. Her heart started to race. She placed her hand over it, even though she knew that was ridiculous. It didn't slow the beat. This was anxiety. She lowered her hand.

She walked quickly to where the others were. "I need to pee."

"Now?" Kelsey asked.

"Yes, now."

"We can't wait. There are people."

"I know. Just give me a six, or whatever you think is right. I'll be back by the next hole."

"Are you okay?" Garret asked.

"Yes. I shouldn't have had beer with dinner." She laughed. "Be right back."

She hurried to the restrooms, hid the comment, and blocked the user.

Not until she was lining up her little yellow ball did the guilt, with more intensity than she'd imagined possible, wash over her again.

Not Lacey.

CHAPTER 37

FIFTEEN YEARS AGO: BLYTHE

*S*carlett made the announcement when they were all at the park, watching their just-turned and about-to-turn one-year-olds crawl and stagger around the grass.

"Guess what!? This is about to be the most magnificent day of your year."

"I doubt that," Lacey said. "I—"

"Okay. Maybe not, the year, but you will be very excited, I promise." Scarlett clapped her hands. "Paul and I won that raffle for his company party—a weekend at a house in Santa Barbara. On the beach! Six bedrooms! And we want to invite you all. No kids. They're old enough to leave them overnight now. Right? Our first weekend without them."

After some angst from a few—Blythe admittedly started it because she wasn't sure her parents would be up to watching the twins for an entire weekend—they all decided it was too good to pass. It was almost once-in-a-lifetime-too-good. When would they be this young and be offered a chance like this again? Their children would survive without their parents for two nights. They would thrive. That was what they all convinced themselves. That's what all the parenting experts said. It was good for the children, and good for the parents to enjoy some time apart. Evie, the other one who wasn't sure she was ready to leave Ben because he'd been premature and she still carried those anxious first weeks in the marrow of her bones, finally decided that she and Isaac needed this.

Blythe's parents said, *no problem.*

Their first night at the beach house had been absolutely perfect. Together, they made pizza from scratch, drank wine, and sat outside around the fire pit, listening to the ocean waves sweeping the shore less than fifty feet away. They talked about their babies and laughed. They went to bed happy and relaxed and refreshed. They enjoyed uninterrupted sleep.

The following morning, just after they spread their towels on the beach, things took a turn.

Jenna lay on her back, a sun hat covering her face, her body slick with sunscreen. She stretched her arms overhead and pointed her toes, then curled them, forcing the tendons in her feet to stand out. "I feel like doing something crazy."

Blythe felt a tiny pinch of concern in her stomach. But alongside it was a thin tremor of excitement. Jenna had always done that for her. It made her feel like a teenager again. As if all the years since she and Jenna had lost touch had never happened. The other three women seemed to fade into the background, taking on the appearance of sand sculptures around her. No one was alive but Jenna, ready to make their weekend more than memorable.

But Blythe was a mother now. So was Jenna. They needed to be—

"Nothing too crazy." Jenna giggled. "I mean, we're moms. And dads. We have to be responsible."

"Yes," Blythe said.

"All grown up," Evie agreed.

"That doesn't mean we can't have fun. Go a little wild," Scarlett said. "We still have a few good years yet. The fun isn't over, right?"

"Absolutely," Jenna said.

"I'm having a great time," Lacey said. "Last night was so nice. I love being here with all of you. And it is good to have some time away from my sweet babe. As much as I miss her. This is so amazing. Thank you, Scarlett."

"I brought something with me," Jenna said.

"I don't want to do anything dangerous," Lacey said. "We have responsibilities."

"And this isn't our house," Scarlett said. "The rules—"

"Shh!" Jenna laughed. "It's not dangerous. It's just a little fun. Take the party up a notch. Who's ever tried E?"

"You're not serious," said Lacey.

"I am," Jenna said.

"I've never done drugs," Lacey said. "And I don't plan to start now."

"It's perfectly safe," Jenna said. "If you do it in a secure and loving environment. Which means, with people you trust. Which is us."

They discussed it for the rest of the morning. By lunchtime, they'd more or less agreed, it would be fun, and different. If they didn't do it now, they never would, and you only lived once, and they *did* trust each other, and they'd never, not a single one of them, done something truly outside the boundaries of normal, whatever that was, which they also discussed while they made sandwiches.

Someone pointed out that all of their babies were weaned. It was safe.

Over lunch, they brought the subject up with their husbands, and by late afternoon, when the first bottle of wine was opened, they knew they were going to do it.

Blythe found herself strangely excited. She wondered why she was so eager. Maybe it had something to do with parenthood itself. There was a need to escape, not only for the weekend, knowing your children were well-cared for and safe. She could sleep late and let down her guard for fifty hours or so, for the first time in well over a year.

When had she ever done something like this? And from what she'd heard, ecstasy had the potential to bring them even closer. It had the potential to re-ignite something in their marriages that might have dimmed over the past year. No one said that last part, but as her friends glanced at their husbands, touched them more than they had in weeks, letting their hands linger on their shoulders, she was sure they were all thinking along those same lines.

While they barbecued the steaks and tossed green salad, cut up fruit and husked corn for grilling, they took the little tablets Jenna had brought with her. Blythe realized Jenna had been confident they would all agree. She wondered when the idea had first crossed Jenna's mind.

By the time they'd enjoyed a satisfying meal, Blythe felt her mood starting to shift. She could see from the easy smiles of her friends, the drifting conversation without any tense words, that the others were experiencing similar sensations.

They went outside and started the gas fire, even though the sun was still above the horizon. They sipped wine and watched the rays spread through the few stratus clouds stretched across the sky. They marveled at the silken texture of golden sunlight settling across the water.

And then it was dark.

They continued talking, but the group broke gracefully into smaller pieces.

Then things grew fuzzy.

Suddenly, Blythe and Miles were the only two by the fire pit. She wasn't sure where the others had gone, or exactly when they'd disappeared. The strange thing was, she didn't really care.

It was nice to be alone with Miles. When did she ever get time alone with her male friends? This was how life ran through your fingers. You spent years with people, and every encounter was chaotic, ending too quickly. It was almost an illusion to call yourself close friends, because all you had were lots of group events filled with small talk and activities. But how well did you really *know* the other people?

Now she had a chance to know Miles as a real person. Someone unique and separate from Lacey. She marveled at the opportunity. She wanted to run and find Jenna. She wanted to throw her arms

CATHRYN GRANT

around her friend and thank her for showing them how much they needed this. It wasn't a drug-tripping experience at all. It was almost spiritual.

She asked Miles how it felt to be a father. To her surprise, although it shouldn't have surprised her at all, because her own emotions felt very close to the surface, as if the prick of a straight pin into her forearm would send them oozing out of her body, he began talking.

His voice was soft. It had a tenderness she'd never heard from him before. Did he speak that way to Lacey? Or was this something new? Maybe he was only this way when he was alone with his baby girl, whispering to her as she cried for comfort in the middle of the night. Or, it was the ecstasy, a drug-induced euphoria, feelings that weren't real.

She wanted them to be real. She loved this.

As he spoke, she looked into his eyes, made brighter by the firelight. She felt as if she could see deep inside his mind. It seemed as if his feelings were right there, visible to no one but her. She was hearing and seeing and feeling things that no one else had seen in him. Not ever.

It was magic. She had a unique skill, an ability to draw this out of him she hadn't known she possessed. He looked as if he wanted to kiss her. He was so grateful she was allowing him to share so much with her, to speak about things he'd never had the courage to reveal before now. He looked as if he felt safe with her, that he could trust her with his deepest, most vulnerable thoughts, knowing she would keep them to herself.

She leaned closer, listening as his voice grew softer. Was this how men felt about their infant children? Did all men feel this way? She had no idea. He sounded as if he loved that little girl so much he didn't have room inside his heart for all the feelings.

Blythe placed her hand gently on his leg, just above his knee. He covered her hand with his own. The warmth flooded her body. She felt as if they were becoming one person. It was divine. Their souls were being joined into a single entity. Their love for their children was binding them together in a way she hadn't known two people could possibly connect.

Then, without being sure how it happened, just as she hadn't been sure how the others had vanished, she was on his lap and they were kissing. Their tongues were entwined, their arms wrapped so tightly around each other, she couldn't sense where her body ended and his began. She felt her bones and muscles melting into him, she felt as if she were taking his entire being into herself.

He shifted and moved his hand up inside the back of her shirt. She moaned softly as the warmth of his skin touched hers. He made a sound that seemed to echo her own, and she thought of Garret, always so quiet when they kissed, when they made love, until the very end.

What was happening? This wasn't ... she wanted to be close to Miles, to know him better, to deepen their friendship. But not this. Not this.

She pulled away from him. "No. We can't. We ... I ..."

His hand slid out from beneath her shirt, both hands falling away from her body completely. He grunted. "I don't—"

"Shh." She stood. "I liked talking to you." She kissed his forehead.

"Yeah. Me too."

She walked away quickly. By the time she reached the wide porch that extended from one side of the back of the house to the other, she was almost running. Had she given him ... had she asked for that? Had she done something? She still felt warmth and love rushing through her chest, but she also felt she wanted to find Lacey. She wanted to hold her close and tell her she was so, so sorry. She wanted to run back to Miles and tell him the same. She wanted to fix it, repair it, make sure she hadn't shattered their friendship and her friends' marriage into a million pieces.

She loved them so much! It was ... she couldn't think about it.

Miles hadn't meant to. Neither had she. Did that mean it was okay? A terrible mistake. The E. They were so sorry. It didn't mean anything at all. Lacey would see that. Lacey didn't have to know. It was almost a dream. Wasn't it?

She couldn't think right now. She was high. She needed to remember that. None of this was real. Her feelings while they were talking, her feelings while they kissed, and her feelings right now, were all the result of the chemicals invading her body. It wasn't real.

Their friendship was real. And maybe the things they'd said were real. But the rest was just ... she couldn't think about it. Not now. Her mind was blurry, and she was still feeling a blissful peace. Mostly. It would all work out. That had been a slight misstep. Everything was fine. Miles knew it was fine, and it would fade into a dream that would dissolve over time. Lacey would never know.

Miles would never tell her. Would he?

In the morning, she would be able to think more clearly. For now, she wanted to enjoy the lingering feelings. She wanted to be with all her friends. They were such amazing friends. She was so lucky to have these people in her life. They would be with her forever. How had she gotten so incredibly lucky? She smiled as she stepped inside the house.

It was such a beautiful home. A magical gift that was bringing them even closer.

In the kitchen, she filled a glass with water and took a few sips. She left the glass on the counter and wandered into the living room. It was empty. She shivered. Why was she so cold? And where was everyone? Maybe they'd gone down to the beach. That made sense. It probably felt peaceful by the water, everyone together.

She would grab her jacket and find them. She hurried down the hall and up the stairs to the bedroom belonged to her and Garret. She went inside and opened the closet. It was on the hook, wasn't it? Then she remembered she'd tossed it on the bed in one of the unused rooms that morning rather than making the trek upstairs. She returned to the first floor and went to the second unused bedroom around the corner from the main bathroom.

She opened the door and stopped as if she'd slammed into a wall of ice. Everything froze. Her fingers on the door handle, her muscles, her eyelids, unable to blink. Her breath seemed to freeze in her lungs, her voice in her throat. Even her blood turned to ice in her veins.

Garret was naked, his back to her, a pair of naked legs around his waist, sounds of pleasure—so soft, yet at the same time, a deafening roar.

She backed out of the room. The voice of her father even louder in her ears now. *Don't react. Think first. Always think first.*

CHAPTER 38

NOW: BLYTHE

*B*lythe knew she and Garret had taken an unconventional journey to healing their marriage. Or maybe it hadn't been unconventional at all. Blythe just thought it was because she didn't know anything about other marriages that had weathered the same storm they'd gone through. It wasn't something people she knew talked about.

She'd read stories online and in books. She'd devoured them. But you never knew if those were the entire truth. The only truth you knew was your own. So it felt unconventional to her.

Sometimes, she looked at Garret and wondered. But mostly, after all this time, she didn't think about it much. Hardly ever. Which meant their marriage was healed. And she'd done it single-handedly. Right or wrong.

The only time she felt that awful night slither to the surface was when Garret seemed patronizing to her. She wasn't sure why that triggered it. She knew the primary reason it had happened was because of the ecstasy. And she certainly hadn't been entirely blameless. She didn't do what he'd done, not even close, but she'd dipped her toe in the water.

And right now, he was being patronizing.

"It's not because of social media," he said. "You make too much of it."

"But why else would they quit? Two clients, in five days? I've never had clients quit unless they were moving away or had some other major life change."

"You don't know what's going on in their lives. Maybe it's something they didn't feel comfortable talking about."

"My clients tell me a lot—about their marriages, their children. About problems with their in-laws. Financial struggles. Issues at work. I don't think there's some dark secret that both of them can't talk about, which made them suddenly decide to ignore their health."

Garret opened the refrigerator and stuck his head inside.

"What are you looking for? I'm trying to talk to you."

"I'm hungry." His voice was muffled.

"Can you wait five minutes?"

He closed the door and turned to face her. "You don't know. Just because people tell you a lot about their lives, doesn't mean they tell you everything."

She sighed. She knew that. She absolutely knew that, better than most people. She narrowed her eyes, searching his face to see if he was trying to make some deeper point that was eluding her.

"It's not because of your social media troll," he said.

"Both of them said he gave them the creeps."

"So?"

"Maybe they—"

"No. You're being paranoid. Of course, they said it was creepy." He walked around the island and put his arms around her, pulling her close. He rested his chin on the top of her head. "Please don't get yourself into knots. I know you're really upset about this. But eventually he'll get tired of it. You're doing the right thing to keep ignoring him."

"I know that."

"Your clients said it was creepy because it is. Anyone would say that. It doesn't mean they quit because of it. You're so consumed by it, you can't see clearly what's going on."

"Don't make it sound like I'm hysterical."

"That's not what I'm doing."

She wriggled out of his arms. "I just think it's really strange that two people quit so closely together. And it feels like more than a coincidence that it was right after another rush of ugly comments. And that both of them, *both* of them, were vague about their reasons."

Garret returned to the fridge, pulled open the door, and grabbed a container of leftover pasta. While he heated the pasta in the microwave, he continued talking, but Blythe was tuning him out. He didn't get it. He didn't see the impact this issue was having on her business because he didn't think social media mattered to begin with.

Why had she brought it up with him? This was why she had her friends. They were her supporters for brainstorming her business plans. Garret was great for working on the financial side, or helping her with scheduling and dealing with difficult clients. But marketing was not his thing. When was she going to stop expecting him to understand the issues around it? She wanted to laugh at herself for even mentioning it.

He was comforting when she was upset that the troll was frightening her, although his solution was backing out altogether. But the rest of it was not his area of expertise. She was just so used to telling him everything. Almost everything.

That afternoon, she sent a group text to her friends. Group texts had become difficult, painful. Each time she added to the thread, she experienced the absence of Lacey like a knife going through her solar plexus. She imagined it was the same for the others. There was an irrational feeling she was leaving Lacey out of their conversation. Their previous group text was a thread that had been running for years. She couldn't recall who had created the first message after Lacey was gone, deliberately leaving her out.

She tapped out her message, telling them about the two clients who had disappeared in the space of a few days, with flimsy explanations. They'd paid their final bills almost immediately, then stopped responding to her messages.

Jenna: That does sound strange, but customers are flakey. Trust me, I know.

Evie: Most aren't, though.

Jenna: More than you'd think.

Evie: Don't put so much negative energy out there, Jenna. It's not helpful.

Jenna: I have a lot of positive energy, too. But I'm just being honest. It doesn't help to lie about it.

Scarlett: What were their reasons?

Blythe: Life changes. I don't think you can be more vague.

Evie: Both of them?

Blythe: One said, life changes. The other said, new priorities, or something like that.

Scarlett: It does seem strange not to prioritize your health, so it's a weird way to put it.

Blythe: It just feels so sudden. And such non-reasons.

Scarlett: I agree.

Jenna: So do I.

Evie: I don't think you should assume, with not very much information. But at the same time, you need to trust your gut. Did you ask them?

Blythe: No. I didn't start thinking about it until after the second one quit.

Evie: Maybe you should ask.

Blythe: Maybe. They were both really definite about saying goodbye, and wishing me the best. It feels annoying to go back to them now.

Evie: It's the only way to know.

Jenna: What will you do if that is the reason? It won't change anything.

Blythe stared at her phone. Jenna was absolutely right.

She laughed bitterly. That thought hadn't occurred to her. She wanted the reassurance that she'd called it right, that she wasn't being paranoid. She wanted them to agree with her that the troll was hurting her business. But what good would it do?

She could use that as supporting evidence in her reports to try to get the issue escalated. But would that do anything to solve the problem? Every single time she reported the user name, screenshots and all, her complaints seemed to vanish into thin air. It was always *under investigation*. She was told she needed to give them time to investigate.

Maybe they just didn't want to do anything. They had far worse problems to deal with. She'd never received a physical threat. There was nothing about violence or truly stalking her in the real world, aside from that picture at the gym and the hint about the swimsuit. They were probably dealing with much more serious issues.

It was all fear and a sense of disgust in her own head, and worries about her business. All the fun had been sucked out of social media. But global, multi-billion dollar social media companies didn't feel any of that. They were dealing with real violence in countries around the world. With bona fide scams, where people lost thousands of dollars and more. With human trafficking and other horrible things that Blythe didn't want to think about.

She left her phone on the end table and crossed the room. She pushed open the bifold doors and stepped outside. She took a deep breath of warm afternoon air.

Trust her gut.

What good did that do? She was trapped by this creep. He was holding her business hostage. Even though her gut told her he'd cost her two clients, there was nothing she could do about it.

CHAPTER 39

*W*hen Blythe turned to come into the house, she was startled to see Garret just inside the open door. How long had he been standing there? She'd been completely unaware of him coming home, of him entering the living room. She'd been unaware of anyone nearby, of someone watching her.

She shivered, rubbing her arms.

"Are you okay?" Garret asked.

"Yes."

"Why are you shivering? It's hot."

"You startled me."

"I didn't mean to. I said *hi*. I thought you heard me."

"I didn't. When did you get home?"

"A few minutes ago."

She nodded. She wasn't going to tell him she hadn't realized it was so late. How long had she been out there? It felt like only a few seconds. She shivered again. She felt her pocket for her phone, then recalled leaving it on the sofa. She glanced at her watch.

"I was talking to Jenna," Garret said.

"Oh?"

He stepped outside and put his arm around her. "Are you sure you're okay? You keep shivering."

"I'm fine."

"So, I was talking to Jenna. And she offered to have Kelsey and Kate over for a weekend. So you and I can get away."

"That's random."

Garret laughed. "Why is it random?"

"She's never done that before."

He squeezed her gently. "Well, now she is. Where should we go?"

"I ... why didn't she tell me?"

He shrugged, tightening his grip.

"It's a little strange. Out of the blue. She's never—"

"Just accept it as a gift. It'll be great. We could go to—"

"But why the sudden offer?"

"Maybe because you're so tense. Why can't you just accept a really nice gesture? You're so wound up about the troll. And She probably—"

"So, it's not random. It's because I'm losing my grip."

He laughed and let go of her. "She's trying to be nice. I'd love to get away for a weekend alone with you. Don't over analyze it."

"I'm not over-analyzing. She's never watched Kelsey and Kate, so we can go away. It's random and you know it."

"People are worried about you."

"What people?"

"Jenna. Me."

"You're talking about me with Jenna? What other people?"

"No one is talking about you! She said you were stressed about the troll, which I am already well aware of. And no one else said a word."

"You said—*people* are worried about me."

"I'm worried. I'm *people*." He laughed, but it sounded hollow. "Where do you want to go?"

"I'm not sure I want to go anywhere. It's not a good time."

"Why not?"

"I just lost two clients. Remember? And I need to ..." She'd promised herself she wouldn't bring up her social media issues with him again. Although he'd started it by mentioning that damn troll. Why couldn't she get that out of her life? She was sick of it. That faceless, formless creep was a bigger part of her life than her husband or her daughters, or her friends. A constant shadow.

She had a good client list. Maybe she should just be happy with that. But there was always some turnover, and if she wasn't getting her name out there, she would face inevitable decline when others moved away, or met their goals and grew past the point of needing weekly coaching.

Garret stepped around so he was facing her. "A weekend away would be really good for us."

"Are we having problems?" she asked.

"No. This is a chance to—"

"It's just not a good time. I already said that. If she wants to have Kelsey and Kate over so we can go away, the offer will stand. We can do it another time. But I can't think about it right now."

He looked crushed.

She didn't feel guilty. For some reason, she felt manipulated. She felt as if Jenna was ... what *was* Jenna doing? This was so strange. She wasn't going away just because Jenna, or Garret, was worried about her. That was her final decision. And she was done trying to explain it. Besides, what was the point of going away and spending the weekend worrying about the troll? It would put a dark cloud over her enjoyment.

She placed her hand on his shoulder and kissed him lightly on the lips. "Another time. I don't want a weekend away because people think I need escape therapy, or whatever idea you and Jenna cooked up. I'm fine." She gave him a cheerful smile. "I'm going to start dinner." She turned and went into the house.

There was a rotisserie chicken in the fridge that she planned to shred for Mediterranean style sandwiches in pita bread with a bit of feta cheese, chopped Kalamata olives, greens, and a chilled Raita she'd made earlier. She washed her hands, pulled out the chicken, and got to work shredding it into a bowl.

When everything was ready, she covered the serving dishes and returned them to the refrigerator. She set the table rather than calling one of the girls to do it. Being alone with her thoughts, or rather, trying to empty her mind of thoughts and focus on the task at hand, was all she wanted right now. No chatter. No effort applied to thinking about anything more complex than folding napkins and placing flatware on top.

She did not know where Garret had gone. He might still be outside. Sometimes he went for a swim before dinner, but she hadn't heard any splashing in the pool. She glanced out the window. The surface of the water was still. He must have gone into the office or was upstairs.

She put on a Blues playlist and went looking for her family.

Kate and Kelsey were lying on the floor in Kate's room, their lower legs on her bed, talking and looking at their phones. She climbed the stairs, calling Garret's name. He wasn't in the bedroom or the small TV room that was their private retreat on the second floor.

As she passed by the hall window on her way back to the stairs, she glanced out. Garret stood near the curb. Jenna's navy blue sedan was parked haphazardly in front of their house. The driver's door was open. Jenna stood in the street, a few feet from Garret, looking up at him. Her sunglasses were on top of her head, pushing her fine, ashy brown hair off her face. She was frowning and gesturing wildly as she talked.

Blythe hurried down the stairs, through the living room and into the entryway. She pressed the handle of the front door gently, opening the door carefully. She stepped onto the porch. Jenna was still talking. Blythe left the door open behind her. She took a few steps across the patio, hoping to catch what Jenna was saying with such focused intensity that she hadn't turned or noticed Blythe creeping closer to the edge of the patio.

Holding her breath, as if that might make her approach less noticeable, Blythe stepped onto the pathway and moved closer to where Garret and Jenna were standing.

Jenna turned her head. Immediately, she lowered her hands to her sides. Her voice became a whisper, caught in the breeze, and then she stopped talking.

Jenna lowered her sunglasses over her eyes. "Hi, Blythe!"

Garret turned.

"What's going on?" Blythe asked.

"Just stopped by to follow-up on my offer. But Garret said you're too busy to take a weekend away."

"Did he?" Blythe glanced at her husband.

He gave her a tight smile.

"Dinner's ready," Blythe said.

Jenna raised her hand in an eager wave. "Talk to you later. Bye-bye." She hurried to her car. A moment later, she was gone.

"What was that about?" Blythe asked.

"She told you," Garret said.

"Mmm." Blythe followed him into the house. All that gesturing and talking hadn't been a simple follow-up. What wasn't he telling her?

CHAPTER 40

JENNA

*J*enna had stopped by Blythe and Garret's house on a whim.

She'd called Garret the day before to suggest that Kelsey and Kate could spend the weekend at her house so the two of them could get a weekend away, but he hadn't gotten back to her. Even though she hadn't checked with Naomi before issuing the invitation, she knew she could talk Naomi into being agreeable.

But then, she hadn't heard a word from Garret. Not even a text. She'd thought he would respond with a list of dates within the hour. He'd sounded thrilled with the idea. That meant Blythe had not been thrilled.

What woman didn't jump at the chance for a weekend away alone with her husband?

Jenna had finally texted Garret, but he hadn't responded. So, she'd driven by their house.

As soon as she'd turned down their street, she realized it was a poorly thought-out plan. She couldn't ring the bell and assume Garret or one of the girls would answer the door. And if he hadn't responded to one text, sending another from her car, sitting out front, wasn't necessarily going to bring him out for a curbside conversation.

She pulled up in front of the house and studied her phone. She wasn't sure why she was so eager to have an answer. She supposed part of it was her usual tendency toward overexcitement and impatience. She wanted answers when she wanted them. She hated waiting, hated not knowing. Besides, it was rude. She'd made a generous offer, and now she was being ignored. If she was going to dedicate a weekend to entertaining three teenagers, she needed to do some planning. She needed the dates.

Opening her text messages, she tapped on Garret's name and tried to think about what she might say to get him to respond immediately.

> Jenna: I'm in front of your house. Need to talk. Urgent.

She smiled. That should do it. Of course, there was nothing urgent about it, and there was nothing she needed to talk about. All she needed was a simple yes or no. And the dates. But it was taunting and teasing enough that Garret would definitely be out there any minute.

And she was right. Ninety-seven seconds later, the front door opened. She had the timer running on her phone, so she knew. She smiled and stopped the timer, opened the car door, and climbed out. She walked to the curb.

"What's wrong?" Garret asked.

"I didn't hear back from you."

"It's probably not going to happen right now. Maybe in a few months."

"Why not?"

"It's not a good time."

"What does that mean?"

"Just what I said—not a good time."

Jenna laughed. "How can it not be a good time? It's summer. It's perfect. It's harder during the school year. And Blythe needs a break. She—"

"We really appreciate your offer. I hope we can take a raincheck, but it's not going to work right now."

"That's really weird," Jenna said. "I don't get it."

He shrugged. "What did you need to talk about?"

She smiled.

"You said it was urgent."

"I wanted to know what was going on."

"Going on with what?" He took a step back from the edge of the curb.

She sensed his annoyance. She didn't want him annoyed with her, didn't want him shutting her out of their lives. She needed all her friends right now. With her business feeling shaky, Oliver's job ... she needed her friends. Support. Strength. She took a deep breath. "I'm really worried about her."

"I know. But she's fine. Truly."

"Are you sure about that? I would be packing my suitcase right now if someone offered me a weekend away."

Garret chuckled softly. "Is that a hint that you want a return offer?"

"No. Oh, no. That's not what I meant." She grinned, hoping to put that thought out of his head. "Most women, any woman, any man, really, would love a chance to get away for the weekend. Am I right?"

"It's nice. But sometimes, staying home and enjoying your kids is nice, too. We only have a few years left with them. Before we know it, they'll be applying for college. Everything will accelerate even more, and off they'll go."

She gave him a grim smile. "She's just been so upset about the troll on her social media."

Garret sighed. "I get it, Jenna. I know she's upset. I need to get going." He glanced at the house.

"Do you think she made it up?"

He turned back. "What?"

She lowered her voice. She wasn't sure why, because the street was empty of people, only the occasional car passing by. All the windows facing the street were closed. "Do you think Blythe made it up? All those horrible comments by the troll? That there was a troll at all?"

He took another step away from her, losing his balance for a moment, then righting himself. He stared at her, his eyes glazed, as if he wasn't looking at her at all. He didn't seem to be noticing her or aware that she was still there. He looked lost inside his own head.

Was he considering her question, or had it sparked something else that he was now thinking about? He looked partially disconnected from reality.

It seemed like a very long time that he didn't speak. Finally, he met her gaze. "I think I saw some of the comments. She showed them to me. I'm fairly sure I remember that."

"But you *aren't* sure. You really had to think about it. That's why you were quiet for so long. You were trying to think back over everything she's said, and you're wondering—is there really a troll? Or did she make it all up?"

"Why would she do that?"

"For attention."

"Blythe isn't like that."

Jenna shrugged. "Maybe she thought it would bring more eyeballs to her posts. Controversy can be a double-edged sword, right? Maybe she thought it would generate more activity. After a while, posting the same type of content gets stale. She started with that bikini shot, which was really different for her. Provocative." Jenna paused, trying to catch her breath after talking so fast.

Garret nodded slowly. "It was ... a little different. But not ... I don't know much about social media and branding and all that."

"Right after that, all the troll stuff started. So I just wonder, if she was trying to get some viral activity going by letting these trolls make wild, suggestive comments and maybe she thought ... I don't know. Sometimes we do crazy things on social media without thinking it through."

Garret stared at her.

"I just wondered, that's all. But if you think you saw some of the comments, I guess it's real."

"Have *you* seen any of the comments from the troll?" Garret asked.

She looked at him without blinking, holding his gaze for several seconds. She glanced toward the front door as something caught her eye. Blythe had come outside and was watching them.

Jenna lowered her sunglasses. "No. I never saw a single comment. That's why I asked."

CHAPTER 41

BLYTHE

*B*efore she had time to call Kelsey and Kate for dinner, the doorbell rang. What did Jenna want now? Blythe went to the front door and looked outside. The detectives were back, waiting expectantly, as if they had no idea what time it was.

Blythe stared out at them, wondering what else they wanted to ask. There wasn't a single thing Blythe and Garret knew about the night Lacey had been murdered that they hadn't already told them. They'd given the times they'd gone to sleep, answered all the questions about the Abbott's relationship, and addressed speculation about imagined dark secrets. What else was there?

She opened the door.

"Hi, Ms. Farrell. We have a few more questions about Ms. Abbott's murder," Detective Banner said. "May we come in?"

Blythe wondered what they would do if she said no. She opened the door wider and stepped to the side.

"Is your husband home?" Detective Madeira asked.

"Yes."

"Will you ask him to join us?"

She gestured toward the living room, watched Detective Banner close her front door firmly, and then went to get Garret.

They returned to the living room to find the detectives seated comfortably on the sofa. Blythe and Garret took the same seats as they had the previous time, giving Blythe an uncomfortable sense of déjà vu along with a feeling that she'd dreamed this scene and, because of that, she should know how it was going to turn out. It was maddening that she had no idea where this was headed.

"We've ruled out Mr. Abbott as a suspect in his wife's murder."

Blythe felt herself gasp—loudly. She put her hand over her mouth, although it was obviously too late. She'd had no idea they thought Miles might have murdered Lacey. How could they think that? Why would they think that? She was aware that was how cops thought. It was a cliché—*It's always the husband, always the boyfriend*. But they'd actually investigated that? They'd considered *Miles* a suspect?

Why hadn't Miles mentioned it to them? He must have been miserable all this time. It was horrible enough to have your wife die, to have her murdered. But that? Blythe looked at the detectives, hoping her face didn't show the loathing she felt.

"We want to circle back and look again at the possibility that Ms. Abbott might have been having an affair."

"Oh, my God!" Blythe said. "Why is this—"

"Calm down," Detective Madeira said.

"I'm calm. I just don't understand why the first thing you do when you're looking for a killer is assume bad things about nice, kind, good people!"

"I'm not going to get into a definition of *good* people," Detective Madeira said. "We're here to ask a few questions. So, let's try to focus on that and we'll be out of here as quickly as possible."

Detective Banner looked directly at Blythe. "You were close to Ms. Abbott. Did she ever mention having an affair?"

"She would never ... no."

"Was there anything that made you suspect she might be?"

"No. Never."

"No unexplained broken appointments? No noticeable changes in her appearance?"

Lacey's sudden decision to end her coaching flashed across

Blythe's mind like the finale to a firework show. She felt as if everything inside her turned white, the room filled with the deafening silence that follows an ear-shattering explosion.

"Yes?" Detective Banner prompted.

Blythe shook her head.

"Nothing? I have the impression something crossed your mind."

"Nothing."

"You looked—"

"It's not related to this." It had only been a few weeks before Lacey was killed. It couldn't ... besides, why were they thinking she'd had an affair? Wouldn't that point right back to Miles as her killer? Did a woman's lover usually murder her? Maybe if she said she was going to tell her husband, or a friend ...

"Ms. Farrell, it looks as if there's something troubling you. Was there a change in Ms. Abbott's behavior that might suggest she was having a sexual relationship outside her marriage?"

"No."

"Are you sure?"

"Yes."

"But there was a change in her behavior?"

"Not really, no."

"Not really?"

"There wasn't. No. Nothing."

"It doesn't sound like you're being completely straightforward with us," Detective Madeira said.

"I am. Are those all your questions?" Blythe scooted forward in her chair.

"No. A few more. If there's nothing you want to tell us?"

"There's not."

Detective Madeira turned to face Garret. "Have you ever had a sexual relationship with Ms. Abbott?"

"No!" Blythe said. "Why would you ... that's not right."

"We're asking Mr. Farrell," Detective Madeira said.

"No," Garret said.

"No kissing? Groping?"

"Absolutely not," Garret said.

"Flirting?"

"No. Do you really think flirting ends up in a horrific murder like Lacey's?" Garret asked. "That's—"

"We're just being thorough," Detective Banner said.

"I would never. Lacey had criticized, and was somewhat negative toward my wife's business on social media. That's not someone I'm going to have an affair with."

Garret looked smug, sublimely proud of himself, as if that settled the matter.

Blythe's stomach heaved. She stared at him, feeling like she might vomit on the carpet any minute. Did he realize what he'd said? Maybe he was more stressed and upset about these questions than she was. Maybe the fact they'd asked him at all had pierced him so deeply, he was babbling nonsense. Maybe he had no idea what he'd just said.

"Garret." Her voice was a whisper, and the moment she'd spoken, she foolishly hoped the cops hadn't heard, but they both turned to look at her.

They'd heard. They'd heard Garret, they'd heard the meaning in his poorly chosen words, and they'd heard her desperate, embarrassed whisper. They'd heard everything.

"You were upset that Ms. Abbott was critical of your wife's business?"

"I—"

"What business is that?"

"I'm a health and wellness coach," Blythe said.

"What is that?" Detective Madeira asked.

"Just what it sounds like," Blythe said. "I coach people to live a healthier, more well-rounded lifestyle. Healthier body and mind."

"I see," Detective Madeira made a note.

After all this, that's what he'd chosen to write down? Maybe she should be grateful.

"How was Ms. Abbott critical of your wife's business?" Detective Madeira asked.

"I don't think any of this is relevant," Blythe said.

"We'll decide what's relevant," Detective Madeira said. "How was Ms. Abbott critical of your wife's wellness coaching business?"

There was no way Garret was going to be able to explain this without it sounding petty. Blythe could already hear the words.

"I don't know the details," Garret said. "She can explain it better."

Blythe stared at him. What was he doing? This was turning into a nightmare. She couldn't believe they were exposing their lives to total strangers like this. None of this had anything to do with Lacey's murder. The detectives were just digging for secrets and dirt because they didn't have any evidence and didn't know where to turn in their investigation.

"Ms. Farrell?" Detective Madeira said.

She hated him. She absolutely hated this intrusive man looking at her as if he had a right to know about the most intimate issues with her friends. Her deceased friend. The friend she'd barely begun to grieve. How dare he!

"It wasn't that big of a deal," Blythe said. "Garret was just making a point that he wouldn't cheat on me. She hurt my feelings a little. That was all. It's not important."

"I already said, we'll decide what's important. Please explain what happened."

"It doesn't matter! He told you he didn't have an affair with her. That's all you wanted to know."

"But he was upset with Ms. Abbott for hurting you."

"Are you accusing me of killing her?" Garret asked.

"No. We're asking questions. You're prolonging this, Ms. Farrell. If you'd answer, we can be finished."

"I promote wellness. Lacey was selling mugs that celebrated a lack of concern for improving yourself. They were feel-good sayings, little jokes on the mugs. She tagged my business. It was nothing important."

Detective Madeira made another note. She wanted to grab his phone and smack it against the side of his head. She wanted them to leave. She didn't want to see either of them ever again. She wanted them to find the person who murdered Lacey instead of talking to her friends and prying into their lives as if that had anything to do with her death.

Finally, the detectives were gone.

When Blythe closed the door, she couldn't look Garret in the eye. She went into the kitchen and opened a bottle of wine. She took two glasses out of the cabinet and splashed wine carelessly into both. She handed one to Garret, who was right behind her. They didn't toast. She still didn't meet his gaze as she took several rapid sips, trying not to replay the last hour in her mind.

CHAPTER 42

FIFTEEN YEARS AGO: BLYTHE

*B*lythe had always been a deliberate person. She wasn't sure if it was her genetic makeup, if it had grown out of her father's constant, gentle, persistent reminder to not *react*, but to *think first*, or if it was a protective coating she'd developed against the bullying she'd experienced. A hard, impenetrable shell she'd developed. She never wanted to respond to a question she wasn't expecting until she'd had time to think it through.

She never, ever agreed to a significant purchase without walking away first to clear her mind.

She never spoke when she was angry or hurt. She let the feelings settle first.

When she'd started her business, she was careful and deliberate about how she'd mapped out her place in the market. She'd studied what other health coaches were doing, making detailed spreadsheets to see what they offered and where their strengths lay. She'd carefully carved out the space for herself where she'd seen gaps left by others.

After she and Garret purchased their first, and only, home, she'd spent nearly six months looking at furniture and carpet samples, paint chips and tile before they'd even started to make plans for upgrades. She wasn't one of those women who walked into a bedroom and started tearing up the carpet with her bare hands, or ran out to the home improvement store on a Saturday morning and had the walls in the spare room painted teal by dinnertime.

In that horrible moment when she'd seen the man to whom she'd given her life—the man who had vowed he would never love another woman, who had sworn he couldn't imagine his life without her—fucking someone else, the habits that had shaped her entire life overshadowed it all.

Despite the E humming in her veins.

Don't react.

She'd quietly closed the door. She walked slowly, deliberately, then faster, running blindly up the stairs to their bedroom. She'd gone inside, closed the door, and locked it. She'd fallen onto the bed.

Think first.

But she couldn't think. Everything inside her had been a solid sheet of pain, a lake frozen from one shore to the other.

The effects of the drug had been punctured in that single moment. All the bliss and lack of concern and boundless, chemically induced love were washed away. She'd stared at the ceiling, her body trembling with cold. But she was too weak to adjust the blankets, so they covered her.

She wouldn't talk about this when her friends were within earshot. When she and Garret weren't in their own home. That was her first decision. She wouldn't risk an audience, and the possibility of others hearing the worst pain of her life coming out of her lips.

And it was absolutely the worst pain of her life. Far worse than anything those girls in high school had inflicted.

Looking back, she wasn't sure how she'd made it through the rest of the weekend. During the long drive home, she'd kept the music turned up loud. Every time Garret tried to lower the volume, she'd insisted she wanted to prolong the good feelings with upbeat music. She couldn't bear listening to him talk, couldn't tolerate the sound of his voice.

At home, she'd buried herself in her babies. She'd touched them and held them, inhaled their scent, cuddling even more than usual, lying beside them on the floor while they played, letting them tumble and climb over her as much as they wanted. Her entire world became her girls, even more than was required with twin toddlers. Because she knew, she'd known that first night, alone in the room of that fabulous house, while Garret finished fucking someone who wasn't her, that she couldn't leave him.

How would she cope on her own with twins?! Babies, still. She and Garret could barely manage them when they tag-teamed, with dinner and dishes and baths and story time and songs and getting them to sleep. They still woke, sometimes more than once, in the night, and never at the same time. They were cutting teeth. And the diapers. Mountains of diapers.

And there was the other thing.

The thing she hated. The thing that shocked her to her core.

She loved that man more than she could believe it was possible to love a man. Still. Even now. Even after what she'd seen. Even after feeling her heart crushed like a piece of rotten fruit. She loved him so much. That's why it hurt so badly. So, *so* badly.

She loved him with all her being and she couldn't conceive of a life without him. She couldn't imagine telling him it was over. She couldn't imagine walking out the door with their daughters, never returning. Or the opposite—watching his back as he walked out for the last time.

The pain of that imagined scene was worse than the other pain.

She felt like a prisoner. The bars of her cell were made of love—red, hot iron bars of love. She couldn't touch them without burning the skin off her fingers.

The more she considered, the more deliberately she walked through her feelings and all the things she wanted to say to him, the more it became clear what she was going to do.

She would say nothing.

The thought of Garret loving her because he felt he had to make up for what he'd done was not something she wanted. The idea of him apologizing, taking pity on her, was despicable. She didn't want to look at every word and gesture for the rest of her life and wonder —*Is he doing this to reassure me, to make me feel loved, to tell me he's sorry? Or is it genuine? Does he truly feel this?*

Is it real?

Of course, he might be doing that anyway. He knew what he'd done.

Maybe what they'd had was damaged forever, because his guilt would make him do those things anyway. But at least he wouldn't be doing it deliberately to *make* her feel better, to make her feel secure and loved.

She'd made her decision.

CHAPTER 43

NOW: SCARLETT

Scarlett had invited the others over for a wine and cheese party—girls only. The date when they'd planned to visit Calistoga, hosted by Lacey, had come and gone without anyone mentioning it.

Scarlett felt guilty every time she thought about it. She didn't want to think about it, didn't want to entertain even a whisper of disappointment. And she wasn't disappointed. That wasn't what she felt. It was a sense of being robbed, not robbed of the trip, but robbed of everything—her friend, their group, their memories. Robbed of a human being they'd loved. Everything had changed and they would never again be able to remember the good times without a pinch of grief. And right now, that grief became so intense at times, she could hardly breathe. No one talked much about that, either.

She knew they all felt it. They talked around it. They occasionally glanced at each other and saw teary eyes. They noticed their voices tremble, or sentences stopped suddenly before they finished a thought because it was headed somewhere they didn't want to go, talking as if her murder hadn't happened. Their brains forgetting, for the briefest moment, that she was gone, and starting to make plans or talk as if she were still there.

This evening would be a distraction. That was all. But it might be a first step. Or not. Definitely a distraction. Maybe that was all they could manage.

No men. Their husbands changed the dynamic. If they wanted to get weepy and maudlin, they could. If they wanted to gossip, they could. The men tended to want to avoid talking about Lacey altogether. Best not to indulge those painful feelings, most of them agreed.

And then there was Miles. She didn't want to think about that challenge.

Eventually, they would all get together again as couples. They would invite Miles, obviously. Would he come? Maybe it would be a family event, making it easier if Miles and Violet could come as a unit, so he didn't feel so alone. She felt the tears rushing to her eyes. She brushed them away and began carrying wineglasses to the living room.

This would be good.

She'd asked Paul to take Angela and Henry to a movie. He'd complained and argued and ended up making such a fuss that the kids seemed to pick up on his resistance by osmosis. Because when she'd mentioned it to Henry, he'd made a sour face and said he would rather watch a movie at home. Angela had said there was no way she and Henry would ever agree on what movie they wanted to see, so there was no point even discussing it.

She'd asked Cooper if *he* would take Henry to a movie. Maybe then Paul and Angela could plan a father-daughter outing. Bowling? Miniature golf? The arcade? No, no, and no. The only word any of them could utter was *no*. It seemed as if they were glued to the house. Agoraphobics, all of them.

Were Henry's idiosyncrasies infecting the whole family?

Or maybe Paul was still upset with her for insisting he take down the post he'd shared from Lacey's memorial. No matter how many times she'd tried to explain, he couldn't understand why she found it so offensive that he'd shared the details of her murder and the memorial with thousands of strangers.

She felt like crying. She wanted the house to herself. Why couldn't Paul support her in this? He should insist that all the kids leave the house for the night so she could have this time with her friends. He should get himself out of the house.

Since when did teenagers prefer staying home over a chance to go out, the evening funded by mom and dad?

"I want everyone to stay in your bedrooms," she'd said. "If you can't go out and let me have this time with my friends, you can at least give me that. No movie at home. I don't want the sound blasting out of the TV while we're trying to talk in the other room."

They glowered and sulked, but they'd agreed.

Evie, Blythe, and Jenna arrived at seven. Scarlett poured wine and passed around the charcuterie board. She rearranged the bowls of guacamole and hummus so they were within easier reach. She adjusted the volume on the speaker so they could hear the music without it drowning out their conversation.

When everyone was settled, sipping their wine, she ducked out of the room to check that her family members were secluded in their rooms. Her children were. Paul was in the family room, phone in his hand, uploading dog photos.

"Why don't you take Jasper for a walk instead of posting pictures of other people's dogs?"

He ignored her.

"I think he'd love a walk."

"I take him out at seven thirty. You know that."

She sighed and returned to the living room. Knowing Paul was within earshot made her feel as if she had to watch what she said. It wasn't as if she kept secrets from him. It wasn't as if she expected any of her friends to share something she didn't want Paul to hear. It was just ... awkward. She felt they were on display.

For the first hour, they talked about their kids. Work. What was going on in the world? Social media. Memes. Movies and TV shows they liked, loved, and hated. They tenderly recalled memories of Lacey. They wondered how Violet was doing and fretted about Miles.

"It's so awful those detectives thought he might have killed her," Evie said.

"It's always that way." Jenna gulped her wine and poured herself a refill. She ran a tortilla chip through the guacamole and took a bite.

"I know," Scarlett said. "But when it's someone you know. It's just ... it's too awful to think about. How can they look at him and even think that?"

Jenna shrugged. "It's their job to be suspicious."

"How was it for you when they came back with more questions?" Jenna asked.

"Accusing her of cheating on Miles," Evie said. "That poor man."

"Why do they assume bad things about the victim?" Blythe said. "It's so unfair."

"Statistically, that's how it works out," Evie said. "It's so hard to believe. But ..." She took a sip of wine.

They waited for her to say more, but she seemed unaware that she'd left her thought unfinished.

"Right away, they assume it's one of her friends," Scarlett said. "It could have been anyone, not that I believe that for a minute about Lacey. She's not the type."

"What's the type?" Blythe asked.

Evie laughed.

"She was pretty open about how great things were with her and Miles." Scarlett recalled Lacey going on and on about how she'd never known sex would get better the longer you were married.

"I just wish they'd do more investigating and less gossiping," Blythe said. "That's what it feels like. Gossip and digging for dirt."

Scarlett nodded. She hadn't thought of it that way, but Blythe was right. She wasn't sure what she thought the police did to investigate a murder, but questioning their friends and trying to imply there must have been an affair didn't seem like part of it. Maybe it was.

"It's no big deal," Evie said. "One question. Five minutes. Done. It's just a check box."

Everyone took a sip of wine as if they were toasting the wisdom of her comment.

"We should talk about something else," Jenna said.

Blythe nodded. She stood and went to the charcuterie board. She cut a piece of soft cheese and placed it on a cracker. "It's hard to think about anything else."

"It is," Evie said. "But we should."

Scarlett glanced around the room. They all seemed ready to move on to another topic of conversation, tired of the slight discomfort that had crept over them.

They began talking about the food, praising Scarlet for the delicious spread. Only Blythe sat back in her chair, clutching her wineglass, looking mildly upset. She almost looked scared.

CHAPTER 44

BLYTHE

The wine party had been really nice, right up until they started discussing the detective's questions about Lacey having an affair. As the party began, Blythe had sipped her wine and let their words flow around her, feeling part of the group, agreeing with everything they were saying, feeling the support of her friends, their shared outrage.

Then it all exploded inside her head.

After, she'd felt as if her face was stiff with fear, that they could all read the panic in her expression.

...no big deal. One question. Five minutes. Done. It's just a check box.

Five minutes?

The detectives had spent an *hour* asking questions and speculating out loud with Garret. It wasn't simply a check box. They were poking around, looking for something. Did they already know something before Garret had opened his mouth and made it even worse? Maybe Miles had said something. Was it possible he'd mentioned their kiss all those years ago? He wouldn't do that. She'd thought, hoped, he might have forgotten all about it. So much time had passed, so much life, so many more important things. And they were high. Surely he hadn't ... maybe he'd told Lacey ... her head was spinning. But Lacey was dead.

Maybe Lacey and Miles both had bad feelings toward her and they'd hidden them with expert care for years. The thought caused a sharp pain in her stomach. She didn't want to believe their friendship had been a lie. It wasn't possible for two people to be that phony, was it? Was she equally phony? She didn't see it that way at all, but ...

She clutched her stomach, feeling as if she might be sick.

After the Uber dropped her off, she tried to unlock the front door, holding one hand to her stomach, the other gripping her key, shaking as she aimed it toward the lock.

Inside the house, she dropped her keys into her purse, locked the door behind her, and tossed her purse onto the bench in the entryway. She kicked off her sandals and went into the family room where Garret was watching the late news.

Her mind was spinning and reeling, the words coming from the TV sounding like senseless noise. Why were the police so interested in Garret? Was it only because of that stupid thing he'd said about not having an affair with the woman who had hurt his wife? Or had they known something when they arrived? She couldn't seem to recall the order in which their questions had unfolded. It seemed as if they'd been sitting in her living room a long time before Garret dropped that little gem.

So was there more? Why was it only five minutes with the others and an entire hour with them? Or was Evie minimizing it? Maybe her friends had made her paranoid for no reason. Maybe it had been almost as long for the others.

"Why did you say something so stupid to the detectives?"

"What?" Garret kept his attention on the TV.

"You made it sound like you *would* have an affair."

He looked at her. "What are you talking about?"

"You made it sound like the only reason you didn't have an affair with Lacey was because she criticized my coaching. And to make it worse, you gave them a reason why you might have killed her!"

Garret laughed. "What went on at that wine party?" He glanced at the TV for several seconds, then back at her. "You sound a little—"

"Turn off the TV."

He looked startled.

"Turn it off. I want to know why you said that. I'm worried what the detectives are thinking. And I want to know—"

"What's wrong with you?"

"There's nothing wrong with me. The detectives spent five minutes with our friends. They asked if they had a relationship with Lacey. Everyone said no, and that was it. But they talked to you for an hour!"

"It wasn't just me. And you kept interrupting, so ..." He shrugged.

"You're a suspect."

He laughed. "No, I'm not."

"How do you know?"

"I wouldn't kill someone because she made a mug that sounds critical of your coaching." He laughed harder. "Don't you hear how crazy that sounds?"

"Turn off the TV. I'm trying to talk to you."

"I'm watching the news. You barged in here and started throwing conspiracy theories at me."

"It's not a conspiracy theory. Five minutes. They spent five minutes talking to Isaac and the others. They talked to you for an hour."

Garret pressed the remote and muted the TV. "It doesn't mean anything. And you did interrupt them a lot."

"Why did you say that? About her criticizing my business? It was weird."

"You sound like you're ... I think you're really stressed, Blythe. Is this troll getting to you more than you realize? You seem really different. I know Lacey's murder is part of it, but you seem ..."

"I seem, what?"

"You seem ... off center."

"What does that mean?"

"Come sit down."

"Why?"

"Because you look really tense."

"I had three glasses of wine. I'm not tense."

"Come here." He patted the sofa.

She perched at the end, several feet away from him, her knees together, her bare toes curled into the carpet.

"What's going on?" He slid his hand along the cushions, reaching for hers. She kept it in her lap. "Is this troll even real?"

"What?"

"Is it real? Is someone making all these disgusting comments on your social media posts, or are you imagining it?"

She bolted to her feet. "*Imagining* it? Is that what you think? Is that what you've been thinking all this time? Pretending to be sympathetic? Instead, you're thinking I'm deranged? Or ... or ... I can't believe ..." She felt a sob filling her lungs, but she couldn't even cry. The outrage of what he was saying made her feel as if she wanted to smack his face.

He stood and came toward her.

"Don't touch me!"

"I'm sorry. I shouldn't have ..."

"Don't." She backed away from him.

"I'm sorry. I'm really sorry. Please let me hold you."

"No." She wrapped her arms around herself. "How long have you been thinking that?"

"No. It just ... I never thought that."

She laughed. It was so shrill, she didn't recognize the sound of her voice. "Clearly, you did."

"I didn't mean to say it."

"You thought it. So you said it."

"Not really. It just ... I'm sorry. I don't understand it any more than you do. And I—"

"So it must be a lie? Since it's so weird and disgusting and it won't stop, I must be making it up? Why would I even do that? No. Don't answer. Because I don't want to hear why you think that's the kind of person I am. Mentally unbalanced, or whatever it is you think."

"I don't think that. Please, please let me hold you. I never should have said it and I don't really think it. Sometimes words just—"

"Do they?" She couldn't imagine words just coming out of her mouth. First, she had to think about them. Somewhere in his mind, buried in his subconscious, he thought she was unstable. Or manipulative. Or whatever sick thing he was thinking about her. Maybe it was simply his pure hatred of social media, assuming it was all some big self-promoting show, never seeing the positive aspects of it.

"Can we take a step back here?" Garret turned and picked up the remote. He turned off the TV and tossed it on the sofa. "You're worried the police think I murdered our friend. You think I said something that implies I might have killed one of our closest friends, and now I said something really stupid and demeaning about you. It was stupid and I don't think it's true. Maybe I'm scared you can think those things about me."

She looked at him, the lines of concern and regret transforming his face into that of a man ten or fifteen years older. What he'd said was heartless and stupid, but mostly stupid. And what she'd said was equally heartless. In no reality that she could conceive of, did she believe her husband was capable of committing murder. Whatever the police were fumbling around with, it was nothing but suspicion and lack of direction.

"Do you think I killed her because she attacked your consulting work?" His voice strained under the weight of disbelief.

"I—"

"Do you think I was having an affair with her? I wasn't." He reached out his hand, tentatively, as if reaching to test a stovetop to check the temperature, ready to jerk his hand away the moment he felt pain.

She shook her head.

"What is it?"

"I just ... they only spent a few minutes with Isaac. And Oliver and Paul. And they were with us for an hour. Or more. I just don't know."

He moved closer and put his arms around her. She let him, but holding onto him didn't make her feel any better.

CHAPTER 45

$\mathcal{N}$othing was resolved when Garret finally released his hold on Blythe. They pretended as if it was. At least she did. She needed to think. She kissed him.

"I'm going to take a bubble bath."

"That sounds relaxing," he said.

"Go back to the news," she said. "You can update me later."

As she moved away from him, he grabbed her hand and kissed her knuckles. He squeezed her fingers, and she left.

Upstairs, she began filling the tub, setting the water slightly hotter than usual to make sure she would have plenty of time to soak and let her thoughts drift.

When it was full, she lit four thick, white candles, turned off the lights, undressed, and lowered herself carefully into the tub. The warm water closed around her like she imagined amniotic fluid might feel. She took a slow, deep breath and closed her eyes for a moment. Immediately, she felt herself relax.

Her body was at ease, but her mind, after the initial sense of peace, began racing again.

She had no one to talk to, and the feeling of isolation was overwhelming. Maybe this was what an infant felt like inside its mother's womb. Utterly alone. A child didn't know its mother was out there, caring for it, loving it, that both parents were eagerly waiting for its birth. Even her twins hadn't known the other was there. They were each encased in their own bubble, unable to see or hear or feel anything outside their own unformed little minds.

If she tried to talk to her friends about this, they would be horrified by what Garret had said to the detectives. Speaking his words out loud, hearing them come out of her own lips, would make them worse. Listening to them rattle around inside her skull was bad enough. Having to look at her friends' faces, seeing the doubt flickering in their eyes, would be too much.

The others would immediately wonder if Garret had had an affair with Lacey. They'd wonder why the police stayed so long. They'd assume that Blythe's doubts meant he was guilty. And if they didn't assume he'd slept with her, they would read into his words, implying he would casually consider having an affair, that the only reason he hadn't was because Lacey had done something unkind to her.

No matter how she tried to explain it, she couldn't be certain that her friends would be on her side.

And it was clear from the conversation she'd just had with her husband, that she couldn't talk about it any further with him. He didn't get it. He didn't seem to recognize the problem. He didn't get how terrible it sounded. No matter how you looked at it, he appeared guilty of something.

She'd never felt so alone. Maybe when she was huddled in the bottom of her sleeping bag all those years ago, alone in the woods. But back then, she'd known that eventually, morning would come. Eventually, the camping trip would end. The bus would take them back to school, her parents would pick her up, and she would be brought home to a safe place. She had her parents. She wasn't utterly alone in the world as she was now.

Tears filled her eyes. The bubbles lost their distinctive shape, turning into a white sea of foam, no longer the beautiful transparent spheres, catching the light, tiny prisms displaying flecks of color.

Was it possible her husband had had sex with Lacey? After everything that had happened, after what he'd done all those years ago? That thing she'd overlooked and then slowly and deliberately forgiven him for? That thing that she'd believed was driven by alcohol and ecstasy? A thing that was so far in the past it was almost as if it had never happened? It was only once. Something that couldn't destroy them because it was a single moment in time, a terrible mistake.

What if it wasn't?

The water was still warm, but she no longer felt its comfort. She wanted to be moving. She felt anxious and twitchy, her muscles screaming for activity.

She stood, rinsed the bubbles off her skin, got out quickly, and opened the drain.

After drying herself, turning on the light, and blowing out the candles, she dressed in yoga clothes and did some easy poses on the bedroom floor. Garret was probably watching sports now. It was unlikely he'd continued with the news—he didn't like that to be the last thing on his mind before going to bed.

She finished her series with her legs together, bending forward, taking hold of the outside edges of her feet, feeling the pleasant burn in her hamstrings. She closed her eyes, focused on relaxing her lower back muscles, and deepened the stretch. After several more seconds, she got up and grabbed her phone.

Propping herself up on the pillows in bed, she checked her social media. She hadn't looked at it all day. She was proud of herself for putting it out of her mind, for focusing on the party and thinking about real life instead of the virtual world for an entire afternoon and evening. It had cleared her mind. She'd turned off her notifications before leaving for Scarlett's wine party.

The first thing she saw was a comment from a stranger, and before she read it, she knew.

TXV793. The name was always, *always* an immediate warning sign.

This was a new screen name, but she had no doubt it was him.

The weird names were almost as frightening as the messages. Knowing that anyone, from any place in the world, could destroy her peace of mind with a few quick taps on the phone and make her feel utterly exposed—a clichéd, creepy thirty-year-old guy sitting in the dark basement of his mother's house with a single lightbulb overhead, to a scummy mafia-like gang member, to a teenager on the other side of the world, or a teenager in the house across the street, binoculars trained on her bedroom window right now.

She shivered, but forced herself not to get up to check. No one was watching her from across the street.

She read the message.

I didn't forget about you. Don't you forget about me.

Blythe threw her phone at the foot of the bed. It hit the bedding and slid close to the edge where it remained.

She put her hands over her face, pressing them hard against her skull. She started crying, keeping the wracking sobs inside, but letting silent tears fall, allowing her shoulders and chest to shake with rage and frustration. Why was this happening to her? What did he want from her?

He never said. All he wanted was to make her cry, to leave her upset and scared, feeling helpless all the time. He wanted her to hate social media. He wanted her handcuffed so she could never share any part of her business or her life again.

It didn't matter what she posted. He was there. It sometimes didn't matter if she avoided posting entirely. He was still there. He wanted to destroy her life from the inside. To make her agitated and uncertain, incapable of focusing on anything but him.

She hated him with all her heart. If she knew him, if she found out who he was and saw him, she wasn't sure what she would do.

CHAPTER 46

FIFTEEN YEARS AGO: BLYTHE

*T*he first time Blythe and Garret made love after that weekend trip, she'd thought she might die. Every touch was torture. She wanted to claw at his skin, she wanted to bite him so hard he cried out for his life. She didn't want to be there. If she could have, she would have detached from her body and watched from a distance, her mind disappearing to another place until it was all over, and she could fall into a deep, endless sleep.

But then, and this was what made her hate him and hate herself —her memories of him, of them, took over. Her body took over, and she found her mind and, finally, her heart following its lead.

She loved him beyond reason. She loved his smile. She loved the way he took her hand at the most unexpected moments. She loved that he liked to cook and often made pancakes on Sunday mornings, and prepared fabulous evening meals on the weekends. She loved his attention to what was going on in every part of the world. She loved his taste in movies and his devotion to basketball. Everything. He was an incredible father. He was enthused and excited about her plans for starting a coaching business once the twins were in preschool.

When he caught her eye at a party, or in the grocery store, her heart still melted and her knees felt wobbly. After all these years.

Every day she reminded herself that what had happened was caused by the ecstasy. Artificial chemicals. She relived the moments she'd had her arms around Miles, her tongue in his mouth, and remembered how, for a while, she hadn't thought about Garret or her marriage or what was important in her life. She hadn't thought about her children or her values. All she'd thought about were the things Miles had said, the things she'd said—the depth of their connection. The sounds of the crickets and the water on the shore. The feel of the air on her skin and the taste of the wine on her tongue, and then, the taste of his mouth.

She reminded herself that Garret must have had a similar experience. And maybe he'd taken more of the drug than she had. She wasn't really sure how that had all played out. It affected different people differently. She had no way of knowing how far away from his rational mind he'd traveled.

One thing was certain—she didn't want a husband who loved her and supported her and showered her with daily kindnesses and touches because he was trying to prove to her that he still loved her. She couldn't live with that. She couldn't look at every glance and listen to every word, dissecting it to see whether or not it was real. This was the right way to handle it. Sure was absolutely sure of it.

And as the memories of that weekend faded, she knew she'd made the right decision.

The only thing was, the other memory hadn't faded as easily.

When she'd walked into that room, when she'd seen him, when her heart nearly stopped, she'd seen something else.

Looking over Garret's shoulder, her eyes wide and wild, staring directly at Blythe, was Jenna.

But was she staring at Blythe? Or simply staring into the sensations rippling through her body? Were her eyes unfocused? What had she been looking at?

Blythe had been in and out of the room so fast, had Jenna been aware of her presence? Had she seen her? It felt like an eternity, but it also felt like less than the time it took to gasp for air before she was backing out and closing the door.

Blythe had never been sure whether or not Jenna had seen her.
And Jenna had never said a word about it.

CHAPTER 47

NOW: BLYTHE

*B*lythe's sleep was disrupted by a dream that felt as if it lasted the entire night. In the dream, she was opening the bedroom door at the house Scarlett and Paul had won in their silent auction. The house where they'd all been stupid enough to take E.

What had they been thinking? They were nearly thirty years old. They were parents. Why had they decided to take a party drug? It was unnecessary and foolish and dangerous. They were lucky nothing worse had happened. Lucky that no one had rushed into the ocean and drowned, or some other unimaginable tragedy.

In her dream, she stood in the hallway, feeling blissfully, blindly happy. She slowly opened the door, a smile on her face. Then she saw them. Garret fucking Jenna as if Blythe didn't even exist.

A knife pierced her heart. A silent scream tore through her body.

Jenna's bulging eyes stared at her, seeing her, not seeing her.

She closed the door.

Then the dream started again. An endless loop. The pain going deeper each time.

She woke exhausted. Her neck was so stiff she could hardly turn her head, but her thoughts were clear, although completely unrelated to the dream—maybe the social media troll had murdered Lacey!

Maybe he'd been stalking Lacey, and she'd never said a word about it. Lacey had ended her coaching sessions right around the time the troll had appeared on Blythe's social media. And that had been right after Jenna was complaining about being stalked. Was this creep working his way through their group of friends?

She slipped out of bed. It was only five a.m. Garret was still in a deep sleep. She wasn't sure what had woken her, whether it was the dream, or the clarity breaking through the repetitive pain of the dream.

She threw on her robe, went downstairs, and made a pot of coffee. While she waited for it to brew, she began scrolling through her friends' accounts, looking for some of the screen names the troll had used. There was no evidence that he'd been active on any of them overnight. If he'd been bothering them earlier, they'd already been hidden and blocked.

Neither Evie nor Scarlett had ever mentioned it, but it was possible they wouldn't, especially if his comments hadn't been as disgusting or aggressive. Everyone was used to dealing with random men sending direct messages, often posing with pets to make themselves look warm and approachable, jumping into women's accounts, pretending they wanted nothing but casual friendship.

She filled a mug with coffee and went into the office. She opened her laptop and clicked on the file where she'd stored the screen shots of the most offensive comments she'd received. She started a text file and entered all the screen names that had been used. She renamed the file with a number, so it was at the top of her files, easily accessible from her phone.

Later that morning, when the girls were both out of the house —Kate feeding pets for a few neighbors who were on vacation and Kelsey at the mall with a friend—she found the card Detective Banner had given her and drove to the police station.

The lobby of the police station was a sterile room with two windows, three metal framed chairs with thin cushions, and a healthy-looking plant in the corner. A uniformed officer sat behind each window. She approached the female officer with dark hair pulled into a bun that perched on the top of her head and thick bangs that covered her eyebrows.

"Hi. I'd like to speak to Detective Banner or Madeira. They're investigating my friend's murder—Lacey Abbott."

"Do you have an appointment?"

"No."

"What's this about?"

"They asked me to get in touch if I thought of anything that might be related to her murder."

"What's your name?"

"Blythe Farrell."

The officer picked up the phone. "I'll see if one of them is available. Have a seat." She lifted her chin to gesture toward the chairs across the room.

Blythe took a seat, although she didn't feel like sitting down. It seemed to suggest she was willing to wait a long time. Now that she was here, she was eager to talk. She wanted them to praise her for her sudden insight. She wanted to see Detective Banner's face light up with excitement when she realized that Blythe might have the answer to who had murdered Lacey.

In a single moment, Blythe had not only found the solution to her own torment, but might be on the way to getting justice for Lacey. The thrill of it was too much to allow her to sit in an uncomfortable chair for twenty minutes, waiting for whatever a police detective did when they weren't out investigating. Which, as far as she could tell from her limited experience, involved talking to friends of the victim. Why had she always thought police work was more thrilling? Now, it seemed like afternoon tea in people's living rooms.

She listened to the officer talking about her in a low voice, hoping to read from her expression what was being said on the other end of the line. It was hopeless. Her face was as smooth as a mask.

A moment later, the door adjacent to the wall where the windows were located opened. Detective Banner gestured for Blythe to enter.

Blythe smiled. She'd hoped it would be Detective Banner. Madeira had seemed more ... she wasn't sure what the right word was. He wasn't aggressive or negative. But he seemed to be more suspicious, although he hadn't necessarily been suspicious, so she wasn't sure what she'd picked up from him. She was just glad it was Detective Banner. She would listen more carefully, Blythe was sure of it.

The detective led her down a hall lined with doors and windows into small offices, past inspirational posters, framed lists of instructions and policies and awards. She opened the door to a small office that was barely large enough to hold the desk, work chair, and a chair for a visitor. Detective Banner went behind the desk. "Have a seat."

Blythe perched on the edge of the chair. The room was cold, and she shivered, even though she was wearing jeans and a sweater over her sleeveless top.

"What can I do for you, Blythe?"

"Someone's been trolling me, stalking me, on social media. And before me, someone was stalking a close friend of mine. You talked to her—Jenna Dale. I started thinking that maybe it's the same creep, and maybe he was also bothering Lacey. Maybe we just didn't know about it."

Detective Banner nodded.

"He was?"

"I don't know. I haven't seen anything in her social media to suggest that, but go on."

"Lacey started to pull away from me a little, a few weeks before she was killed. And you assumed she was having an affair. But maybe someone was harassing her. She was feeling upset about how she looked, feeling like her appearance was being ... judged or criticized."

"Okay."

"And maybe this troll ..." Blythe tapped her phone to open the file with the screen shots. She handed it to the detective. "These are some of the messages posted on my profile. I wondered if Lacey had ugly messages sent to her, or posted on her profile that we didn't know about. Maybe ... could this person have ..." She felt her voice growing softer, weaker. As she said the words out loud in the small room, hearing them fill the space, without interruption from the detective, they sounded unimportant.

It sounded more like a cause for someone taking her own life than a motive for murder. Why would a troll who was making Lacey's life miserable want to kill her? But how could you know what someone like that was thinking? They were sick, deranged individuals. They didn't think like normal people. That was the whole point.

"I thought there was a way for you to look at her blocking history. And to be honest, it makes me wonder if I should be more concerned. If my life might be in danger."

Detective Banner looked up from the phone with a sharp movement. She handed the phone back to Blythe. "A lot of upsetting things happen on social media. It's filled with trolls. Fifty percent of it is bots."

"But this isn't a bot. It's—"

"I realize that," Detective Banner said. "But it still has a very dark side. I'm sure you're aware of that."

"I am."

"I understand your concern. And the messages are disturbing. Have you reported them?"

"Yes."

"That's the best approach. But none of them are actionable threats."

"They're not?"

"No. And we've been through Ms. Abbott's social media and all of her electronic communications. There's nothing to suggest she was targeted in the way you're thinking."

"Oh. Then what do you—"

"As you said, her behavior changed recently. Several people mentioned it. We're still looking into the possibility she was having an affair. It's the most plausible explanation, and the most likely motive for the manner of her death."

"But she ... I can't believe ..."

Detective Banner gave her a grim smile. "Sometimes, we think we know our close friends, but we don't know their secrets. It's hard to accept that, and a sudden death can be shocking and upsetting for more reasons than one." She paused for a moment. "Thank you so much for being alert to all possibilities. It's important. Don't let this prevent you from bringing anything else to our attention." Detective Banner stood and held out her hand.

Blythe stood. She shook the detective's hand, feeling as if she'd been propelled into following the other woman's lead by a force that was outside her control.

"I really do appreciate you coming in," Detective Banner said.

"You don't think I'm in danger?" Blythe asked.

"Probably not. Just keep a record. If it escalates, you can file a police report."

"Okay. Thanks."

Blythe left, feeling foolish and slightly angry. She was confused by the two emotions that didn't fit together. She still wondered whether she was in danger, despite the brush-off.

CHAPTER 48

In the parking lot of the police station, Blythe lowered the window. She adjusted the seat back and closed her eyes. She'd been so confident the information she had outlining the troll's harassment and threats would solve everything. Part of her motivation had been self-serving, she'd known that. She'd thought the police would use their sophisticated tools to uncover the identity of her troll. He would be arrested and tried and imprisoned, giving her back her life, setting her free from the constant anxiety and growing fear.

It would be a life marred by a thread of grief that would run through it forever, but at least a life where she could relax and run her business, interact online with her friends and colleagues without this constant anxiety and panic, this feeling of dirt under her fingernails.

Now, she was back in the same place. Almost worse. Definitely worse than when she'd woken up a few hours earlier, because now her hope had been taken away.

After several minutes with her head spinning fruitlessly around the conversation she'd had with the detective, she started the car and drove to the gym. An intense workout would clear her mind. She grabbed her gym bag out of the back of the car, grateful she'd left it there after her client session the previous afternoon. Her workout clothes were relatively clean since she'd only worn them for coaching.

She went into the locker room, changed her clothes, and started with forty-five minutes on the treadmill, setting it at a steeper incline than usual. She would push herself hard enough that the exertion might stop her from brooding over what the detective had said about their continued focus on looking for a man who'd been having an affair with Lacey, assuming a breakup or the threat of exposure had driven him to kill her.

It was a sickening, horrible way to kill someone. It was strange that he'd had a plastic bag with him. They'd said she'd already passed out from drinking, making the act of killing her less difficult. There were two empty champagne bottles beside her lounge chair. One in the ice bucket, one sitting on the ground. Miles had told the detectives he'd only consumed a glass and a half.

Was it possible Garret had been having an affair with Lacey after all?

The question slammed against the inside of her skull like a fist. She had no idea why it had returned. She couldn't figure out if it was distrust that had lurked inside her for fifteen years, despite her belief that she'd fully dealt with it. Instead, had it lain there like a cancerous cell, biding its time? Or was she simply paranoid and distrustful because of the constant assault from the troll, over-anxious because of how the police had behaved?

There was nothing she could pinpoint in her relationship with Garret or in the way he'd been with her that suggested he'd been having an affair. It was all Lacey. She'd absolutely changed, treating Blythe like someone she couldn't bear to spend time with anymore.

Maybe Garret had come onto her and Lacey was disgusted with Blythe because of that? Maybe there wasn't an affair, simply an inappropriate move by her husband. Maybe Lacey had threatened to tell Blythe about it?

She felt sick.

She slowed the treadmill until she was walking, then stopped it.

She wiped the perspiration off and moved to the weight machines. After she'd finished the circuit, she showered and drove home.

She found Kelsey, Kate, Naomi, and Cooper in the swimming pool. They weren't diving and swimming, splashing at each other as they had when they were kids. Instead, they were lined up, their arms crossed, resting on the edge, their bodies half-floating behind them as they talked. Cans of soda sat in front of them on the slate that surrounded the side of the pool closest to the house.

She settled in the living room with a sparkling water and a slice of lime. She opened her phone and stared at her accounts, listening to the voices of her daughters and their friends amplified by the water, coming through the open doors.

Without pausing to think about it, starting with her most recent post, and working her way back in time, she turned off the comment feature. It would silence all her clients, mute anyone interested in coaching, even going so far as to prevent anyone from inquiring about her offerings unless they were interested enough to send a direct message. Many didn't want to make that perceived commitment right away. They preferred casual questions in the comments. Now, that was no longer possible, at least for the foreseeable future. But it was the only way to stop him.

She felt utterly defeated. She wondered if posting at all was even worth it. She would still be there for people to contact her directly, but the social, casual interaction—the entire point of social media —was now eliminated. She wanted to cry. She tossed the phone onto the sofa beside her with enough force to send it skittering toward the opposite end.

She shifted her position, so she was partially reclining, and focused her attention on the voices of her kids.

Of all things, they were talking about social media. And their parents. She wasn't sure if she wanted to laugh or cry.

"They're kind of obsessed with it," Kate said. "Except my dad. He hates it."

"He doesn't hate it," Kelsey said. "He just likes people better in real life."

"They act as if they *invented* it," Naomi said.

"They sort of did." Cooper's voice was a low drawl, designed to be funny.

The girls laughed.

"It's to promote their businesses," Kelsey said.

"Yeah, we know. God, do we know," Naomi said.

Cooper laughed. "Not very social then, is it?"

"I love social media," Kelsey said.

The others agreed they liked TikTok. Instagram was okay. They liked taking pictures, sharing pictures. Videos were cool.

"What's going on?"

Blythe looked up to see Garret standing in the doorway. The sight of him was a shock to her system. She felt her body grow cold. She was suddenly aware that she needed to know, without any doubt, whether or not something had happened between him and Lacey. He'd been so upset the other night, asking in that accusing tone if she thought he was having an affair. It had been more of an attack on her—as if she had no right to think that.

When she'd kissed him and told him to return to watching the news, he'd taken it as an apology for hinting at such a terrible thing. At least, she was pretty sure that's how he'd taken it. Because since then, he'd behaved as if everything between them was fine. So had she.

Now she knew things were not fine.

He sat beside her and took her hand. "Are you okay? You look really upset." He glanced toward the open doors. "Are the girls okay?"

She nodded.

"Are you?"

She shook her head. This was not the time. Not with their daughters right there. Naomi and Cooper. Within half an hour, Oliver or Jenna would arrive to pick up Naomi. But that was beside the point. Any time when Kate and Kelsey were within earshot, awake even, was not the time to let loose the monster preying on her thoughts.

247

It was right there. The thing that had happened all those years ago, and Lacey's sudden decision to stop with her coaching, and her murder, and Garret's bizarre comment to the detectives. The troll ... although that might be completely unrelated. All of it was filling her mind to capacity, ready to explode.

"I just ... I shouldn't. This is the wrong time," she said.

"What *is* it?" He squeezed her hand. He turned awkwardly so he was facing her. "Tell me what's going on."

"I just don't ... I forgave you once, but I don't know if I can do it again." A suppressed sob tore at her throat, and she let out a strangled cry.

"You forgave ... what? What are you talking about?" His voice trembled slightly.

She wondered if he knew *exactly* what she was talking about.

And then she heard a voice.

"Hellooo? Are you here? Blythe? It's me ... both of us. Oliver's here too."

Blythe heard the front door close, although she hadn't been aware of it opening. One of the kids must have left it unlocked. Jenna and Oliver were in the house, and now they would be swept up in family energy for the next few hours.

CHAPTER 49

*A*fter Jenna and Oliver offered to get pizza for all the kids, Jenna also insisted on texting Scarlett. She invited the entire Nevin family to join them, which meant that within less than an hour, Blythe and Garret's patio was humming with twelve people along with the Nevin's dog, Jasper.

Paul considered Jasper a member of the family. Scarlett smiled when he said this, never agreeing or disagreeing, so it wasn't clear where she stood on that belief. Jasper was well-behaved, usually finding a shady spot in the backyard where he'd lay on his side, watching what was going on. He never begged for food. Blythe liked that about him. It made her want to offer him food.

Scarlett and Paul stopped to pick up the pizzas on their way. When they walked in the door, a tantalizing aroma entered with them. The teenagers immediately gravitated to the kitchen, hovering around the island as they waited for Blythe and Garret to put out plates and napkins.

Kate and Naomi arranged patio furniture, and soon they were all seated outside, nibbling pizza. The kids drank soda, and the adults sipped wine and beer. It was a perfect summer evening.

Blythe looked at her friends and their teenagers and pre-teens in the dimming light, knowing she should be filled with utter bliss and gratitude. Instead, she didn't think she'd ever been more miserable. Except maybe that night in the woods. Or that other time, when Jenna had disappeared. Or that night when she'd seen Jenna naked with her husband. The night Lacey was murdered ...

So maybe she'd had several moments of absolute devastation in her life. Maybe this one would heal and fade as well.

But right now, it felt as if her life was falling apart. Her heart ached. She was still grieving for Lacey and those feelings were so complicated, she couldn't describe them even to herself. She hated the tension in the air right now. Their friends seemed oblivious to it, chattering and biting cheesy dough and talking, drinking wine, laughing. Glad to be enjoying themselves after what they'd been through.

She had a guilty thought that it felt as if they were secretly getting together without Miles. By not including Evie and Isaac and their kids, it was easier not to invite Miles. But it made sense this way. Jenna's and Scarlett's kids were the ones who had been here ... She sighed and took a sip of wine. She wouldn't overthink it.

Lately, she was overthinking everything. Did that mean she was overthinking this thing with Garret and Lacey?

The problem was, it made absolute sense. It explained Lacey's behavior. It sort of explained Garret's ridiculous, confusing comment to the police. A comment he couldn't seem to clarify. It explained the fact that Lacey had been murdered, although she didn't want to think about that. It wasn't possible that Garret could do something so horrifying, so evil. That wasn't the man she knew, the man she loved. She was insane to even let it pass through her mind.

How could a woman who lived in a nice quiet community like theirs, a woman celebrating her success with her husband in their backyard, wind up murdered? It was unbelievable. It just didn't happen. A stranger, if that's what it was, wouldn't even know they were out there. No one had broken into the house. Nothing was stolen. There was no way a hardened criminal would have been prowling the streets, wandered into her backyard, pulled a plastic bag over her head, and held it there until she stopped breathing.

She shuddered. She took a large bite of pizza, hoping to hide the convulsions of her body. She chewed it slowly, but found it almost impossible to swallow.

She glanced around. No one was looking at her.

She could not believe Garret was cheating on her. She couldn't. She didn't want to believe it. That had been a onetime, drug-fueled mistake. That's what she'd always believed, and she was certain she still believed that. It was just that all the things that had happened made it seem so ... plausible. The pieces fit. They made sense.

Holding her glass up to the fading light, she stared at the liquid. She tipped it slightly, letting the wine slide up the sides. It looked so sleek and soothing. She took a sip. It had grown warm. She took another long, comforting drink.

"Do you want more?" Garret was beside her with the bottle. His voice was clipped. Polite, but unfriendly. Decidedly unfriendly. Why had she let those words out when she'd known they would be surrounded by people? Even if she hadn't known they'd wind up with a pizza party, she'd known the kids would be around.

"Yes, thanks." She should give him a reassuring smile, but she couldn't. She held out her glass.

When he was gone, she took another healthy drink, eager to numb her thoughts.

The truth was, she had no idea what was going on. Something had been bothering Lacey. Something big. Maybe *she'd* been the troll. Maybe they'd been having an affair, or had sex one time, or not done anything at all. He'd hit on her. Whatever had happened, something had happened ...

She swallowed more wine.

Maybe ... maybe Lacey was insanely angry. She made the mugs, mocking Blythe's business. She tagged Blythe's coaching page, trying to damage her business, chase away clients. And then, or first, or at the same time, Blythe couldn't even remember now when it had all happened, Lacey had decided to really sabotage things, so she'd started making those horrible comments.

And then, the comments had stopped when she was murdered. Because the comments definitely stopped for a while after she died.

But then, they'd started again. Why?

What if it was Garret? Maybe it was never Lacey!

Maybe he hadn't cheated. Maybe Lacey was just Lacey, and she was upset and on a mission for body positivity. Maybe Garret was the troll because he didn't like Blythe posting that picture of herself in the bikini. He never liked her being on social media. He complained about it all the time! He said it took her away from their family. He said it sucked up her time, it distracted her. He said she obsessed over it.

He'd been so upset during their anniversary dinner. He'd wanted her to delete her account.

Would he do something like that? Was he that cruel?

He'd never understood why it mattered to her business. He thought she would do just fine without it. He was absolutely certain he was right, and he told her that all the time. What better way to get her to close her accounts than to harass her anonymously until she couldn't take it and decided it wasn't worth it?

Would she ever forgive him? If he'd done something so cruel and sneaky to her? Could she forgive him for that?

CHAPTER 50

$\mathcal{T}$he moment the door closed behind Jenna and her family, the last to leave, Garret turned to Kelsey and Kate. "Will you clean up, please? Your mom and I need a breather." He grabbed a half empty bottle of white wine from the fridge, their two glasses, and nudged Blythe toward the doorway. "Thanks, girls."

Blythe found herself in the living room, Garret behind her, his hand at the center of her back, guiding her toward the hallway and the stairs to the second floor. There was no escape. He was going to keep her awake, sitting beside him, pressing her for an answer until she told him. Now, more than ever, she wondered how she'd allowed the words to slip out. After all these years. It was the grief, the stress. Everything building inside her like a volcano, until a small crack opened and something had to ooze out, warning of the eruption to come. But why *that*?

Fifteen years. She'd happily and easily kept it to herself for fifteen years. And she'd been at peace with that decision. She'd never regretted it. Garret had proven her decision right every single day. After that trip, he'd been everything she'd wanted in a husband—an attentive, creative, eager lover. Not that this was the first thing, but it was definitely up there on the list. She'd been thrilled to see how their sex life became better, something she wouldn't have thought possible with twin toddlers, after what had happened, and with several years of marriage already behind them. He'd supported the launch of her career with unbelievable enthusiasm. He'd taken on near-equal share in household tasks and he'd been an engaged and nurturing father. He was that before, but it seemed to grow deeper every year.

And now, she'd blown it all up in a single moment of panic and uncertainty.

She could lie. But where would that put them going forward? And what if it did turn out he'd cheated with Lacey? If the police uncovered definitive evidence of that, the thing with Jenna might get exposed. Besides, she didn't want lies to start defining their relationship. She didn't want that to become who she was, who *they* were. If they survived.

Not telling him what she'd seen had never felt like a lie.

The whole night in that house, the drug-induced euphoria and shock felt like a dream at this point anyway. It had never really been a lie. It was a bad dream that sometimes felt as if it had been only that—a dream, a nightmare. A surreal experience that faded over time.

Garret placed the wineglasses on coasters. He poured a small amount of wine into each one, then placed the bottle on a third coaster. He settled on the loveseat, waiting for her to join him.

She could plead exhaustion, kiss him lightly on the lips, and escape to the bathroom to get ready for bed. But it was only eight thirty.

"What did you forgive me for?" He asked. "Once?"

"I ..."

"It sounded ... ominous," he said.

Blythe laughed. She picked up her wineglass and took a sip.

"Will you sit down? And please don't laugh, it wasn't meant to be funny."

She remained standing. "Ominous?"

"Yes, ominous. You said you forgave me once, as if there's some massive sin I committed. And now, there's some other terrible crime that's hanging over me and it's so heinous you don't know if you can forgive me? What the hell does that mean? What's going on? Please sit down."

She took a sip of wine.

"I want to know what's going on with you."

This was it. She had to tell him, or lie. Tell him or put him off. Tell him or ... She had no idea what her other choice was. Could she manage to divert him? To convince him it had been nothing, that she'd misspoken? The way he was looking at her, she didn't think so.

"Do you think I murdered Lacey? You must know I was kidding when I said that. But you've been acting like a zombie. It's as if you're not even here. You need to tell me what the hell is going on. Did someone say something at the wine party?"

She looked at his face, the expression of frustration. Concern? What was he thinking, really? Had it crossed his mind at all that she might be thinking about that night with Jenna?

In the first months after the weekend away, she'd often wondered if *he* would come to *her*. He didn't have to know she'd seen them to confess what he'd done. Some evenings, she'd found herself waiting all through dinner, brooding as they played with Kelsey and Kate, rolling balls across the living room floor. Giving them baths and putting them to bed. Was this the night he would tell her what he'd done and beg her to forgive him?

She didn't want that, but she wondered if he would. And she wondered if a tiny part of her did want that. Shouldn't he want to tell her? The conflicting thoughts confused her.

Over time, her confusion had dissipated. Finally, she stopped waiting for him to say something. He wasn't going to. Knowing he planned to let it fade away helped her relax and look to the future. She could put it behind her and enjoy what they had. She could frame it the way she chose—focusing on the effect of the drug, remembering what it had done to *her*. Living out her forgiveness inside her own mind without having to explain or discuss or analyze or tiptoe around each other.

Now, she wondered if it had entered his mind after all these years.

Or maybe he'd forgotten entirely.

Was it possible that after the drug had worn off, he'd had trouble remembering whether it was real? She had no idea. The mind did strange things. Memories were elusive and often inaccurate. They changed shape over time. Sometimes your memory of a memory became its own thing, and often, you forgot what the truth really was.

"Are you going to talk to me or not?" Garret asked.

"I ..."

"What the hell did I do that makes it such a difficult decision to *forgive* me?" He stood and crossed the room. He tipped his wineglass and swallowed the contents in a single gulp. "If you think I'm capable of murder, I ..." He glared at her, hurt and disbelieving. "Stop giving me the silent treatment. You threw that out there." His voice rose slightly. "Now, you're just going to stand there and stare at me? Turn it into a guessing game?"

"Don't shout," she whispered. "The girls will—"

"I'm not shouting. I just need you to stop staring at me like I'm a murdering psychopath and tell me what's going on." He walked to the table, refilled his glass, and took a sip. He moved around the table and sat down again.

There was no way out of this. Whatever he was imagining was worse than the truth. She'd walked into it and now she had to finish. She sank onto the loveseat next to him. "I forgave you for having sex with Jenna when we took ecstasy that night. But if you had an affair with Lacey ... or if you and she were the ones trolling my social media, I don't know if I—"

"You ..." He put his glass on the table. He put his hands over his face and bent forward, resting his elbows on his knees.

The room was silent for several minutes. She heard his breath as he labored slightly to draw it through the gaps between his hands.

After a while, his shoulders seemed to collapse, his head bent lower.

What was he thinking? Was he making up excuses, trying to think of a way to explain, wondering how she knew? Was he thinking about fifteen years ago, or Lacey?

Finally, he straightened and lowered his hands. His eyes were red, his face stricken with grief. "I'm sorry," he whispered. "You should have told me. Why didn't you tell me you knew?"

"We were happier this way."

"Until now," he said.

CHAPTER 51

THIRTY YEARS AGO: JENNA

*J*enna's mother was pissing her off. She did that a lot lately.

The newest thing was that Jenna wasn't allowed to go to school. All because of their big fight on Sunday. Now, Jenna was basically a prisoner in her bedroom. She could look out the window and see kids walking to school. She knocked on the glass, but from the street below a third-floor apartment, no one heard.

She was a prisoner because her mother had actually locked her in her bedroom. She'd screwed a sliding lock on the outside of the door.

"It's to keep you safe," her mother said.

"From what?"

"I don't want anything to happen to you. Right now, you need to rest. It's better to spend some time at home by yourself. Your brain needs to calm down. You're thinking too much, kitten." Her mother kissed her forehead. "Knock on the wall if you need me. I'll hear you right away."

Then, her mother went out and closed the door. A moment later, Jenna heard the lock slide into place.

It must be illegal. You weren't supposed to lock up your daughter in her own bedroom! Or anywhere.

The fight hadn't really been a fight. It was more of a not-listening. But the only one who'd been angry had been Jenna. Her mother mostly cried and tried to tell her things weren't *right*. Gaslighting her.

Jenna flopped onto her bed. Her mother did not listen. She didn't believe anything Jenna told her. It was infuriating.

The cheerleaders were trying to get her. She'd told her mother that. They were working on a plot to get her drunk, hook her up with Chip, and get her pregnant. He was a dealer. And not just weed. Bad stuff. Everyone knew that. Her mother knew that.

But she didn't seem worried about Chip at all. Or what the cheerleading squad was up to.

"They're not plotting anything," her mother said. "You need to stop thinking about them."

"I can't stop, or they'll win! They have it all planned. They want to bring me down. They want to keep me from getting my scholarship! Don't you see that? If I get pregnant, that's it. No scholarship. Done. I'm fucked."

"Please don't use that word. You won't get pregnant. Don't have sex. Or if you do, make sure he—"

"They're going to mastermind me into it. Everything is arranged."

She'd explained it over and over, but her mother would not *listen*. She just stared at Jenna, then she started crying. After a while, she went out to run errands.

The next morning when Jenna woke up, the new lock had been screwed onto the doorframe.

A week went by. Her mother had gone to the school and spoken to Jenna's teachers. She came home with a folder of assignments from each of Jenna's classes, providing work she could do at home for a week to stay caught up.

"A week!?"

"For now. We'll see."

"Why are you doing this to me?"

"It will pass, but for now, you're not ... some of the things you're thinking need time to fade. Your mind needs to settle back into a more ... into a normal rhythm."

"What things?"

"Just rest. Read one of the library books I got you while I make dinner." Her mother left the room, securing the lock outside the door.

Twenty-seven minutes later, according to her digital clock, Jenna heard the apartment doorbell, followed by her mother's voice. It was easy to hear what she said, as well as the visitor's voice, in their small apartment.

"I just wanted to see if Jenna's okay." Blythe's voice was shrill, filled with anxiety. If Jenna's mother wanted to worry, she should worry about Blythe.

"Does she have the flu or —"

"Jenna isn't here," her mother said.

Jenna wondered if she should scream. Blythe could rescue her, couldn't she? How would she do that? Blythe could push past Jenna's mother and unlock the door. But then what? Her mother would never let Jenna leave with Blythe. She might even call the police. She'd done it once before. Of course, when the police showed up, she sent them away. But this time, she might not.

"Where is she?" Blythe asked.

"She went to visit her dad. She'll be back in a week or two."

"Why is she visiting her dad in the middle of the school year?"

Her mother didn't answer.

"I thought she never ... I thought she only went at Christmas. I thought he wasn't ... I don't know," Blythe said.

"That's why it's so great that she'll have some extra time with him." Her mother laughed. It sounded so fake, but Blythe wouldn't pick up on that. "Thanks for stopping by. I'll let Jenna know."

Jenna heard the door close.

She should have screamed.

CHAPTER 52

NOW: JENNA

*J*enna was shocked to see that Blythe had turned off the comments on her social media. It was such a drastic move. After weeks of complaining about being trolled and harassed, she'd finally done something. It was a little unusual for Blythe. Or maybe it wasn't. She wasn't a complainer. She must have gotten sick of dealing with it—decided it wasn't worth trying to keep her page pristine.

It must be nice to feel as if you could post content without feeling the need to allow interaction through the comments. It must be nice to be so successful you didn't have to worry about using every tool and option at your disposal.

Jenna couldn't imagine turning off her comments. They were the lifeblood of her social media presence. How else would she interact with her current and potential customers? Her sales would plummet. Until they became serious buyers, that was how people expressed interest in her jewelry. They asked questions about the designs and sizes, the availability and pricing. They asked questions about shipping and custom orders. The comments were a virtual conversation with customers walking into her shop.

Obviously, it wasn't quite the same for a health coach, but still, it must hurt. Unless you were so successful, it didn't matter.

She thought about calling Blythe, or texting, to try to make her feel better about this obvious defeat. But how? What could she really say? The degrading comments must have embarrassed or upset her so deeply, she was afraid they would do the same to her customers.

Jenna picked up her phone to check Blythe's latest post.

It was a photograph of a strawberry smoothie sitting on her nightstand, the beautifully made bed, blurry in the background. Across the image, she'd written the word—*Yum!*

The comments were off, but something else had happened.

The post had exploded without them. It was mind-blowing. She'd posted it less than an hour ago, but she already had thirty shares. Thirty! Jenna was lucky to get seven or eight shares in twenty-four hours. How could Blythe have thirty shares in such a short time? And for something so meaningless? A smoothie? It said nothing. It meant nothing. But everyone loved it. That was proven by the 1,732 smiling and heart emojis. It was mind-blowing. Soul-shattering.

Jenna could not believe what she was seeing. She wanted to refresh the page, thinking there was some kind of glitch and the likes and shares from another account had somehow attached themselves. At the same time, she was quite sure things like that didn't happen.

She locked the screen, so she didn't have to look at it. Tears flooded her eyes and spilled out. It was so unfair. Blythe didn't even need more clients. There were only so many hours in the week, and coaching took time. It wasn't as if she could coach all 1,732 people who loved that smoothie.

Of course, they loved a yummy-looking smoothie. Who wouldn't?

Jenna's hand-crafted jewelry was gorgeous. Everyone said so. It was delicate and downright seductive. That's what she'd been told. And her photographs were stunning.

So, why? *Why?*

After dinner, while Naomi loaded the dishwasher, and she and Oliver sat on the back patio sipping tea, Jenna pulled out her phone.

"Look at this."

Oliver took the phone she was holding out to him. "What am I looking at?"

"Blythe's post."

"A smoothie. Yum."

"Are you reading it, or saying that?"

"What?" He held the phone toward her.

"She has almost two thousand likes."

He glanced at the screen. "Nice." He held it toward her again.

"Why does that happen?"

He sighed. "Not this again."

"Why?!"

"An algorithm. Timing. It struck a chord. Hot day. People are hungry. I have no idea. We've talked about this a hundred times. No one knows why."

"It's not fair."

He put his hand on her leg, squeezing it gently. "You never know what's going to hit. And she's not asking people to buy anything, so it's easy to like it. You can't compare."

"Yes, I can." Her voice was shrill. So loud, the neighbors could probably hear, but she didn't care. She did not care at all, even if Oliver was glancing toward the fence.

"Well, you shouldn't." His voice was lower, trying to counter hers.

"Don't tell me I shouldn't care about it! I care about it very much! It's my livelihood. My life! Our second income! You should care too! You shouldn't be so ..." She waved her hand in the air. "So dismissive."

"I'm not being dismissive."

"You are!"

"Calm d—I didn't intend to sound that way."

"You sounded exactly that way. If you lose your job! If we can't

... if things ... the world is sliding out of control ... my social media is under-*performing*!"

"You're doing okay."

"I'm not!"

"Your social media isn't doing okay? Or sales?" He rubbed her leg. "Or ..."

She batted his hand away.

"Jenna."

"What?"

"Should I ..." He stood.

"What?"

"Have you been taking your meds on schedule?"

"Don't. Don't you dare tell me I'm a nutcase."

"I didn't say you were a nutcase. I've never said that. Ever." He sat down, leaning forward in his chair, placing his hand firmly on her thigh again. "You seem wound up."

"I'm not."

"You seem really upset. And you seem—"

"I'm not allowed to be upset that a fruit smoothie is more popular than artistic, beautifully crafted jewelry? I've poured my heart and soul into my designs!"

"You're shouting." Oliver stood and took the phone out of her hand. "Let's go inside. I'll rub your feet and we'll take a quick check of your meds. Maybe you missed a few days by mistake. Because of Lacey and the memorial and—"

"Stop talking to me like I'm incompetent! I know how to take medication! It's on the label." She stood, shoving him away from her. "Why are you being so mean to me?" She was crying now. Why couldn't he understand? Why didn't Blythe understand? She was supposed to be her best friend.

Friends for life. After all Jenna had done for her when they were kids. *Everyone* in their group was supposed to *support* each other. Why didn't they support her? Why didn't they promote her posts more? It was so unfair. She ran into the house, feeling crazed, as if she had to do something, had to take action right now, but there was nothing.

She stood in the kitchen, breathing heavily. After a few minutes, she went to the fridge and got out a bottle of wine. She poured a small glass for herself and sipped it quickly. It did help her calm down. Oliver was right. She needed to calm down. Although he would be upset when he found her drinking more than their agreed-upon single glass of wine a day. He would say that wasn't the solution. She took another sip.

CHAPTER 53

BLYTHE

*B*lythe was curled at one end of the loveseat, and Garret was sprawled at the other. Without speaking about it, they seemed to have agreed they wouldn't be going to bed until they'd worked through fifteen years of secrets.

"How did you ... how did you know? Did Jenna ...?" Garret looked at her, his lips parted, his eyes wide with obvious fear that he wasn't going to like the answer to his question.

"I saw you."

"How?"

She could see his mind racing, trying to remember a night that had grown blurry the moment darkness began to recede. All of them stumbling into the kitchen the next morning, craving coffee, famished and uncertain about what they'd experienced.

At first, Blythe had had trouble sorting out what had been created by the chemicals playing with her brain cells, what had been pieces of her troubled dreams, what had been the result of racing, incoherent thoughts that felt like dreams, and what had been real. She'd wondered if the others felt the same. She'd looked at her husband, at her recently reconciled best friend from childhood, and wondered what they remembered.

More times than she could remember, she'd asked herself if

Garret had been aware she'd walked into that room. Had he heard the door open after all, but not turned to look? *Had* Jenna seen Blythe watching them and told him later? These were questions she'd turned over in her mind so many years ago. But they were also questions she hadn't had time to brood about for hours on end because she'd been busy.

She had twin babies. She hardly sat down during those years. If Kelsey wasn't running as fast as her tiny legs could move toward the other end of the house, shrieking with glee because she wanted to pull the toilet paper off the roll, then Kate was yanking open the kitchen drawer and flinging all the plastic lids across the tile like she was practicing the discus throw.

Cooking and washing dishes, trips to the park, reading stories over and over and over, consumed her days. She fell into bed at night and was asleep before she had a moment to reflect on what she'd done that day. She hardly had time to capture their photographs into memory books.

Her monthly date nights with Garret had been filled with conversation about their daughters and his job. As the girls got older, they talked about pre-school, then sports and other activities, and Blythe's fledgling coaching business.

It wasn't as if she'd buried it. She didn't think she'd buried it. She'd made peace with it. She'd thought it through logically and decided her love for him outweighed one wild, drug-crazed act.

That was the bottom line. She loved this man.

"How?" He repeated. "How did you see me? When?"

"I was looking for my jacket. I went into the bedroom and you were with Jenna." Her voice was so low, so soft, she wondered if he'd heard her.

"And you ... you watched us?" His voice was raw with pain. He looked as if he might be sick.

"No. I ... for a second. But I ... no. I left."

"Why didn't you say anything? How could you not tell me?"

She shrugged. "I needed to think. You know how I am."

He stared at her. "I just can't ... we should have talked about it."

267

"I didn't want to. I decided the E had a lot to do with it and ..." She wasn't going to tell him about Miles. Maybe she owed him that. And maybe, at some point, she would. But for now, she wasn't. She owed that to herself. Didn't she? Maybe it wasn't fair, but that was her decision. For now.

"It would have been better if we'd talked about it," he said.

"Why didn't *you* tell *me*?" she asked. "If you think it was so important to talk about. You could have told me. But you never did."

He stared at her, his eyes watery. "I ... I wanted to. I did. A hundred times. A thousand times. But every time, you looked happy or content, or you were tired, or ... there was always a reason. The wrong reason, I know. I know that. I didn't want to spoil ..." He choked, his voice breaking. "... everything. Even though I knew I already had. I would watch you being such an amazing mother. The best." He wiped his eye. "I would think about how much you loved me. How I didn't deserve your love. You would look at me with so much love, so much love—" His voice broke again. "I couldn't rip that off your face."

"We both made a choice."

"The wrong one," he said.

"Was it?"

"I think so," he said. "Because now you think I did so much worse. I don't even know what you think. That I had an affair with Lacey. That I didn't have an affair with her? That I murdered her? That I wrote disgusting things on your social media? You think I'm the worst piece of scum on the earth."

"No."

"All those thoughts have crossed your mind. You've said all of them."

Hearing him speak back to her the irrational accusations she'd made, filled her with sadness. Why did she think those things? Because she was confused and frustrated and grieving? *Had* she buried that pain after all? She thought she'd made a logical decision based on loving him so much more than feeling betrayed and hurt.

Right this minute, she had absolutely no idea how she felt or what she thought or how she'd come to this place in her life. Looking at her husband, his grief-stricken face, she couldn't begin to imagine him cheating on her.

There was absolutely no way in the known universe he was capable of murdering someone. What had put that thought into her mind? A few rude and aggressive questions by two detectives who were blindly searching for answers. They were poking every tender spot they could find, hoping to puncture the right one, causing an outpouring of bile that would expose their killer.

She laughed. And the last one. Garret hardly knew how to use social media. She wasn't sure he would even know *how* to set up multiple accounts to initiate a trolling scheme like the one that had been launched against her.

"Why are you laughing?" he asked. "There's nothing funny here."

"It's not. I realized you probably don't have the skills to be a social media troll."

He glared at her. "That's the only checkmark in the my-husband-isn't-a-cold-blooded-killer column?"

She sighed. "No. What you said to the police was really weird. It sounded off to them. You could see it in their faces. It has them more interested in you. And ... I don't know. The troll has been really disturbing. It scares me. So I'm having a lot of irrational thoughts." She closed her eyes. The room was utterly silent.

At some point, Garret had closed the door. She assumed Kelsey and Kate were still watching TV. Most nights during the summer, they drifted to bed on their own. It was a preview of their future— being a couple again. No kids. Would they make it? Was this a turning point?

"I thought I forgave you years ago," she said. "Not thought ... I *did* forgive you. And it was quick. Within a few months. Maybe less. I loved you. I *do* love you. But maybe it was simmering there, and when I thought about how strange it was the Lacey quit her coaching sessions, and that she was murdered. It's all so far outside anything I've ever experienced, I couldn't make sense of anything. So maybe it was still there. I don't know. But I haven't been thinking about it for all these years. I honestly have not. I love our life. I love you." She slid to the center of the loveseat.

Garret came toward her. He pulled her onto his lap. "I'm so, so sorry," he whispered into her hair. "That night was so weird, so ... I felt like I loved everyone. I'm not even sure how it happened. I don't want to make excuses. There is no excuse. I just don't know. But I'm so sorry, and I was sorry the next morning and for so long. After a while, it started to feel like it never happened. And so many times, I almost wondered if maybe it didn't happen."

She knew what he meant. She knew exactly what he meant.

"I love you more than anyone, or anything, in the entire universe," he said.

"I know." She wrapped her leg around his waist, and her arms around his neck as he pulled her closer and kissed her in a way she was sure he'd never kissed her before.

Later, just before she climbed into bed, she checked her phone. At the top of her feed, was a post from Paul. He was often at the top with his wildly loved dog pictures and videos. But this was a video of Cooper and Henry when Henry was four. Henry was eating a chocolate ice cream cone, his nose completely covered in melted ice cream. Just as Henry looked as if he was about to cry, the clip gracefully ended, preserving his dignity. The title simply said #ThrowbackThursday.

Blythe smiled, added a heart, and went to her last post.

The fruit smoothie had loves and likes and shares beyond anything she'd ever experienced. But something new had happened since she'd last looked at it. There were over fifty angry faces glaring at her—red and filled with loathing.

She gasped. She turned off her phone, powered it down, and went to bed, curling her body around Garret's.

CHAPTER 54

THIRTY YEARS AGO: JENNA

*J*enna knew her mother wasn't going to be happy when she found out what Jenna had done, but she had no other choice. Chip was the father of Jenna's baby and he belonged with her.

If her mother had listened when she told her those girls were plotting to use him to get her pregnant, then this wouldn't have happened. Her mother had only herself to blame. That's what her mother was always saying—*You have only yourself to blame.* Her mother loved that saying.

"Shh," Jenna said when she heard her mother's key in the lock.

"Why?" Chip asked.

"Let me handle this. She doesn't know you're moving in."

"No shit?"

"It'll be fine. Just let me handle it."

Jenna went into the living room. "Chip is moving in. The baby will be here in two months, so we can't waste any more time." She glared at her mother, daring her to argue.

Her mother sighed and dropped her purse onto the couch. "There's no baby, Jenna. Please. And no Chip."

"Hey," Chip's voice was a low purr behind her.

A look of horror rippled across her mother's face as Chip

grabbed the back of Jenna's neck and pulled her head toward him. Jenna wanted to laugh. Her mother thought she was always making stuff up. She thought she needed to lock her in her room until the *episode* passed. She'd refused to believe there was a plot to steal Jenna's scholarship. She didn't believe the cheerleaders were out to get her. And she hadn't believed they were masterminding a way for the drug dealer to get Jenna pregnant.

"I said to wait," Jenna said.

"Who are you?" Jenna's mother asked.

"Bry, short for Brian, but everyone calls me Chip. Thanks for letting me crash here. For the baby."

"There's no baby!" Jenna's mother said, loudly enough for Chip to let go of Jenna's neck.

Chip held up his hands. "Okay. Cool. Don't want to get involved in that." He shrank back toward the hallway.

Jenna's mother turned toward her. "He can't stay here, Jenna. You know that."

"He has to."

They talked in circles that night. As they always did, because her mother never, ever *listened*. She never believed Jenna. And it looked like she didn't believe much of what Chip said, either. He ended up sleeping on the couch.

He continued sleeping on the couch for three weeks. Jenna and her mother argued for three weeks. Her mother cried for three weeks.

Then, one morning they woke, and Chip was gone. So was their TV, her mother's laptop, their phones, and her mother's wallet.

Two days later, Jenna's mother came into her bedroom with Jenna's suitcase.

"You need to pack some clothes," she said.

"Why?"

Her mother sat at the foot of the bed. She wrapped her hand around Jenna's ankle, rubbing the bone gently with her thumb. "I thought I could take care of you, baby. I thought I could love you enough that the monsters would leave you alone. But you need to go someplace where you can get better. Where people can help calm your thoughts. And find some medication that will ... I don't know. This place is nice. You'll still do schoolwork, but you'll get to do things you love—like painting and drawing. Yoga."

"What are you talking about?" Jenna asked.

"You need some help. More than I can give you." Her mother began crying softly. "My love isn't enough."

"I don't need help. I'm having a baby and I can't be going—"

"We'll work that out. Just pack your suitcase. Okay?" Her mother left, securing the outside lock behind her.

Jenna didn't pack her suitcase. She sprawled on the floor, face down, breathing in the dust from the carpet, trying to remember when she'd last vacuumed, trying to determine whether she could smell Chip's footprints.

The doorbell rang, and she knew, as if she could see through her locked door, past the living room, and through the front door, onto the balcony outside their apartment, that Blythe was standing there. Blythe must be so lonely without her. Blythe hardly knew how to have fun without her. She wasn't sure who to talk to or where to go without Jenna to give her ideas. She hardly knew how to live without Jenna.

Jenna heard her mother open the apartment door. She wriggled across the floor, close to her bedroom door, where she could hear better.

"Hi, Blythe. Before you ask, Jenna's gone. She went to live with her dad."

Jenna wondered if she should scream. Now would be the time to scream for Blythe to rescue her. But Blythe wouldn't. She would be upset. Very upset. But what would she do? Would she fight off Jenna's mother, come into the apartment, unlock the door, and set her free? Then what? Would she invite Jenna to live with her?

Maybe the place where she was going would be nice. She did love to paint, and there was nowhere to paint in the apartment. Her art class at school was never long enough.

"I thought her dad didn't want her around much?" Blythe asked.

"He's changed."

"Why didn't she tell me?" Blythe's voice was pleading, whining.

"She didn't have time. I'm so sorry. It was such a rush." Jenna's mother laughed. It sounded fake.

"Why would she just disappear like that? Will she visit you?"

"I'm not ... at some point. Yes."

"She's my best friend. She wouldn't disappear and not tell me."

"I said I'm really sorry. She didn't have time. It was so hectic. Can I give you a hug, honey?"

"No. I want to see her."

"I'm sorry. It's ... that's not possible. I can give her your address. Maybe she'll write. But I can't promise."

"She has it." Blythe sounded like she might cry.

When Blythe was gone and the front door was closed, Jenna pressed her forehead against the floor as hard as she could. She probably should have yelled goodbye to Blythe. She wasn't sure why her mother didn't want her to say goodbye. She wasn't sure why her mother had lied to Blythe.

But she wasn't sure about anything, so she could just add that to the list.

CHAPTER 55

NOW: BLYTHE

*A*fter Blythe had seen Jenna staring at her over Garret's bare shoulder, seeing or not seeing her, Blythe never knew which. It had taken months before Blythe could look her best friend in the eye again.

When they'd first reconnected just weeks before their daughters were born, it had felt like magic. A reconnection orchestrated by the universe, if there was such a thing. Despite the betrayal of Jenna disappearing to live with her father without saying goodbye, her failure to ever write a single letter, Blythe had let all that slide away. They'd been teenagers. And Jenna had been caught between parents who lived in different states. She had a father she'd missed terribly. There were probably a lot of things Blythe didn't understand about her.

Wouldn't she jump at the chance to live with her father if she'd hardly seen him for six or seven years? She couldn't even imagine such a thing.

She and Jenna would have a fresh start. She would remember all the good things about Jenna. The fun. The wild, crazy, exciting experiences that could only be had with Jenna. And she would remember that Jenna had saved her life. Literally. She could have been torn to pieces by a mountain lion because of what those girls had done.

The weekend away hadn't been that different in some ways. Jenna was the one who brought the E. She was the one who urged them to try it. What was the harm? You only lived once. They'd never get another chance to be young and still able to see their care-free lives in the rearview mirror.

Just as she'd weighed her love for Garret, a love that filled her heart no matter how much pain occasionally pressed against it, she did the same with Jenna. She forgave her. The drug and what it did to her thinking. How it took her mind out of reality. How the sensations in her body must have overpowered everything, as they had for Blythe. How it mimicked love as if love was nothing but an all-encompassing cloud of boundary-free emotion and passion. There was that.

And there was always that memory of the flashlight in her face, then Jenna's eyes, asking why she was alone in the woods, burrowed into that sleeping bag, surrounded by absolute darkness without another human being in earshot until Jenna showed up. And the friendship she'd given Blythe after. Wild, unrestrained, absolute friendship.

Still, after she'd seen her with Garret, there were times when Blythe felt a sliver of cold loathing snake its way through her heart. She tried not to let it rise to the surface, but it did. And Jenna felt it. Even the others in their group may have felt it. Blythe was never sure.

She wasn't sure why it had been easier to forgive Garret than Jenna. Maybe because she loved him so much more, in such a differ-ent, all-encompassing way. Maybe because Jenna had already betrayed her once. Even though Blythe's logical, adult brain under-stood, the young girl inside her still felt the betrayal of that day Jenna had vanished without saying goodbye.

Looking at the fifty angry faces on her smoothie photograph, she wondered if she should have cut out the poison then. The moment she'd seen Jenna lying naked with the man Blythe loved.

It was entirely possible that Jenna had attracted that troll with her wild behavior. She'd always been impulsive. As kids, as teenagers, it was fun. So much fun. Thrilling to never know what she was going to do next. At the weekend party, it had been fun, until it wasn't.

Now that Jenna was expressing her creativity in her jewelry, raising her daughter, had she changed? The wild side wasn't evident. It hadn't been for a long time, and Blythe wondered why she'd never thought about that until this very moment.

Where had that fun-loving-to-a-point-on-the-precipice-of-danger side of Jenna gone? Was it only motherhood that had changed her? It was possible that her devotion to her artwork had subdued that part of her. But it was equally possible that it had gone underground and bubbled up elsewhere.

Social media and the internet had transformed since they were in their twenties. It was a different world.

It was possible that after the E-fueled party, when all of their friends, Blythe and Garret included, had agreed—*Interesting experience, but never again*—that Jenna had found other outlets.

Had Jenna realized she could no longer count on her friends to indulge her wild ideas and cheer her on when she wanted to take risks? She certainly wouldn't involve her daughter. As far as Blythe knew, Oliver wasn't a thrill-seeker.

Enter, the internet.

Maybe Jenna had other accounts. Maybe she had all kinds of online friends and communities. There was no way of knowing what kind of people she'd hooked up with. Blythe knew nothing about her friends from the time she'd been living with her father, for that matter. Maybe she was still in touch with those people.

There could be a whole other world where Jenna lived and gave free rein to the side of her that Blythe had been so in awe of as a teenager. The side that had frightened her. And the side that, if she was honest, she'd admired. But mostly, she'd been a little scared. All the time.

Had that Jenna attracted the troll? And when he got tired of

Jenna, he found Blythe. Did Jenna *know* the troll? Had he breached the boundary between cyberspace and reality? Was there some reason he'd gone after Lacey and murdered her?

Blythe bit down so hard on her lip she tasted blood.

CHAPTER 56

ANONYMOUS

Some people consciously use social media as a diary. But there's no lock and key. There's no parchment paper and quill pen and a candle burning on the desk, dripping wax onto the page. They think they'll save and preserve the best parts of their lives in a digital timeline.

Do they ever go back and look? Or just rely on the algorithm to spit out memories once a year?

Across the board, people will post anything. Offensive, sick, outrageously fun. Lame and inane. Half of them just post ads for whatever they're selling. So why is it social? It's commercial. They try to make their ads sound social, which is so sad. Do they honestly think no one sees through that?

Lots of people dance. That's cool. Who doesn't like watching people dance? Who doesn't like watching cats do wild, hilarious things? Who doesn't love all the crazy things people do? But who has their phone set to record video twenty-four-seven? That's what I'd like to know. I usually don't even have my camera ready.

They say stuff they would never say in a hundred million years to someone's face. Cursing, calling names, cutting them down to size. Winning verbal wars, or so they think. So witty and clever, regurgitating what ten thousand other people have already said.

Fourteen billion pictures are posted on social media every day. That's 420 billion pics a month. The human brain only has one hundred billion neurons. It blows the mind to think of all those photographs. It makes your eyes explode. Everyone sees them. No one sees them.

Scroll. Scroll. Scroll.

Too many people see some of them. And not enough people see others.

A life can be crushed because there aren't enough likes.

A soul can be terrorized with too much exposure that turns dark when all the haters crawl out of the muck.

People put up pictures of themselves looking good. They put up pictures of parties and they pick the ones where they look good. Maybe their friends look less good. Maybe their friends look like shit.

Teenagers who are still half-children are mauled by words and disappear inside their heads. Some of them never come out again.

Pictures of houses and vacations, adorable kids and parents, weddings and parties. Engagement rings glittering in the sunlight. People post photos of the people they're crushing on and the people they're married to. Until they're not.

It's unvarnished truth. And it's lies.

CHAPTER 57

SCARLETT

Cooper had been holed up in his bedroom all evening, skipping dinner because he'd complained he was feeling queasy. He was playing video games. When Paul had pointed out that video games might make him more queasy, Cooper had put on his noise-cancelling headphones, closed the bedroom door, and locked it, according to Paul.

"Now that he's in college, don't you think he should be developing better manners?" Paul asked.

Scarlett nodded, but didn't respond. She didn't want to argue about Cooper's manners. He would grow out of it eventually. She was far more concerned about Henry. And Cooper was so good at keeping Henry calm and engaged. She loved that about him, loved what a protective brother he was. She loved that Cooper was never phased by the fact that his sister and brother had a different father. As far as Cooper was concerned, they were his siblings, period. He never used, and never wanted to hear, the term *half-brother* or *half-sister*. He thought it was a ridiculous and irrelevant distinction.

Henry was also hunkered down in his bedroom. Scarlett was less calm about that situation. She'd tried to convince him to watch a movie with her and Angela, but no matter what she suggested, he thought it was too lame, too scary, too boring, too violent, or he'd already seen it. She suggested a board game. He rolled his eyes.

She'd thought about taking the two of them bowling, but Henry could be unpredictable in places with a lot of people. It might be fun, it might terrify him and reduce him to tears, a shivering bundle of nerves, or worse. She shuddered, thinking about their last trip to the arcade. Henry had crawled under one of the games, grabbed the legs of the machine, and refused to come out. When another child tried to play the game, he shook the machine violently until the father of the other child had called security. Two security personnel had pried his fingers loose and dragged him out as if he were a dangerous criminal.

So Henry was in his room reading, which she supposed she should be happy about. And she and Angela had a bowl of popcorn between them as they scrolled through the movie selections, trying to make up their minds.

"I'm taking Jasper out," Paul said.

Scarlett nodded. Paul took Jasper for his evening walk every night at seven thirty—winter, spring, summer, fall, rain, wind, temps still in the 90s during a heat wave or dipping into the 30s during a cold snap. But she appreciated her husband's faithful reminders. She turned and smiled. "Enjoy."

A moment later, they were gone.

She and Angela lost themselves in a YA adventure film that was sending Scarlett's emotions on a roller coaster ride she hadn't expected. She was glad she'd let Angela make the selection. It was a great choice, and she felt like she was bonding with her daughter without forcing it.

The movie was reaching its climax and the popcorn bowl was long empty when Angela grabbed the remote and paused the action. "Is that Jasp?"

Scarlett turned.

There was a faint scratching sound at the front door, followed by a whimper. "Why is he ... is that him?"

Angela stood, tossing the remote onto the sofa.

There was another whimper and more vigorous scratching sounds.

Scarlett stood and followed Angela to the entryway. Angela opened the door.

Jasper bolted into the house, dragging his retractable leash behind him. He butted his head against Angela's legs, then circled her and Scarlett, forcing his way between Scarlett's legs, rubbing her calves. He repeated this several times, then sat whimpering, looking at them. A moment later, he stood and began circling and head-butting again.

Angela rubbed his head. "What's wrong, Jasp? What's going on? Where's Dad?"

"Why would he let him go?" Scarlett asked. "That's not ..." She hurried back to the living room. She picked up her phone and called Paul. It went to voicemail. She sent a text.

> Scarlett: Where are you? Are you okay?

She opened the *find my friends* app and tapped Paul's image. It showed him in the middle of the park, quite a ways off the path, but who knew if that was right. When they were driving along the coast, the app sometimes showed their car drifting out over the ocean.

She returned to the entryway.

"My phone says he's still at the park. I'm going to look for him."

"I'm going with you," Angela said. "Maybe Cooper—"

"He's not feeling well. And someone should stay with Henry. Go tell them we're leaving."

"We should hurry." Angela's voice trembled. "I'll just text Cooper. Dad would never let Jasper go."

"I know," Scarlett whispered. "I know."

Angela picked up Jasper's leash, taking out her phone to text her brother with one hand while Scarlett grabbed her purse off the hook.

They opened the back hatch of the mini SUV to let Jasper in and climbed into the front seats. Scarlett hit the gas too hard, and the car shot out of the driveway, rocking slightly. She gripped the wheel so hard, her hands ached. Paul was too young for a heart attack or stroke. Wasn't he? Had he been mugged? No one had ever been mugged at the large, wooded park with multiple play areas, picnic tables, and vast stretches of grass for sports.

"I'm scared," Angela said, her voice weak with the press of tears she was holding back.

"Me too," Scarlett said. She should be reassuring her daughter, but there was so obviously something wrong, lying about her feelings wouldn't make it better.

As if to echo their fears, Jasper whimpered.

They parked haphazardly at the curb, got Jasper out, and began hurrying toward the center of the park, Scarlett looking at the tiny disk displaying Paul's photo on her phone, showing his location.

At first, they walked quickly, Jasper tugging them forward as if he wanted to lead the way, as if he knew exactly where he was headed. Then, they were running.

Paul's image on her phone hadn't moved. That wasn't good.

It was easy to run on the flat, smooth path, but even with the well-placed lights, there were deep shadows between the lampposts. Off to the sides, it was impossible to see more than the inky black smudges of trees and the occasional picnic table.

Scarlett saw Paul before her phone indicated he was nearby. The phone slid out of her hand, landing on the pavement as she felt a horror unlike any she'd ever experienced take hold of her.

Paul lay on his side, one of the pathway lights providing a ghastly illumination of his body. His head was thrown back at an unnatural angle, his eyes were open wide, staring at nothing, and his mouth gaped like a dark pit. A large pool of blood surrounded his neck and shoulders. It looked more black than red, even with the lamp casting its white pool of light over the glistening liquid.

A guttural scream came out of her, filling the night sky. She heard Angela scream, echoing her own cry. Jasper howled as Angela knelt beside her father, hugging his legs, shaking him slightly as if it might force the life back into him, as if he were sleeping and she could wake him.

Scarlett put her arms around Angela, trying to pull her away, but Angela clung more tightly to her father's legs, sobbing and screaming. "Daddy! Daddy! Wait. Please, wait. You can't leave me!"

Scarlett felt as if her heart were being ripped out of her chest. She saw her whole life falling apart. She wasn't sure if she felt empty because her husband was gone and she was left alone forever, or if the pain of seeing her daughter's heart shattered was too much for her to ever be able to take a breath again. She would never be able to heal her daughter's heart. She would never be able to fix what had just happened.

Angela's life would never be the same. Henry. Cooper.

How could she keep going? None of their lives would be the same.

How would they live without him? How could she do anything without him? She hadn't kissed him goodbye! She hadn't told him she loved him. She'd ... she couldn't even remember the last thing she'd said, what they'd talked about at dinner, the last time they'd made love. The last time she'd told him she loved him at all. The last time they'd really, truly kissed. The last time she'd looked into his eyes and seen him, noticed him.

And now he was gone. He couldn't be dead! It wasn't possible.

She stopped trying to pull Angela away. She collapsed against her daughter's back, holding onto her, sobbing. She felt Jasper come close, resting his head on her shoulder, pushing his nose against her neck.

CHAPTER 58

BLYTHE

*B*lythe could not believe a police detective was back in her living room again. When they hadn't returned with any more suspicions about her husband, she'd thought they were done. She'd thought the police were finally conducting a proper investigation into Lacey's murder, an investigation that might include looking for evidence of online harassment as she'd suggested.

How was it possible that another one of her close friends had been murdered? It didn't seem real.

And the first thing the police did was start knocking on doors. She felt as if the detectives *wanted* one of them to be guilty. They *wanted* to find an ugly secret or expose a scandal. Maybe the detectives wanted their own names in the news, their photographs on social media, just like everyone else.

This time, Detective Madeira had come alone.

"Where's Detective Banner?" Garret asked.

"Divide and conquer," Madeira said as he stepped into the entryway.

They settled in the living room. The detective leaned forward, his hands on his knees. "So. Had Mr. Nevin ever mentioned anyone he was having trouble with? At work, or any neighbors?"

"No," Garret said.

Blythe shook her head. "Do you think it's the same person who killed Lacey?" she asked.

"Do you?" Detective Madeira asked.

She was startled by the question. Was it a trick? Was he trying to get her to tell him something about her friends? Or was he genuinely interested in her opinion? "I don't know. It seems ... maybe it's a gang, or something?"

"There's no known gang activity at that park. Or in this neighborhood."

"But it could be a gang," Blythe said.

"Neither murder has the characteristics of a gang killing."

"They have characteristics?" Garret asked.

"Yes. So you're not aware of any disagreements between Mr. Nevin and his neighbors?"

"No. Paul was an easy-going guy," Blythe said.

"Everyone says that about their friends," Detective Madeira said.

"It's true," Blythe said. "He loved dogs."

"I've heard. Had he mentioned any concerns about walking alone at night?"

Garret laughed. "Not around here. Not with a dog."

"Why not around here?"

"It's very safe."

"Why do you say that?" Detective Madeira asked.

"You just said it is," Blythe said.

"Because it is," Garret said. "Our teenage daughters even go out at night sometimes. They walk home from their friends' houses."

"Is that right? Alone?"

"In groups," Blythe said. "But still."

"Every area has some crime," Detective Madeira said. "In some, it's more blatant and prevalent than others. I was referring to gang activity, but you shouldn't lull yourselves into a false sense of safety. I noticed you have a security camera."

Blythe and her friends had talked about security cameras. Scarlett and Paul had one, but it hadn't kept Paul safe. Lacey and Miles didn't, and it might have saved her ... would her killer have been deterred? Or found a way around it? Garret had mounted their camera at the front of the house. It captured most of the front yard, but it was possible to get to their left side gate out of camera range.

It felt slightly creepy having it. She didn't really like it, and Lacey had laughed at her when they'd had it installed. Evie had rolled her eyes, but two years later, they'd installed one as well.

Still, never in a million years had she expected a killer, or more than one killer, in their neighborhood. Never. She supposed the camera had partially been to keep the twins safe, although what she was keeping them safe from, she couldn't really say. Was it only to protect their possessions? That seemed downright sick, thinking about it now, with two of her friends gone, two families grieving. One teenage girl without her mother, and now, three children without a father.

Detective Madeira continued asking questions about Paul, about his hobbies and habits. He wondered what Garret and Blythe might know about his financial life and whether he engaged in gambling or owed money, whether he used illegal substances.

At least he wasn't asking about affairs. Yet.

"Did Detective Banner tell you about the troll I have stalking me on social media?" Blythe asked.

Detective Madeira looked at her, waiting for her to say more.

"Did she tell you I went to the police station? To show her the ugly comments I've been getting?"

"No. She hasn't mentioned it. You think this is related?"

"I don't know. But I've had someone leaving ugly comments on my social media. I can show them to you. Some of them ask for naked pictures, stuff like that. Some of the comments suggested that he knew where I lived. I wondered if this person could have been bothering Lacey and we didn't know about it. I thought Detective Banner could look at her social media accounts to see—"

"And how would this relate to Mr. Nevin's murder?"

"I don't know. But it's really creepy. And I just ... it's a crime. And these are crimes. Paul was really active on social media, so maybe ..." She realized there was probably no connection at all. She wanted to help. She really did. Madeira sat there asking so many questions, but none of them had any connection to Paul's life. It was as if the detective were talking about a total stranger. "Maybe this guy—"

"Nothing was found on Ms. Abbott's social media. And we'll be looking at Mr. Nevin's, of course. But it seems unlikely. There are all kinds of trolls on social media. You know that. They rarely cross over into real life. Those kinds of crimes are when a person known to the victim is harassing them online. Not a stranger."

"Oh."

"Has he threatened you in any way?"

"Not ... he made it look like he knows where I work out. That felt threatening."

Detective Madeira tapped a note into his phone. "Not a true threat, but disturbing, I agree. It's unlikely it's related. As I said, we'll be checking Mr. Nevin's social media. Did he ever mention being stalked or harassed online?"

"No," Garret said.

"No," Blythe said.

"Okay. Anything else? Does anyone you know own a handgun? The Nevin family claims they do not. Is that accurate, as far as you know? A .45 caliber. One of the bullets was recovered."

"One?"

"He was shot twice. They definitely wanted to make sure the job was completed."

Once again, he seemed so eager to immediately think bad things about her friends' families. Why would he want to know if Scarlett owned a gun? And why would he have to emphasize that they *claimed* they didn't? Couldn't he just believe them?

She did know someone who owned a gun. But that had been years ago. Did they still? Millions of people owned guns. Did that matter here? Why had he asked? Was she supposed to tell them about that gun she'd seen all those years ago, after her friends had proclaimed their aversion to wanting guns in their homes?

Why was he assuming this wasn't a random stranger? A kid high on drugs? A gang. He was so sure it wasn't a gang.

"He wasn't robbed?" she asked.

"No."

"And you think ... just like Lacey, you think someone he knew killed him? Why?"

"Because in that park, in this area, without a robbery, it's unlikely to be a random shooting. No other crime was in progress, so it wasn't someone running from another scene that he might have witnessed."

"Oh."

She looked at Garret. He was studying her, as if trying to understand why she was asking the questions she was, as if he sensed she was about to say something.

"Do you own a handgun?" Detective Madeira asked.

"No," Garret said.

"Do you know if any of the Nevins's friends or neighbors own one?"

"So many people do, does it really mean—"

"Not as many as you'd think. Only a little over a quarter of Californians own guns."

Blythe could feel Detective Madeira looking at her. She was avoiding meeting his eyes. It was a strange question. Why had he asked? It didn't seem normal. It seemed like the police should be looking for the person who wanted to kill Paul, not just someone who owned a gun. That made no sense. But just as they had with Lacey, he was fixated on the killer being someone Paul had known.

"Why do you always think it's someone they knew who killed them?" she asked.

"As I explained, random crimes have certain similarities, or characteristics. Most people are killed by someone they know. Do you know if any of their friends or neighbors own a handgun?"

"I ..."

"It's an easy *no*," Detective Madeira said. "So I'm going to assume that's a *yes*."

"It was a long time ago," Blythe said. "So I don't know if they still have it."

"How long ago?"

"Fourteen ... fifteen years ago. I saw a gun at our friend's house. But I—"

"When?" Garret asked. "Where? Whose house?"

"Jenna and Oliver's. I was in their study, and I saw it in a drawer."

"Jenna and Oliver Dale?" Detective Madeira asked.

Blythe nodded.

"Thank you," the detective said.

When he was gone, Blythe and Garret stood in the entryway. They stared at each other, neither one speaking.

CHAPTER 59

JENNA

*J*enna looked out the window and saw the two detectives standing at the front door. They couldn't see her from where she stood in the living room. Why had they come back? She and Oliver had answered all their questions. It was infuriating that they felt they could just show up whenever they wanted. They never texted or called to say they were coming. They just walked up to the front door, and she was supposed to invite them inside, smile, and answer their questions.

It was rude. It was so unfair. This was her house. Her time was important. She was a busy person. They acted as if she had nothing else to do, as if her day was so easy to interrupt. And it was almost always at dinnertime or in the early evening. Family time.

She could pretend she wasn't home, but Cooper was over again, his truck parked in the driveway, so they knew someone was here. And if she didn't answer the door, Oliver would. Even if she could convince Oliver not to answer, if she could get him to see how fucking rude this was, Naomi and Cooper would eventually come out and open the door because she knew the cops would keep ringing the bell until someone answered.

Flinging open the front door, she let it slam against the wall. She didn't care. She knew this wasn't good, that they were back. There was no reason to talk to them. All their questions about Paul's shooting had been answered with simple *yes* or *no* responses. They'd only stayed for fifteen minutes, if that.

"What's up?" she asked.

"May we come in?" Detective Banner asked.

"What's this about?"

"Is Mr. Dale home?"

"Yes."

"We'd like to speak to both of you."

"About what?"

"Will you get him, please," Detective Banner said.

"Why won't you tell me what this is for?"

"We'd like to speak to both of you."

"Is this about Paul's murder? Because we already told you—"

"Please get Mr. Dale, if he's available." Detective Banner gave her a crisp smile.

Jenna turned, leaving them standing outside, the door open. She wondered if they would walk into the house without an invitation.

When she returned with Oliver, who had asked the same question she had, they were still outside.

"Come in," Oliver said. "What's this about?"

"It should only take a few minutes," Detective Banner said.

They walked into the living room, everyone awkwardly stepping to the side, no one wanting to go first. Everyone but Detective Banner sat down.

"Do you own a handgun?" Detective Banner asked.

"Yes," Oliver said. "But—"

"What kind?"

"A forty-five."

"We'd like to see it."

"Do you have a warrant?"

"Do we need to get one?"

"I ..." Oliver looked at Jenna.

She shrugged. She hadn't shot Paul. She wanted to laugh at the idea of Oliver shooting anyone. Ever. He was the gentlest person she knew.

Before they were married, he'd lived in San Francisco. After a break-in at his apartment, and coming home to catch the men still there, he'd wanted one. For protection, he'd said. She could never imagine him actually using it.

When they'd first bought this house, he'd kept it in a drawer in the office. But once Naomi was walking, Jenna had told him they needed to be safer. Since then, the ammunition had been stored on the top shelf of the bookcase and the gun was kept in the storage closet in the same room. Essentially, it was now useless for protection. She'd almost forgotten they still had it.

Oliver stood slowly. "Why do you want it? I know that's an absurd question, but why?"

"We need to check if it's been fired. If so, we'll run a—"

"No one here used that gun. It's never been out of the house. It hasn't been fired since I learned to use it almost twenty—"

"We'd like to check it out. Please show me where it is. We can get a warrant, if you prefer."

Oliver glanced at Jenna. She shrugged again. She felt relieved. Their faces when she'd looked out the window seemed threatening. This was nothing. No one had fired the gun. Everything was fine. She gave Detective Banner a little smile.

Detective Madeira put on rubber gloves, and he and Oliver left the room. When they returned, the gun was in a plastic bag that seemed to have appeared out of nowhere.

"Where were you Thursday night between seven thirty and nine, Mr. Dale?" Detective Banner asked.

"I didn't ..." Oliver cleared his throat. "I had a headache, and I went to bed early."

"And you, Ms. Dale?"

"I was working on my jewelry. Remember? I own a jewelry making business? I'm an artist." She smiled.

"You weren't together?"

"We were both home," Jenna said.

"Was your daughter home?"

"Yes. She was in her bedroom."

"So all of you were home, but there was no actual contact among any of you?"

"We were home," Oliver said.

"No one went out," Jenna said.

The detectives didn't ask any more questions, but seemed dissatisfied with their answers. They left, saying they would let them know the results of the tests on the gun.

Jenna and Oliver collapsed onto the sofa when they were gone. Oliver took her hand.

"Do you want a glass of wine?" she asked.

"Jenna ..."

She sighed. She could really, really use a glass of wine. Maybe later, after Oliver got absorbed reading a book. Or much later, when he was in bed.

He squeezed her hand. He cleared his throat. "Uhm. You know, I don't remember you coming to bed until really late that night."

"I *said*, I was working on my jewelry." She'd also been enjoying a glass of wine without his hovering, judging, over-protective presence. Two glasses, actually.

"I was awake until almost twelve," he said.

"I got really caught up in it."

"Mmm." He released her hand. He leaned forward, resting his forehead in his palms. When he spoke, his voice was muffled. "I heard the front door. Twice. And saw headlights ..."

"You can't hear the front door from our bedroom. God, Oliver. And headlights? There are *headlights* going down our street all the time. What are you saying? Do you think I murdered Paul? Are you out of your mind?" She laughed. Then she laughed harder, hearing herself slipping into a tone of near-hysteria.

CHAPTER 60

BLYTHE

*B*lythe woke to seventy-nine more angry faces on her smoothie post.

A scream roiled in her gut. She put her hand over her mouth, unsure if it was a scream, or bile that had lain there for weeks. Without stopping to think, she tapped the post, swept her finger across the screen and deleted it entirely.

Nothing was worth this. Garret was right. For now, at least, she had plenty of clients. She had her newsletter mailing list. She would interact with her existing clients. The rest of it ... she just couldn't.

Two of her friends were dead. She didn't need this.

She closed the app, left her phone on the bed, and went downstairs to make coffee.

After breakfast, she drove Kelsey and Kate to the high school for their welcome back to school event. They'd already signed up for classes, but the day would be filled with music, outdoor games, dancing in the gym, and a chance to meet their teachers.

Despite their thrill when school had ended in late May, they burst out of the car as if they'd been wrongfully deprived of everything that mattered in their lives for the past two months. Blythe smiled, feeling a wave of positive emotion she hadn't experienced in days. Even though the good feelings were fifty percent, if not more, about their friends and social life and had nothing to do with learning, she was glad they loved going to school.

She pulled away from the curb and drove to the gym, where she was scheduled to meet two clients. By the time she returned home, she had the distinct feeling her life might be returning to normal. She ate half a turkey sandwich, standing at the kitchen door, gazing out at the backyard. She took a sip of water and heard her phone buzz with a text message.

The text from Jenna was frantic.

> Jenna: YOU HAVE TO COME OVER RIGHT
> NOW. SOMETHING TERRIBLE HAPPENED.

Blythe messaged back, asking Jenna what had happened. There was no reply. She sent a second message with three question marks. Still no reply. Knowing it was a waste of time, she tapped Jenna's number and waited for it to ring. After two rings, Jenna's recorded message began, talking about her jewelry and her delight in receiving Blythe's call.

Blythe's phone vibrated again.

> Jenna: Don't CALL me and TEXT me!! I need to
> SEE you.

Blythe slid the phone into her pocket. She finished drinking her water. She didn't have anything urgent that needed to be done. She didn't like acquiescing to Jenna's hysteria, but at the same time, Jenna sounded ... not good. She wasn't due to pick up Kate and Kelsey for another two hours.

She went upstairs, brushed her teeth, ran her fingers through her hair, and put on a fresh coat of lip-gloss.

Driving to Jenna's, she tried to imagine what terrible thing might have happened. Was the troll bothering Jenna again? She should have thought to check Jenna's social media before she left.

She pulled to the curb, turned off the car, and walked slowly to the front door. For some reason she didn't understand, her finger trembled as she reached out to press the bell. What was she expecting? Something worse than the troll? Had the detectives upset her? Jenna had manic, almost hysterical moods occasionally, although not as often as she had when they were younger. But this, she'd never been like this. Demanding a visit, sending a message in all caps. Maybe that awareness was what caused Blythe's hand to shake.

The door opened.

Jenna's face was free of makeup. Her hair looked as if she hadn't washed it for several days. She wore a white spaghetti-strap top and jeans. The top emphasized her collarbones and the hollows around her shoulders, making her appear bonier than usual.

"What's wrong?" Blythe asked.

"Do you want a glass of wine?"

"No thanks."

"I'm having one."

"Go ahead. I'll just have water, thanks."

"Whatever." Jenna disappeared. She returned with half a glass of white wine and half a glass of tap water, which she handed to Blythe in a rough gesture that caused the water to splash up the sides of the glass.

Blythe took a sip and sat down. "What's wrong? You look really upset."

Jenna remained standing. She sipped her wine. "You probably don't know, but we have a gun. We've had it for ages. Those detectives found out somehow. I have no idea how, because no one knows we have it. At least I ..." She took a sip of wine. She put the glass down and looked up at the ceiling.

"How *did* they find out? That's really weird. I have no idea how they knew. I need to look into that. I should have asked them! Anyway, somehow, they found out ... maybe they were looking through my house without a warrant when we were out of the room or something the last time they were here. Or maybe they came by when Naomi was here alone. If they did, they're going to find themselves sued. I need to ask Naomi."

She picked up her glass and took a tiny sip of wine. "They found out, and they took it and they're testing it because they think it was the gun that killed Paul! They think one of us *murdered* him! Can you believe that bullshit?!"

She was talking so fast. She was ... she sounded angry. Blythe supposed she would be equally angry if she were in Jenna's position. Would the police tell Jenna that Blythe was the one who had reported the gun? She wondered if she should tell Jenna right now. It would be better than Jenna finding out from one of the detectives. Surely that was private information. Wasn't it? She took a sip of water.

"Can you believe that? I did not kill him! Oliver did not kill him!"

"Do they think Naomi—?"

"Don't you *dare* say that!" Jenna shouted. "How can you even *think* that?"

"I don't think that. I wondered if they—"

"They better not. We'll sue them for that too."

"I don't know if you can sue the police."

"You absolutely can." Jenna swallowed the rest of her wine. "I need more wine. Are you sure you don't want any? Oliver gets pissed off if I have too much, but I'm so stressed, beyond stressed. I really need it. I think I'm justified. Don't you?" She turned and started out of the room. "I'll be right back. I have to get another bottle out of the wine fridge. It's in the garage." She laughed. "Oliver thinks it's better not to have it too *easily accessible*."

Blythe sat back on the sofa. She rested her head against the cushion for a moment, stretching her neck. She sat up and turned her attention to the digital picture frame on the end table. She watched, almost in a trance, as it moved through pictures, the settings too short, flicking through photographs every fifteen seconds or so, barely giving her enough time to absorb each one.

She stared, not blinking, as if the rapid change of the photos were doing her blinking for her. A picture of herself and Jenna came up. They were standing on the beach, their feet in the water. It was that gorgeous Santa Barbara house they'd stayed at a lifetime ago. Jenna was grinning maniacally, wearing nothing but a towel wrapped around her. Blythe wore a black, one-piece swimsuit that was too small for her, cut high on her legs.

Seeing the swimsuit opened a door in her mind that she hadn't known was there. It all came rushing back.

The comment from the troll—*Wear the black one.*

That weekend. Other pieces that had been lost in her memory, buried by what had followed that night when they'd gleefully swallowed their tablets of E.

Blythe hadn't packed a swimsuit that weekend. She'd still felt self-conscious about her body after giving birth to twins. She'd figured splashing around in the waves in shorts and a tank top would be fine. But Jenna wasn't having it. And Jenna, being Jenna, in one of her manic moods, had stripped off her black bathing suit, shoving it at Blythe. She'd run into the water naked, diving under a wave, surfacing, taking a few strokes, then turning and calling out for everyone to join her. She wouldn't shut up about giving up her swimsuit until Blythe agreed to put it on.

Was *Jenna* the troll? It wasn't even a question.

Wear the black one.

She'd never owned a black swimsuit in her life. That was the only time she'd worn one. It was either one of her other friends, or it was Jenna. Evie? Never in a million years would Evie do something so cruel. Scarlett, or one of the men? None of them were petty enough to even think of something like that. And they would never remember that moment, never remember the swimsuit after all these years.

But Jenna? Jenna who had been so upset about the troll, accusing Blythe of dismissing her fears about being *stalked* on social media?

She turned her attention away from the digital frame, which had now advanced through another ten or fifteen photographs. Jenna stood in the doorway holding a full glass of wine.

"What's wrong?" Jenna asked. "You look like you're going to pass out. Are you okay?"

Blythe stared at her.

"What?" Jenna asked.

"Are you the one trolling my social media?"

Jenna laughed, her voice shrill.

"You are."

"I don't know why you would think that. And right now, social media is the last thing on my mind. Those detectives—"

"It's you. There was a comment telling me to wear the black swimsuit. *The* black swimsuit. As if the troll had *seen* me in a black swimsuit once. I've never owned a black swimsuit. And just now, I saw a picture of us at that house in Santa Barbara." She gestured toward the digital picture frame. "I remembered when you took off your suit and gave it to me because I didn't bring a swimsuit."

Jenna laughed.

"Why would you do that? Why have you been terrorizing me? I've been scared out of my mind! You ruined social media for me. You almost ruined my business. *Why?*" Blythe choked back a sob.

"I didn't—"

"You did."

Jenna took a sip of wine.

"And you followed me. Didn't you? You followed me at the gym!"

Jenna shrugged. She peered into her wineglass. "You acted like it was no big deal that I was being stalked." She spoke in a mocking tone—"Oh, just block them. Ha ha."

"Were you even being stalked? Or did you invent that?"

"What difference does it make? We're supposed to *support* each other. All of us. And you haven't *supported* me!" Jenna's voice rose.

"Yes, I have."

"Not like you said you would. You said you would promote my work."

"How petty. How insanely petty can you be?" Blythe cried.

Jenna took a large swallow of wine. "It's not petty! It's my life!

My art. My soul. It's *our* life. Oliver's job is hanging by a fucking thread! I told you that. It's our whole lives. And it's what I created, and you ignored it like it was nothing."

"I support your posts all the time. Why are you being so childish? If I wasn't doing enough, why didn't you ask me?"

"I did. And you blew me off. I did everything for you, my whole life. I saved you from those bullies. I'm your best friend. I was always your best friend. I was your only friend, Blythe. You wouldn't have made it through high school without me. And you said you would support my business. I have talent, and no one knows that because my stuff doesn't get attention. It doesn't go viral."

"I can't *make* it go viral," Blythe said. "That's ridiculous. Viral means—"

"People follow you. The others do what you do, and you're so slow to comment and you don't—"

"You're being ridiculous. So you terrorized me and trashed my posts and did all this?" Blythe stood.

"You owe me!"

"I *owe* you?"

"Yes. I saved your life in high school. I made your life fun and exciting. And I saved your marriage. You knew I saw you come into the room that night." Jenna was screaming now. "Garret was *into* me. He was so hot for me. You wouldn't believe what he said to me. And how he was looking at me that day. You didn't even bring a swimsuit when we were going to a luxury house at the *beach*. So yeah, I gave you mine, but he was looking at me when I was naked. Me! That bullied girl still lives inside you, doesn't she?" Jenna laughed, her voice shrill, piercing. She took a long swallow of wine. "I had to get your attention."

"You thought trashing me on social media would make me support you?"

Jenna shrugged. "You needed a wake-up call."

"I can't ..." Blythe crossed the room. She walked toward the entryway. Her mind was racing. She wasn't even sure what she wanted to say. "You're crazy."

"I'm not crazy. They said I should never let someone say I'm crazy. It's not healthy. I'm ill, just like when you get the flu or cancer. It's the same. I take my medication. I just had to stop for a while because it gets so fucking boring. And I can't drink wine when I take the medication and Oliver watches me like a hawk. So yeah, maybe I'm a little wound up. I get wound up. But I like wine, and I think I deserve a few glasses now and then, so I stopped for a few days. Big deal." She took a swallow of wine.

"And if you were my friend, we could have had a nice glass of wine *together*, and worked this out like adults. But you're acting like that meek bullied little junior high girl or whatever. But the thing is, I'm a really good artist and I deserve *attention*. And everyone said they would support each other on social media and help promote our work. And it hasn't been equal. Not even close. Starting with you."

Blythe turned and walked through the entryway. She opened the front door and stepped out into the glare of the afternoon sun.

CHAPTER 61

JENNA

*J*enna and Oliver fought about her medication for the next three days. He knew she wasn't taking it, so there was no reason to lie about it. At first, she'd been able to get away with it, but once she'd been off it for this length of time, there was no hiding it. She didn't care. She needed a break. She was tired of the sameness, the lack of creative energy. Maybe this was why her social media had no pizazz. Maybe this was why it languished and didn't go viral. There was no passion, no energy coming through.

Those pills they forced down her throat turned her into a bland, boring nobody.

She hadn't heard a word from Blythe, who was busy sulking about being trolled. It hadn't hurt Blythe's coaching business one little bit, so Jenna wasn't sure what she was so upset about. Even without posting anything, Blythe's older posts kept magically floating to the top like pool toys that you couldn't force below the surface, beautiful pink rings gliding across the water, attracting hearts and shares because no one was allowed to leave comments, Blythe was so paranoid.

Eventually, she would get over it.

Jenna realized she probably shouldn't have said all that about Garret wanting her. That had been a mistake. It probably fanned Blythe's insecurity. But it was important to have things out in the open. It wasn't good keeping that secret between them for all these years. Once Blythe calmed down, they could talk about it like responsible adults.

After Blythe admitted she'd been a terrible friend, Jenna would give a genuine apology for saying that about Garret. She would admit that Garret had been so high, he'd hardly seemed to know who she was. He hadn't really said much of anything. She'd made that up. It was amazing what you could make up and people would believe you, if their mindset was in the right place. Or the wrong place. Depending on how you looked at it.

And now those cops were back. At least she could be sure that was good news. The gun had not left the house for over a decade. No one had fired it and now the detectives would have to admit they'd jumped to conclusions. She smiled. She'd washed her hair, put on makeup, and was wearing a sundress. She looked great. A profuse apology would be nice, but she doubted she would get that.

Having the gun back where it belonged, having them leave and promise never to return with their nosey, gossipy questions would be apology enough. She stepped into the hall bathroom and gave herself a gracious, charming smile that said—*I understand you're desperate to close your case.* She gave her reflection an air kiss and went out to join Oliver in the living room. She was glad Naomi wasn't there—hanging out at Cooper's house, for once.

"The bullets that killed Paul Nevin match your gun," Detective Banner said.

There was no greeting, no thank you for making time to see us. Just a blunt delivery of information that couldn't possibly be true.

"That's not right," Jenna said. "The gun has not been out of the house since we bought it. Almost sixteen years ago."

"The ballistics test doesn't lie," Detective Banner said. "The only issue is, the gun was wiped clean of fingerprints. Which is also an indication it has been used. Because we would have expected to find your fingerprints, Mr. Dale, and possibly yours, Ms. Dale."

"I didn't shoot him!" Jenna said.

"No one said that. Calm down," Oliver said.

"Are you aware of anyone else being in your home? Was it loaned to anyone?"

"No!" Jenna said.

"Let's go through your activities again the night Mr. Nevin was killed."

"Why?" Jenna asked. "I didn't kill him. I never left the house. I was making jewelry. I told you that. I didn't shoot him. I would never do that. I've never shot a gun and I don't like you implying I did. I would never murder someone on purpose and you have no right to assume just because of some stupid test that I did that—"

"Jenna!" Oliver stood and came to where she was sitting. He placed his hand on her shoulder. "My wife has a ... please don't take what she's saying seriously. She has some mental health challenges, and she's chosen to go off her medication for the past week or so. Part of her illness can involve some psychotic—"

"I'm not crazy! You're not supposed to say that word! I'm not psychotic. I didn't kill him and I don't have to explain where I was. I don't have someone watching me every fucking minute of every day. No one does and just because someone gets killed doesn't mean I suddenly have an alibi or whatever and it's not my fault I was making jewelry by myself!" She was screaming now. They were all staring at her, but she didn't care. This wasn't right. She couldn't breathe. She literally could not breathe. Just like—Why was this *happening*?! Why were they treating her like this? "I would never take our gun and shoot someone. I would never kill someone on *purpose* and Lacey died because she was drunk and she was acting like she was some great brilliant artist for putting stupid sayings she made up on mugs from a factory. And I just put that bag over her head for one minute, to get her to shut up for two fucking seconds and how did I know she was going to stop breathing and fucking *die* on me?!"

"Jenna! Oh my God, Jenna. What are you saying?" Oliver gripped her wrist.

She was sweating. She definitely couldn't breathe. The room was so hot. Why was it so hot? She needed a glass of wine. And why wouldn't Oliver let go of her? She hated it when he held her like that. As if she were some wild animal that needed a leash or something. Like he wanted to put her in a cage. Like her mother did. Locking her in her room. Then taking her to that place. It was a nice place, but they still locked her up and there were bars on the windows like she was in a cage!

There was nothing wrong with her!

And that Lacey with her stupid, ugly cheesy mugs made twenty thousand dollars in one *day* with some lame, supposedly self-affirming, saying she made up like she was some brilliant *guru*. It was so monumentally unfair!

"I didn't shoot him! You have no right to come in here and act like I shot him. Or someone in this house shot him. Who even told you we have a gun? How did you know we have a gun? Did you snoop through our house when we weren't here? *Did* you?"

"Oh, Jenna," Oliver said.

Oliver sounded like he was crying. Why was he crying? He was trying to pull her to her feet and hug her. She didn't want to be hugged. It was too hot. The sweat was pouring off her. God, it was hot. She needed something cold to drink. She needed fresh air. She wanted those cops out of her house.

She didn't have to prove anything to them. She was tired of everyone acting like she had to explain where she was and what she was doing, watching over her medication, making her take pills, watching how much wine she drank, telling her she shouldn't do this or that or the other thing. They were all so boring. You only get one life, why did it have to be so *boring*? Why couldn't she have some fun?

She was a brilliant artist, and no one noticed that. Lacey with her stupid mugs and T-shirts making thousands of dollars for a bunch of tacky stuff that ended up at yard sales. Laughing at her.

Telling her she needed to chill and let it flow and maybe it would happen for her.

She had to make Lacey stop talking. So she did.

CHAPTER 62

BLYTHE

*B*lythe sat in a beige chair in front of a mostly beige table in a small room with beige walls. In two minutes or less, she would be seeing Jenna. She would be allowed fifteen minutes to talk to her, and she wasn't sure whether the things she wanted to say would take three minutes or three hours.

The only decoration in the room was a small black camera staring at her from the corner of the ceiling. There was a red light, but she wasn't sure if that meant it was already recording her, or if it would begin blinking when it was recording. The fact that what she said would be listened to by strangers, possibly by Jenna's attorney, repeated to Oliver, potentially analyzed, was nudging her toward keeping most of her thoughts and feelings to herself.

She heard footsteps in the hallway. A moment later, the door opened. Jenna walked into the room. The female guard who was with her remained in the doorway.

"Fifteen minutes," the guard said.

Jenna wore navy blue cotton pants with a drawstring waist and a navy blue T-shirt. Her hair was clean, brushed back into a limp ponytail. She looked tired. "I'm not sure why you're here."

"I wanted to see how you're doing," Blythe said.

"Now you've seen."

"I want to hear how you're doing," Blythe said.

Jenna shrugged. "So you can tell everyone?"

"No. I ... can I hug you?"

"It's not recommended."

Blythe remained in her seat.

Jenna was still standing near the door.

"Are you going to sit?" Blythe asked.

"What do you want?"

Blythe was determined not to apologize. She had nothing to apologize for, but for some reason, that was the feeling that welled up inside her. The human desire to offer condolences, that universal *sorry* that sounded like an apology even when that wasn't the intention.

I'm sorry you're hurt, sorry for your loss, sorry your life is coming apart. I'm sorry I told the truth.

The word didn't really mean any of those things, did it? What should she say? She'd thought she had it worked out in her mind, a three-minute statement, and a few words to add, depending on what Jenna had to say. She realized now, she'd assumed Jenna would have a lot to say. She hadn't expected this subdued, slightly angry person she was facing. It was clear Jenna didn't want to talk to her. Maybe there was nothing left to say.

She was not apologizing for failing to perform to Jenna's absurd expectations on social media. Or for telling the detectives about their gun, which had apparently pushed Jenna to the breaking point, leading to her rambling, inadvertent confession to Lacey's murder.

All the other apologies owed were on Jenna's side. Where was the apology for having sex with Garret? And alongside of that thought, Blythe felt a whisper of anger. At the same time, she wasn't here to talk about that.

She and Garret had been through it all. They'd talked again about that night—every detail. He'd told her about his state of mind and assured her Jenna's taunting about his desire for her was manic delusion. Blythe had told him about kissing Miles. They'd compared what they could remember of their experiences while they'd been under the influence of ecstasy. They'd talked about how lucky they were that nothing too awful had come out of such a foolish decision.

Another time, while she and Garret enjoyed a leisurely dinner at a secluded table on the patio of their favorite restaurant, she'd relived her friendship with Jenna during her junior high and high school years. She felt like she'd let go, finally, of her sense of obligation that Jenna's protective friendship decades ago meant that Blythe *owed* her. Friendship wasn't about stacking up debts and keeping score.

Jenna was still staring at her, as if she were indeed waiting for an apology.

Well, Jenna was wrong. That bullied girl did not live inside of Blythe any more. The only remaining fragments of that girl were the shadows of her experiences that had shaped her compassion for other people. She was a strong, confident woman.

Following her father's advice for all these years—thinking deliberately before she spoke, refusing to squander her power simply to score a verbal point, or before she had time to carefully consider all her thoughts and feelings—had indeed made her strong.

"Did you just came here to stare at me? You wanted to see what a killer looks like?" Jenna asked.

"No. I'm not sure what to say."

"You only have fifteen minutes and you've wasted five sitting there with a blank look on your face."

"Don't *you* want to talk about anything?" Blythe asked.

"Nope. I didn't kill Paul. Everyone says I did. But I didn't. And I didn't mean to kill Lacey. She acted like she was as talented as me! She wouldn't stop saying that. All I did was try to get her to shut up." Jenna shrugged. "Just for five minutes."

Blythe shivered. "But she'd passed out. She wasn't really talking. She couldn't—"

"Don't tell me how it was. She kept talking and talking and even when she slumped over, she still had that smirk on her face, and I knew she would start up again any minute. You weren't there. You don't know."

Blythe felt sick. She wanted to cry, but she held her breath for half a second, keeping it inside. "I wish you'd told me you were taking medication."

"Why? It has nothing to do with you."

"Things might have been ... I don't know ... different."

"What things? You have no idea what you're talking about." Jenna looked down at her hands, rubbing the edge of her index finger as if she were checking for a hangnail.

"Oliver said your attorney is going to try to argue for diminished capacity because—"

Jenna let out a barking laugh. "Long shot. A total long shot."

"I hope it works."

Jenna shrugged. "Doesn't matter if I'm locked up here or locked up in my brain on drugs. 'Cuz if I'm not in prison, they'll be watching me around the clock to make sure I take my pills every single day, so ..." She laughed. "I should go. There's a schedule here. Might be time for a pill. Or lunch. Or exercise. Or another pill." She cackled. "It's always time for something." She knocked on the door.

The guard opened it, and a moment later, Jenna was gone.

That night, Blythe and Garret took the twins out for pizza.

As she bit into her final slice, Blythe looked across the table at Garret. Kate was beside him, staring down at her pizza, diligently picking off each delicate slice of green pepper, placing it on the edge of her plate.

Blythe chewed slowly, then took a sip of beer. "I've made a decision."

"Drum roll ... you're having a fourth slice?" Kelsey said.

Blythe laughed. "No."

"A second beer?" Garret pushed his chair away from the table.

"Be serious. It is serious."

Garret repositioned his chair.

"I'm getting off social media."

"Slow down," Kate said. "That's not possible."

"I think it is," Blythe said. "I'm going to make my coaching word of mouth only. I'll still have my newsletter, so I'm still going to launch the video classes I'd planned. But I don't need social media for that."

"But what about your friends?" Kelsey asked. "You mean just for your business, right? I mean, that's cool. It's supposed to be *social*, right?"

"No. I'm deleting everything."

"Living in reality," Garret said.

"That's not possible. You can't pretend it's 1989," Kate said.

"I'm not pretending."

"Everyone is on social media. Even people your age. It's how people *socialize*," Kate said.

"I know," Blythe said. "And maybe, in a year or two, I'll reconsider. But I have two dead friends and one in prison, and it feels like it's because of social media."

"That's not why," Kelsey said. "That is so *not* why."

"No, probably not. But it didn't help, and I really need to clear my head. I think I can be a more focused coach without it. I'm honestly not sure I need it."

"People will think you're dead," Kelsey said.

Blythe felt ill, thinking of Lacey's dormant accounts. Paul's thousands of dog photographs and videos, now archived.

Garret laughed. "No one thinks I'm dead."

"You at least have a profile," Kate said. "She's *deleting* them."

"It's what I'm doing. In fact," Blythe smiled and took a sip of her beer. "It's already done. And I don't feel dead at all. I feel more alive than I have in a long time."

CHAPTER 63

ANONYMOUS

I was a beautiful child. There are a thousand pictures on my step-father's social media to prove it.

I had blonde hair that looked white in the sunlight and the most *stunning* blue eyes. Everyone said so. There wasn't a single photograph in which I didn't look like an *absolute angel*. I had a *charming* smile and was *always looking directly into the viewer's eyes.*

I do have excellent eye contact. It makes people believe I'm trustworthy, that I'm a good person. And mostly, I am.

But what that man did to my brother, technically, my half-brother, although I never cared about those labels, to his very own son, made me sick to my stomach. I lived with it for a long time. I lived with it and I lived with him, until I couldn't any more.

Henry was crying out for help. In the end, there was no one to help him but me.

The therapist couldn't help him. My mom couldn't seem to help him. And my step-father—I do care about *that* label—that dude sure wasn't going to help Henry, because he *made* him that way. They were all so blind. They were all so busy scrolling through social media, they couldn't see what was happening in the real world.

All my step-father wanted was his dopamine hit from the *likes* and the *loves*, the comments and the shares. So he put us up there. His boys. Every day. Twice a day. Three times a day.

Smile.

Let me get a picture of that.

Do it again so I can take a video.

Didn't matter if we were smiling. Crying. Looking great, or looking like tools. Didn't matter what we wanted or how we felt.

Up went the pic onto social media.

I didn't care. But once Henry was old enough to realize what was going on, he cared. He cared a lot. He fucked the freak out.

Henry started getting weird. Really weird. Grabbing the phone and throwing it. Hiding. Refusing to pose for pictures. Then he got weirder. He thought people were always looking at him. He *knew* people were always looking at him, looking in his bedroom window, staring at him when we went out of the house.

It didn't help that people acted like they *were* always looking at him.

My parents' friends would come to the house. *Henry, did you have fun at the beach?*

Henry would stare at them like God Almighty had walked in the front door. How did they know? How did that man know he went to the beach? He wasn't there. Was he watching? Could he see him? Was someone always watching him? It terrified him.

Henry, It's great that you have a big boy bed now. How exciting!

Henry ran to his room when that happened. He dove under the bed, shaking and crying. He was right! That woman was looking in his bedroom window at night. How else could she know he had a new bed?

And my step-dad kept taking pictures. Paul put his hand on Henry's shoulder and held him in place. He begged him to smile. If he didn't smile, Paul took the pic anyway. *People will love this, kiddo. They'll see those big, wide blue eyes. You're a good sport.*

But after a while, Henry couldn't be photographed with a hand on his shoulder. He went wild, thrashing and kicking. His fits were epic. He wouldn't tell them what was wrong. I wasn't sure if he even knew himself what was wrong.

It took me a while to put it together.

I hated all the photos, all the posting for the world to see.

It felt like my step-dad was pimping us out to grow his social cachet. For what reason? His ego? Bored? Lonely? I really had no idea. I asked him to stop. He laughed and told me not to overreact.

It's the world we live in.

Everyone does it.

Get used to it.

There is no privacy.

I told my mom that Henry might be falling apart because he didn't like being used like that.

He's not being used, she said. *Don't be dramatic. Paul loves you two. He's proud of you.*

I told her it was creepy. I said it might be making Henry crazy.

Don't try to analyze the situation, Cooper. That's the therapist's job.

After that, I kept my mouth shut.

I got older and my step-dad kept posting pics of me and my sister, but Henry was out of the picture, so to speak. Finally, my step-dad gave up and switched to dogs. The dogs didn't know what was going on, so he could invade their privacy all he wanted.

But Henry wasn't getting better. He was still afraid of his own shadow. He hardly wanted to leave the house. The therapist got nowhere. They tried drugs, which just doped him up. They took him off the drugs. He wanted to stay in his room. The more I watched him shrink inside himself, the more pissed off I got.

When Naomi started showing off her dad's gun to me, I had a little fantasy flash through my head about shooting Paul. It was nothing at first, but then it came back. Every time Henry did something weird, every time he crawled under the bed, I thought about that gun.

I looked at Paul's social media and I saw how he fawned over all those women gushing about his dog pics and I got more and more pissed off. I didn't snap like some people do. I just thought more and more about taking that gun. Naomi was a little obsessed with it, but not as much as I was.

She loved that she knew where it was. She loved holding it. She thought it was funny that her parents were absolutely sure it was hidden, and they were so certain she didn't know about it. When she went to get us a bag of chips and sneak some beers, it was easy to take it and put it in my backpack.

After you've fallen asleep every night for six or seven months, imagining yourself pointing a gun at someone and pulling the trigger, actually doing it doesn't feel all that unusual. In fact, it feels normal. So one night, I did it.

I really did think about taking a picture of his bleeding body and posting it on social media. But I didn't. As much as I would have loved to make the point, to make people stop and think, just for a minute, I didn't do it.

I wouldn't risk going to prison, because Henry needed me.

A NOTE FROM CATHRYN

Thank you so much for reading *Like. Love. Hate.* I absolutely loved writing this book and I hope you enjoyed reading it. Discovering these characters' complicated relationships with social media, and more importantly, with each other, felt very much like spending a few weeks talking with my family and friends about how we communicate, and miscommunicate.

I appreciate every single person who chooses to read my books. It means so much to me that you spent a few hours of your life inside my stories, living with my characters.

I love hearing from readers. If you want to get in touch, you can reach me at the social media links below or contact me through my website at cathryngrant.com

If you want to be the first to know when new books are released, sign up for my new book release mailing list here. You'll receive a free short story featuring the main character in my Alexandra Mallory series.

Best wishes,

www.cathryngrant.com

ACKNOWLEDGMENT

Thank you to Mark Freyberg of The Freyberg Law Group. As a former criminal prosecutor for the Bronx County District Attorney's Office and longtime New York City defense attorney, he provided valuable insight to ensure some of my police procedure and legal details were accurate.

I've always worked to research my novels to ensure factual details don't interfere with the fictional experience. Sometimes things slip through the cracks, and several readers have helped fix those over the years!

It's great to have an expert like Mark on my team going forward.

ABOUT THE AUTHOR

Cathryn is the author of over thirty psychological suspense novels, including the ALEXANDRA MALLORY series featuring a sociopath you can't help but love. Readers have called the series "addictive".

The things that torment us in real life—obsession and revenge, guilt and envy and longing—are endlessly fascinating in fiction and she never grows tired of writing stories about characters struggling to overcome the worst.

Cathryn also writes ghost stories because who knows what lies beyond our senses—The Haunted Ship Trilogy and the Madison Keith series of novellas.

When she's not writing, she's usually reading, walking on the beach, or playing golf, going way out of her way to avoid hitting her ball in the sand or the water. She lives on the Central California Coast with her husband and her cat, Cleopatra.

You can get in touch with her by email, find her social media links, or sign up for her monthly newsletter at cathryngrant.com/contact. As a thank you for signing up, you'll receive a free short story about Alexandra Mallory.

www.ingramcontent.com/pod-product-compliance
Lightning Source LLC
Chambersburg PA
CBHW070845260626
47170CB00007B/2506